A Highlander
of Her Own

ALSO BY MELISSA MAYHUE

Thirty Nights with a Highland Husband

Highland Guardian

Soul of a Highlander

MELISSA MAYHUE

A Highlander of Her Own

POCKET BOOKS
New York   London   Toronto   Sydney

Pocket Books
A Division of Simon & Schuster, Inc.
1230 Avenue of the Americas
New York, NY 10020

POCKET and colophon are registered trademarks of Simon & Schuster, Inc.

For information about special discounts for bulk purchases, please contact Simon & Schuster Special Sales at 1-800-456-6798 or business@simonandschuster.com.

Cover design by Min Choi
Cover art by Alan Ayers

Manufactured in the United States of America

ISBN-13: 978-1-60751-727-6

As always, to Frank, my own personal Happy Ever After
And
To all my readers, for the wonderful notes
and emails you send. Truly, you make writing
the most fun I've ever had!

Acknowledgments

I owe special thank-yous to the following people:

Alianore [Kathryn] and the helpful folks at the Edward II forum [www.edwardii.justforum.net]

Anne Helmenstine, Ph.D., About.com Guide to Chemistry—for her expertise in chemistry and her helpful explanation of the differences between blue vitriol and green vitriol!

Louise Suit, EdD, RN, CAS, Assistant Professor, Nursing, Regis University, for her input on how wounds might heal and their lingering effects.

Chris—for the weapons training and showing me how to safely use an assault rifle—and allowing me to actually shoot the thing [with photos to prove it!!]

Megan—for always being ready to discuss the best last book we've just read.

Elaine Spencer—for being my fantastic agent!

And I couldn't forget Megan McKeever—for all her help and support. You are the best!

The precise quote Ellie vaguely remembers is:

"Water, water, everywhere, nor any drop to drink."
—from *The Rime of the Ancient Mariner*
by Samuel Taylor Coleridge

Prologue

Dallyn Aí Lyre, High General of the Realm of Faerie, strode down the long golden passage, his well-shined black boots gliding noiselessly over the sparkling marble floors in the Hall of the High Council.

Something was not as it should be. That much he could sense.

He took the stairs up several flights to the dignitaries' floor, following a series of twists and turns to the very back of the massive building. More than once he stopped to test the air, to listen, to *feel* for any who might follow.

At last, satisfied he was alone, he approached the carved wooden door that was his destination and knocked. Three quick raps, as instructed.

The door swung open slowly, admitting him to the private chambers of Pol Aú Revyn, hereditary High Prince of the Fae.

"You wanted to see me, your highness?"

Pol turned from the large window at the end of the room, a smile fleeting over his face before he crossed the room toward his visitor, his arm extended in greeting. "Yes, my friend. Thank you for coming."

Dallyn clasped the arm proffered to him. "Is something wrong?"

With a wave of Pol's hand, the massive wooden door closed silently. "Have a seat. Would you care for a drink?"

Shaking his head in refusal, Dallyn took the offered chair. He reminded himself of the necessity of patience when dealing with this man. "Is something—"

"Possibly," Pol interrupted, sitting down across the table from Dallyn. "I have fretted over this since returning from Mairi Rose's wedding. Since I find that I cannot let it go, I have decided to seek your assistance in the matter."

Apprehension blossomed in Dallyn's heart. Prince Pol did not seek the counsel of others lightly.

"When Mairi came to my glen and demanded her gifts be returned to her, I must admit I was somewhat shaken."

"To be challenged by a slip of a girl? I am sure you were, your highness." Few in the High Council would challenge the prince, let alone a young woman with only a touch of Fae blood.

The Prince smiled sadly. "Not because of her challenge, but rather by the knowledge of my own massive oversight. The thought of all those young women I had abandoned. I was so sure of myself for so long." He shook his head, a haunted look in his eyes. "In any event, as I said, I was shaken by the knowledge of the enormity of the mistake I had made and I think—that is, I suspect I might have . . ." Pol stopped, chewing on the inside of his mouth as he studied his hands.

The Prince lifted his head and met Dallyn's gaze before he spoke again. "No. The time has come for me to accept responsibility for all my actions. I committed a grave, unthinking error. You do understand that I restored all Mairi's gifts to her? All that she would have had if I had never interfered with my dratted blessing?"

Dallyn nodded. Though he was confused about where Pol was headed with this conversation, he felt sure that whatever it was that bothered the Prince was also the source of his own feeling that something was not as it should be.

"Yes, well, as I said, I was shaken, so I did not stop to think through my actions at the time. I simply responded to Mairi's request and restored that which should have been hers."

"But surely you have no reason to suspect Mairi would be a threat of any sort. She is the Soulmate of a Guardian. I have no doubt Ramos will see to her safety."

Pol shook his head rapidly. "No, no, not Mairi. It is the others who concern me."

"*Others?*" The tendril of apprehension grew as Dallyn voiced the word. "What others?"

Pol rose from his chair to pace the length of the room. "Mairi's demand that her gifts be restored was not for herself alone. She wanted the gifts restored to *all* those like her. All my descendants who had been ignored by the original blessing."

The ramifications of Pol's statement hit Dallyn, curdling his stomach.

"These are women who have no idea?"

"Exactly." Pol's steps drew to a halt at the large window, his back to Dallyn. "In my youth, in my anger, I was so sure of myself. When I blessed my own daughters on that day, I did not envision any omission. I never once considered the words I had used. *'The daughters of my daughters.'* Not one time in all these centuries did it occur to me there would be sons who would have female children. Young women who were as much of my blood and Rose's as any child of a daughter."

When Pol turned, the sorrow on his face caught Dallyn by surprise.

"Confronted with the magnitude of my error, I simply reacted, compounding what I had already done. You must find them, Dallyn. Find them and help them. Save them from what I have done to them."

Dallyn gripped the arms of the chair where he sat, the polished wood cold beneath his hands. "Do you know where we might begin? You told me once you had maintained a connection to your descendants."

The Prince's lips tightened, his head shaking almost imperceptibly. "To the line of one of my daughters only, I fear. I've no idea what happened to the offspring of the other two. They have never visited my glen so I can only assume they have no knowledge of me. And after all these generations? Their numbers could be staggering."

Willing his legs not to shake, Dallyn rose from his chair. "I will begin at once, your highness." With a respectful dip of his head, Dallyn walked out the door of Pol's chambers.

His mind raced as he made his way out of the Hall of the High Council. An unknown number of women roaming the Mortal Plain with the powers of the royal line of the Fae suddenly activated. And none of them with any understanding of what had happened to them.

Worse yet, none of them would know anything about how to control those powers. Or about the threat they faced from the Nuadians.

Dallyn had no idea where to begin the search. The best he could do would be to dispatch his Elite Guard. They would need to be vigilant now.

It was a matter of watching and waiting for whatever happened next.

One

Dun Ard
Scotland
December 1295

The clipped fall of boots on stone sounded loud in the deserted hallways of Dun Ard. Though few would be up and about at this early hour, Caden MacAlister had no doubt his cousin would already be hunkered over the estate accounts in his solar as he was each and every morning. Blane MacKiernan, Laird of the MacKiernan, taught the importance of hard work by setting an example.

Caden paused at the heavy wooden door, unconsciously running a large hand through his tousled dark copper hair as he gathered his wits and his courage. He had considered his alternatives time and again. This must be done.

He rapped his knuckles sharply against the door, the

vibrations echoing in his stomach. Or was that simply nerves?

"Enter."

He pushed open the door and approached his cousin's desk. "I've come to a decision and I must speak with you." Quickly. Before he lost his nerve.

Blane looked up from the work spread in front of him, a smile creasing his face. "Very well, Caden. Have a seat and share yer great decision with me."

Caden shook his head, declining the offer to sit. He thought better on his feet. "You must choose one of my brothers as your heir. I'm no longer fit to be the next laird of the MacKiernan." There. He'd said it. It was done.

His cousin leaned back in his chair, studying the hands he steepled together. At last he looked up, a confused frown replacing his earlier smile. "I had thought you cared for our people and this land."

"I do. And that's why I ask you to choose another as yer heir." Even though this was all he had ever really wanted.

"Explain yerself."

"The next laird should be someone who'll love this place, these people. Someone who'll look after them, improve their lot in life and pass it all on to his own son to do the same." And he would never be able to do that.

Blane nodded. "Exactly what I've chosen you to do, lad."

"I canna, Cousin. After what's happened with Alycie, I ken now I'll no ever wed. There will be no sons to succeed me."

He would never have a wife. Alycie had found the

idea of marriage to him so repulsive she had betrayed his sister and cousin in order to escape him, almost causing their deaths. He would never again put his family in such jeopardy. Nor would he trust another woman. Alycie was now happily installed in the convent on Iona as she had wanted, and he would remain unmarried as the fates had obviously intended.

"Yer young yet, Caden. Mayhap one day you'll change yer mind on this."

"No. I'll no allow any other lass to be forced to face marriage to me. I've made my decision, just as you made yers all those years ago."

Blane rose from his chair, coming around his desk to place a hand on his young cousin's shoulder. "I chose never to wed because I feared any son of mine would carry the madness of my father and my brother. I would no risk exposing Dun Ard and her people to that tragedy again. Yer situation is entirely different. You take too much blame upon yerself, lad."

Caden shook his head. He deserved the blame. He knew his limitations. Of the three MacAlister brothers, he saw himself as the least desirable to a woman. He had neither Andrew's pretty face nor Colin's warrior abilities. He wanted only to manage Dun Ard. To find new ways to help their land and their people prosper. And while one day he would have been the laird of the MacKiernan, that alone wasn't enough to hold a wife. He'd learned that from his experience with Alycie.

No, Caden knew he was not meant to find the happiness of a mate in life. And though he had never known why his cousin remained unwed and childless, he suspected that Blane revealed his reason now in an attempt to provide solace. Solace he didn't deserve. "Still, I dinna think . . ."

"There's no a need to think on this, lad. I willna choose any to be my heir other than you. I've invested too many years in you and you've learned too well the duties of a laird. You'll go off to school as we'd planned, and when you return you'll pick up where you left off. You are my heir and that's my last word on the subject."

"And when I never wed? When I have no sons to continue the line?"

Blane smiled again, squeezing Caden's shoulder before he dropped his hand and walked back to his chair. "If that is the way of it, then you'll do as I have and choose someone. Perhaps one of yer brothers' brats will succeed you, aye? Now off with you. I've work to do before I take my morning meal."

Caden waited, unsure of what to do next. He'd struggled for weeks trying to make the right decision. And now that he finally had, Blane had dismissed his concerns as minor.

"Go on," Blane encouraged. "Oh, we're still going out to inspect the sheep pens later this morning, are we no?"

"If that's yer wish," Caden replied, leaving the room and shutting the door behind him.

He was almost embarrassed at the relief he felt, knowing at least part of his life would continue as he'd always hoped. He would have Dun Ard to live for.

And as for his own heir?

Just as Blane had said, Drew and Colin would marry and have sons. He would simply have to wait and watch to see what time would bring.

Two

The quick clip of worn cowboy boots resonated joyously in the short hallway, bouncing off the hospital green walls of the clinic. It was all Ellie Denton could do to keep from skipping down the hall. So great was her relief as she pushed through the swinging door into the aged waiting room, she had to resist the urge to hug the elderly receptionist standing by the front desk.

"Them test results come out okay, Ellie?"

"Yes, ma'am, Miz Waller." Ellie gave in to the urge and threw her arms around the little old woman, who giggled like a schoolgirl.

"I'm real glad you got yourself some good news today, honey," Ethel Waller murmured, reaching out to tuck a stray lock of hair behind Ellie's ear. "You sure do got your mama's pretty black curls." Then she giggled again and fanned herself with her thin, blue-veined hand. "But you got them green bedroom eyes straight from your daddy. Lordy, if he wasn't the handsomest man I ever did see." Ethel patted Ellie's arm before returning to her chair behind the front desk. "You be real careful driving home now, you hear."

"I will, Miz Waller. Thank you."

That's what came from living in the same small town her whole life. Everyone knew everything about her as if they were all family. Still, Ellie was grateful for the good news, too. Anything good in her life was way past due.

As she walked down the dusty sidewalk toward the little store where she'd parked her old pickup, she was determined not to let even the busy noise of the little town darken her mood. Soon enough she'd have to deal with all the unpleasantness life had thrown in her path the past few weeks. For the next couple of hours she just wanted to savor the one positive she had been given.

The tests were all negative. Whatever this thing on her chest was, it wasn't skin cancer.

Doc Hill had offered to set up an appointment with a skin specialist in Dallas, but Ellie had declined. She wasn't sure how she was going to pay Doc Hill, let alone come up with money for some expensive big-city doctor. At this point, if it wasn't going to kill her, by necessity it fell to the bottom of her list of priorities.

The little bell above the door jingled merrily when Ellie walked into the old store.

"Well, I'll be! You're looking right happy there today, Ellie. Haven't seen you smiling like that since before—"

The old man behind the counter paused and coughed to buy himself some time before lamely finishing. "Yes sir, you sure do look nice today."

Ellie knew what he'd been going to say. Since her mother's death, nothing had been worth smiling about. Until today.

"Thank you, Mr. Paul. How's Herman?"

"He perked right up after you were out to the house. The wife couldn't believe it. Nobody could ever get that cat to take pills like you did, Ellie. Darndest thing I ever did see. You sure got a special way with animals." The old man nodded to himself.

"I'm just glad I could help."

Special way with animals? Mr. Paul didn't know the half of it. She used to think she had a gift, an empathy for all four-legged creatures. But recently that *gift* had turned into something else altogether. Something bizarre and frightening.

Either that or she was going stark, raving mad.

"Sure is hot today. Bet we're in for a storm tonight."

"I wouldn't doubt it," Ellie agreed, wiping her hand along the back of her neck. Even pulled back in a ponytail, her long, heavy hair stuck to her skin in this heat.

Ellie walked to the far shelf, studying the canned goods. Something portable and cheap was what she needed. Something she could keep in the pickup until she decided what to do.

Don't think about it now.

She had, after all, promised herself a couple of hours' reprieve.

"Vern Peters was in earlier," the shopkeeper called

from the front of the store. "He said when he drove past your place there was a truck out there looked an awful lot like Ray Stanton's."

Just the mention of that man's name made Ellie's stomach turn. Her reprieve was over. Time to face the chaos her life had become.

"Yes sir, Mr. Paul, that's his truck alright. He showed up yesterday. Heard about mama's death and seems to think he has a right to take over the place."

Ray had been sitting on the porch, his filthy boots propped on the railing when she'd come in from checking on the sheep.

"Oo-whee, girl! You always did fill out a pair a jeans like nobody else." He'd taken a long drag on his cigarette, then tossed it to the porch and ground it out with his heel.

"What are you doing here?" Some small part of her had known the minute she'd pulled off the road and seen his truck.

"Now, Ellie darlin', is that any way to talk to your old daddy?"

"You're not my father. Now get off my property." She didn't want anything to do with the loser her mother had made the mistake of marrying five years ago. A marriage that hadn't lasted twelve months.

"Oh, I don't think I'll be leaving anytime soon. Way I see it, with Nora passed, this is rightly my property now. I talked to the sheriff and he agrees. I've decided to move back in. But don't you worry your pretty little head. You can stay if you want. I'm sure we can work out something you can do to earn your keep around here."

The conversation had gone straight downhill from there. Finally, with Ray's laughter and taunts ringing in her ears, Ellie had run to her pickup and sped away, leaving gravel and dust heavy in her wake.

There was no point in her going to see the sheriff. He was Ray's brother-in-law.

Peanut butter, bread, a toothbrush, soap, some canned goods. A can opener. Ellie gathered items she would need and headed up to the counter, trying to calculate just how much cash she would have left.

She paused to look longingly at the rack of paperbacks at the front of the store. Her favorite author had a new Highlander romance out, but for now she'd have to content herself with rereading the one she had out in the truck.

Reluctantly she turned her back on the books and piled her selections on the checkout counter.

"As I recall, your mama never did rightly divorce ol' Ray, now did she?"

"No sir, Mr. Paul. She didn't." Nora hadn't left a will, either.

"That's a damn dirty shame. I guess that good-for-nothing bum sees this as his golden ticket. You gonna fight him on it?"

"I'm not sure."

Fight him? Oh, she could take him to court. Probably could win if she got herself a good lawyer—which she couldn't afford. And Ray? His older brother was a big-shot attorney over in Austin.

"Well, it don't seem right to me." Ben Paul shook his head, then peered over his reading glasses. "You going back to College Station in the fall? You gonna be a vet like your mama wanted you to?"

"Right now I can't say. After those developers were

out from Dallas, Mama and I had talked about selling off some of the north pastureland so I could finish school, but now . . ." Ellie let the words drift off.

Between her mother's death and Ray claiming rights to the ranch, the likelihood of her being able to sell off part of the land was pretty remote. Finishing school would have to wait.

The shopkeeper added up the items Ellie set on the counter. "That'll be thirty-seven fifty."

She dug into the pocket of her jeans and pulled out her last two twenties, returning the meager change in their place.

With a wave, she left the store and loaded the two brown paper bags into the seat of her old pickup before heading out of town.

School? Who was she kidding? Until all this mess with Ray was straightened out, she had exactly two dollars and fifty cents to her name. And not even a place to sleep tonight.

After dark the night before, she'd returned to her house and snuck out back where the load of wash she'd done was still hanging on the line. Thank goodness she'd at least been able to get a clean change of clothing to wear into town today.

For now she headed to the same place she'd spent the night before, out to the far pasture on her land. To her favorite place by the river that flowed across a corner of the property.

Pulling her pickup to a stop under the dappled shade of a huge old mesquite tree, Ellie climbed out and walked over to the riverbank, breathing in the familiar smell of the place.

This had been her favorite spot for as long as she could remember. It was quiet here. Peaceful. A private place where she had always come to think, to plan, to daydream.

She grabbed her new bar of peach soap from the bag of groceries, peeled out of her clothes and dove into the river. The cool water closed over her, washing away her worries for the moment, along with the grime of the day.

"A clean body means a clean mind," her grandmama had always said. Ellie hoped that was the case now. She needed her thoughts to be clear in order to plan what she would do next.

Heat hung in the air, even as dark approached. In no time she was dry, except for her hair. After putting on her jeans and a clean T-shirt, she ran a comb through her curls before using an old bandanna that had been lying on the floorboard of her truck to tie her hair up into a ponytail. It would be a mass of long tangles tomorrow, but she had more important things to worry about now.

Reaching under the seat of the old Ford, she pulled out her favorite romance novel, the pages worn from the number of times she'd read it to escape into the fantasy of the Scots Highlands. Reading had long been her refuge whenever she was unhappy.

And "unhappy" certainly was hovering over her tonight.

Things had gone so wrong lately. Her mother's death had been the first. Less than a week later this awful red mark had showed up on her chest. Then there were all the strange games her mind had started playing on her. Now Ray was back.

Ellie finished up her cold canned dinner, not wanting to start a fire and draw attention to her location. She bagged her trash and tossed it into the bed of her pickup before sitting down at the foot of her favorite mulberry tree. From here she could hear the fish break the surface of the water to gobble down the dark berries that fell from the limbs hanging over the river.

In the far distance, thunder rumbled and lightning jagged a path to the ground, flashing a bright white in the growing dark.

There wasn't enough light left to read, but just having her book in her lap was comforting. She stroked her hand over the cover as she tried to come to some decisions.

She couldn't live out here in her pickup forever. What was she going to do? More specifically, what was she going to do about Ray taking over her home?

That slimy worm!

She hated the man. He was even worse than all the chauvinistic cowboys she'd grown up around. This lowlife had broken her mother's heart and now he had the nerve to show up and think she would forget all he'd done? He was so full of himself. Sitting up there on the porch yesterday, leering down at her, making his dirty little insinuations about what she'd have to do to stay in her own home.

"I'll have you know I already earn my keep around here, Ray. I work this ranch, which is more than you ever did in the short time you were here."

He stood up from his chair and pushed the sweat-stained straw cowboy hat back on his head. "You need a man, honey. And I don't mean for working those damn sheep. I can be that man."

"Don't flatter yourself. You think I'd be interested in a man my mama kicked to the curb?" Ellie laughed, masking the fear she felt.

Ray's eyes had hardened at that. *"Look around you, missy. You got some secret true love out there somewhere who's gonna come riding up to your rescue? One of them bare-chested guys from those books you and your mama used to read?"* He'd laughed at her then, a thin mean bark of a laugh. *"I don't exactly see you beating guys off with a stick, Ellie. You're too goddamned picky for your own good. But that's getting ready to change. You want to live in my house, you're going to do what I want, the way I want it. Matter of fact, I'm thinking you could peel out of them jeans and we could start right now."*

She'd run then. Jumped in her old truck and raced away. Straight to this spot, where she'd cried until she'd finally fallen asleep.

But that was yesterday. This morning she'd gone into town and gotten the best news she'd had in months. It was the start of a whole new chapter in her life.

Now she would . . . what?

What could she do? The frustration of feeling so completely powerless in this situation almost had her in tears again, but she fought it down. She would think of something, some way to deal with this. Her mama always did say she was stronger than she gave herself credit for.

She leaned her head back against the massive tree trunk and closed her eyes.

When she was younger she would come out here, stare up at the stars and dream of her perfect man—her "true love" as Ray had called him. He would show up in her little town and sweep her off her feet. A man with whom she could be as happy as she remembered her mama and daddy being together.

In those days she had truly believed he was out there somewhere and that wishing on a falling star would bring him to her.

Thunder rumbled again, much closer this time.

"Even the gods are laughing at that idea," she muttered, watching as the lightning drew closer.

Whoever her dream man had been, he certainly wasn't any of the boys she'd dated around here. They were all alike. They talked about how their "little woman" belonged at home, raising babies and cooking meals. Barefoot and pregnant, as the old saying went, sure wasn't the life for her. Especially not with a man who thought he had the right to tell her what she should be doing all the time. She'd had more than enough of that from the guys she'd known all her life.

Besides, she didn't want a man. She would never be weak like her mama had been. She wouldn't settle for the first cowboy that came knocking just because she wanted love so badly. Wouldn't go looking for some man to take care of her. She could take care of herself.

Still, the old fairy-tale dream wouldn't fade that easily. Just for this one moment she allowed herself to feel that dream again. To want. Wouldn't it be wonderful? If such a man really did exist?

"That's still what I'd wish for," she whispered. "To find that one man who's meant for me, my true love, wherever he is." She glanced down at the dog-eared book lying next to her and smiled. "A Highlander of my own would be totally cool."

The spot on her chest began to tingle and she unconsciously rubbed at it as she watched the lightning cut through the dark. A quick count to the next peal of thunder told her the storm was still miles away, but she could already smell the rain on the gentle breeze.

The tingle grew stronger and she felt the hair on her arms stand up as the next bolt of lightning met the ground within feet of where she sat.

"That's weird," she muttered, rising to her feet.

Green lightning? She'd seen a whole lot of thunderstorms in her twenty-three years, but she'd never seen the like of that before.

She forgot all about counting to the next clap of thunder when lights of all colors began to twinkle and flash around her.

"What the . . . ?"

The breath was sucked from her lungs as she felt the sudden rush of forward momentum and the stomach-dropping sensation of a free fall into nothingness. A rainbow of lights flashed and danced in a frenzy, circling about her, passing around and through her, all as she felt her body speeding through an eerily green-lit emptiness.

A thought about the storm being too far away for lightning to have struck her flashed through her mind just before her world faded to blackness.

Three

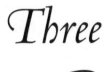

DUN ARD
SCOTLAND
1304

*H*urts.

"Who's there?" Ellie awoke in the dark, cold and disoriented, her eyes at first unable to focus, sensitive from the bright flashes she'd experienced. With the sound of a hard, steady rain beating above her head, it all came rushing back to her. As impossible as it seemed, she must have been struck by lightning. What else could explain all those crazy lights she'd seen? Still, as best she could remember, the storm had been miles away. It made absolutely no sense.

Hurts.

Someone was here with her. It was a plaintive voice, vaguely familiar, as if she'd heard it, or one like it, before.

She opened her eyes as wide as possible, willing them to adjust quickly to the dimly lit surroundings as she stretched out her hand, feeling around her.

Her fingers encountered a large, furry mound.

Hurts.

"Hold on. I'll help you."

Where had she heard that strange, reedy voice before? Not heard, exactly. Nothing out loud. More like sound and pictures floating inside her head.

"Oh my God!"

Now she remembered. The day after the mark had shown up on her breast, her mind had started playing horrible tricks on her. It had happened for the first time out at the Pauls' ranch when she'd been so sure she'd heard their cat speaking in her mind as if through mental telepathy. Mental telepathy with pictures.

And it had continued to happen ever since.

Ellie jerked her hand back and bolted upright, immediately wishing she hadn't as a pain shot through her head and waves of dizziness assailed her. Raising both hands to her temples, she concentrated on not passing out as shivers racked her body.

None of this made any sense. Could the pain and the dizziness and the cold shivers all be the aftereffects of a lightning strike? She didn't remember ever having heard anyone describing feeling like this after such an experience.

Trying to calm herself, she breathed in deeply, an exercise that quickly told her she wasn't anywhere near her river any longer.

In fact, the smells that assaulted her nose were those of a barn. It even felt like hay under her hands when she reached back down. With her eyes adjusting to the dim light, she recognized she was in some kind of a stall and standing next to her was what had to be the largest dog she had ever seen.

Help.

The largest, most pitiful dog she had ever seen, she quickly amended.

After only a moment's hesitation, she crawled toward the animal and, reaching out, she gently stroked her hand down his side. Something was wrong. The dog was in pain.

Ellie had always had a natural affinity for animals. For years she had worked summers as an assistant to the vet in their county, helping with the animals in his care. Recently, though, since the mark had shown up, her affinity had become something else all together. Something scary. Scary to the point where she'd been avoiding all animals other than the sheep on her ranch.

People didn't "hear" animals. Not normal, sane people anyway.

But this pitiful creature needed her, his pathetic plea reaching her heart. She couldn't turn her back on him.

"You poor baby. What's happened to you?" she crooned as she continued to softly stroke the thick, wiry fur. Her fingers rippled over every one of the dog's prominent ribs. "They sure don't overfeed you, do they?" she murmured, exploring down the dog's front legs.

He stood quietly until her hand reached his foot.

Hurts.

"I know." She focused on the picture in her mind. This was the source of his pain. "I'll be careful. Let me have a look." She lifted the paw, wet from the dog's licking at it.

Embedded in the pad of the dog's foot, right between his toes was a large thorn. She might have missed it in the dimly illuminated stall if not for her mental visions of the animal's pain.

Another wave of dizziness washed over Ellie as she grasped the thorn between her fingertips, and she paused, waiting until she felt it pass. It took two tries to pull the barb from the dog's flesh, but in the end the thorn gave way.

Good!

The word exploded into her mind, propelled on a wave of sheer gratitude and happiness.

At the same moment, the dog toppled her over, pinning her shoulders to the ground, joyously licking her face by way of thanks.

Unable to lift her arms or move out from under the dog's weight, she tossed her head to the side to escape the brunt of his large wet tongue. It was then she saw the huge man emerge from the shadows, an enormous sword held out in front of him.

Ellie followed her natural instincts at that point and screamed for all she was worth.

Caden MacAlister sloshed through the mud of the dark courtyard on his way to the stables, muttering under his breath. He pulled his plaid tightly about him to ward off the cold, heavy rain.

This was a prime example of the sort of task he hated most.

Of course, he could have sent one of his men to take

care of the problem, but he refused to send anyone to carry out a duty he wasn't willing to perform himself.

Blind Tavish had brought one of the deerhounds here to Dun Ard to be destroyed. The creature had refused to run on the last hunt and turned on the old man in the feeding pens. While Tavish was difficult at best in his dealings with people, he had a soft heart for the hunting dogs and would not put one down himself. Not even one that had attacked him.

No, instead the old man, with the aid of the lad who helped him care for the beasts, had tied the dog up and brought him here for the laird to deal with. But Blane was away on much more important business, leaving this chore to Caden.

As if *he* relished the task of harming an animal. Even one gone mad. It was for this reason he had delayed coming out here for the last couple of hours.

Still, according to Tavish, the animal threatened the safety of the people, and that made it Caden's responsibility in his cousin's absence. A responsibility he took seriously. After all, one day he would be laird. He could not afford to feel compassion for the animal awaiting him.

"It's naught but a beast gone mad. No different from any other wild creature threatening my land," he mumbled to himself.

Entering the stable, he lowered the woolen plaid to his shoulders and shook his head, dislodging the droplets of rain that clung to him. A small fire burned in the contained pit of the stableboy's chamber, casting a poor, flickering light over the interior of the barn but adding little warmth.

All thoughts of pity for the unfortunate beast fled Caden's mind as he neared the stall where the maddened animal had been placed.

He drew his sword in response to the scene confronting him. A lad lay beneath the crazed beast, pinned down by his great paws. Apparently he had arrived just in time since even now the young man screamed in his terror.

Caden moved forward slowly, keeping his eyes on the enormous dog, hoping to calm the boy with his words.

"Hold still, lad. Dinna move a muscle and I'll bring the beast down before he's time to hurt you."

"You'll do *what*?"

The frightened boy's strangled reply sounded more child than man, but Caden couldn't afford to spare him a glance, his attention locked firmly on his four-legged adversary.

Another foot forward, carefully, slowly so as not to panic the beast into attacking the boy. Only a little farther and he could open the gate to the stall.

"You keep your distance, mister!"

Before Caden could reach the gate, the boy pushed the dog away and rose to his knees, throwing his arms out in front of the beast, the flickering light glinting off his face.

Caden froze.

Not *his* face. *Her* face!

With her body outlined in the glimmer of firelight, there was no mistaking the feminine curves, in spite of the odd clothing she wore that had led to his initial mistake. It was a woman trapped in the stall with the maddened animal!

Caden no longer doubted or pitied. He would do

whatever was necessary to rescue the woman. He had only to slip into the stall. To maneuver himself in between her and the animal that threatened her.

"Rise to yer feet slowly, lass, and work yer way this direction. Dinna make any sudden movements to provoke the beast to attack." He kept his voice low and calm, with the intent to soothe—both the beast and the woman.

She lifted a hand to her face, pressing the heel of her palm to her forehead for a moment before speaking.

"What's wrong with you? This poor creature isn't about to attack me."

Hand on the gate, Caden paused to reassess. The beast did seem almost as intent on protecting the woman as she was in protecting him. Still, Tavish knew his animals and Caden knew Tavish.

"The dog is maddened. Now move away from him, lass. He's already turned on his keeper this very day."

She faced the animal, putting her arms around him and resting her forehead against his side.

"Would that be the keeper who half starves this poor creature? Or the boy who mistreats him, teasing him with bits of food?" She glared up at Caden. "The same keeper who never bothered to check this animal for injury when he wouldn't run? I don't blame this poor dog one bit. I would have attacked the bastard, too."

The image of this slip of a lass confronting the grizzled old dog keeper almost brought a chuckle along with it, but Caden stifled the urge. This was no time to find humor. The woman was in danger whether she knew it or not.

He lifted the latch, easing himself through the gate

into the stall. He kept his movements slow and delib-
erate, worried as much about the woman's response as
that of the dog. Perhaps he could distract her and get
her away from the animal before it was too late.

"The beast is injured?" The deerhound didn't appear
hurt, but neither did it appear to be maddened.

"He had a large thorn in his footpad. Any fool who
bothered to check could have found it." A shiver racked
her body and she drooped back down, as if leaning on
the dog was all that kept her up on her knees.

"Are you hurt, lass?"

All thoughts of stealth vanished and he crossed the
ground between them in two steps, leaning down to grip
her arms and lift her to her feet. She stumbled against
him and for an instant he could swear the scent of fresh
peaches washed over him before she pulled away.

"I . . . I don't think so." She put both hands to her
head again. "But I'm so confused. Nothing here looks
familiar. Who are you?"

"Who am I?" She had mettle, he'd give her that.
"The better question is who are you and how have you
come to be in my stable?"

"Ellie Denton and . . . I'm not exactly sure how I got
here. I think I might have been struck by lightning."

Lightning? Not on a night such as this. Perhaps her
mind was touched. It would explain much about her behavior.

"No likely in this weather, lass. We've all but snow
this eve. Now come away from the beast and we'll get
you up to the keep." The dog appeared calm enough for
the moment. This woman, this *Elliedenton*, was his more
immediate concern.

"Snow?" she squeaked, her eyes large.

"Aye. Come along." He grasped her arm again, drawing her toward him.

Immediately the great dog tensed, pushing in front of Ellie, growling and baring his teeth.

"Shh," she soothed, her hand on the beast's head. "I feel like we can trust this man. At least, I hope we can." She rubbed the back of her other hand over her eyes before looking up at Caden. "I'm going to have to take a chance on you, cowboy."

Her words startled him. What was this madwoman going on about now? "Aye?"

"Promise me you won't hurt this animal."

"Yer hardly in a position, lass, to be . . ."

"I need your promise to protect him or I can't leave him." She lifted her hand toward Caden, stumbling as she started forward.

He reached her as her legs gave way and swept her up into his arms, resting her head against his shoulder, the smell of peaches wafting around him again.

"Verra well. You have my word." Why he'd agreed to her ridiculous demand, he couldn't say. Perhaps for no other reason than it seemed so important to her.

"You swear it?" she mumbled, her eyes closed.

"I said as much, did I no?" He shook his head in irritation as he tossed the end of his plaid up over her head, preparing to go out into the night. "No that you've any reason to question my—"

Her soft fingers unexpectedly stroking down the side of his cheek struck him mute.

"Thank you." Her eyes fluttered shut but a tiny smile remained even as her hand dropped.

He shook his head and started toward the door of the stable, surprised at what had just happened.

Surprised at himself.

"You've the luck of the Fae about you tonight, beastie," he called over his shoulder as he headed out into the night.

He ducked his head against the cold rain, clutching his bundle tightly against his chest. Now that he thought about it, the whole of this evening had the feel of the Fae to it.

Four

"I suspected I would find you up here. She's sleeping peacefully at last."

Rosalyn MacKiernan MacAlister's words danced across the high windswept parapet of Dun Ard, ringing in Caden's ears. He felt more than heard her steps across the rain-slicked stones, so the gentle touch to his shoulder came as no surprise.

"She's a Daughter of the Fae."

"Are you sure?" He didn't know why he even bothered to ask. If anyone would know, it would be his mother, a Daughter herself. Perhaps it was because it would be so much easier if she were wrong. "Did she come here from the Faerie Glen, do you suppose?"

His mother pushed a bundle toward him. "Do any of these have the look of our Glen to you?"

A faint peach scent wafting up through the cloth confirmed what he held without his having to examine the contents. The clothing *Elliedenton* had worn. He could almost imagine the feel of holding her, the warmth of her body still clinging to the damp bits of cloth, though, of course, that was ridiculous.

"They've no the look of anything I've seen before." Nor had the woman who'd worn them. "If no the Glen, then where could she have come from?"

"You dinna for one moment suppose the Fae confine themselves or their exploits to our fair Glen alone, do you? They would have no reason for such." Again his mother softly touched his shoulder, directing his attention up to the spot in the night sky where she pointed. "Do you see that one wee star shining his light from among those clouds?"

Caden nodded, remembering all the times he had studied the sky with his mother from this very spot. "Aye."

"We see only him, but we ken the existence of all the others we canna see. It's the same with the Fae, son. They walk the lands among the mortals, whether we see them or not."

"As you say." Other Fae, like the Duke and his brother who'd come to Dun Ard nine years ago, threatening those dear to Caden. Exposing what he should have seen on his own. Changing his life forever. "Why do you suppose she's here?"

"I'd say she's another tossed through time. And I've the feeling she's here for a reason." Rosalyn adjusted the plaid she'd wrapped about herself, pulling it tighter against the cold, blowing mist. "Though whether the reason is hers or ours, I've no a clue."

"Ours?" Caden turned to search his mother's face. "What need would we have for a descendant of the Fae to appear on our doorstep?"

Both his mother's eyebrows rose before she answered.

"It's no a secret that the Fae do what they do for reasons of their own. Reasons that often are no clear to us until their plans are well in motion." She paused as if an idea had just occurred to her, a half smile lifting one corner of her mouth. "Perhaps they, like yer own mother, believe it's high time the MacAlister men went about the business of finding their life mates and starting a family."

A familiar litany from his mother.

"You believe she's been sent for Colin or Drew?" It would be good to have one of them settled and about the business of providing a MacKiernan heir.

Rosalyn shrugged and turned her back toward the door. "Time will tell. You'd best come in soon, lad. Yer no going to solve the problems of the world staring at the heavens this night."

He nodded his agreement absently.

At the doorway she stopped. "And I suppose we'd best dispose of that bundle as well. There's enough trouble in our lives without worrying about having to explain those strange things of hers."

"Dinna fash yerself, Mother. I'll do what needs to be done."

He meant that. About the woman as well as the bundle in his hands. If she were here for good, so be it. But he'd learned his lesson about the Fae nine years ago, along with an even more potent lesson about the hazards of trusting women.

His people, his family, Dun Ard. They were all he had. All he would ever have. He'd allow no Daughter of the Fae to endanger any of them.

He'd do what needed to be done. And discovering the true reason for *Elliedenton* being here was first on his list.

Five

Stark, raving mad.

Ellie's insides fluttered as she scrutinized the seemingly normal movements of the woman who had awakened her earlier this morning in this horribly strange place. It wasn't last night's dizziness that tied her stomach in knots now. It was the shock of being trapped in this unbelievable nightmare.

Rosalyn bent over the fireplace, busily chatting as she worked. She was a tall, older woman, but lovely in the way beautiful women age. Only up close could Ellie see the streaks of silver shot through the pale blond hair the woman wore pulled back into a long, heavy braid.

Beauty aside, someone in this room was without a doubt crazy as a bedbug—and Ellie didn't much care for the idea that it might be her.

"My nephew's wife, Cate, used to fix this brew for herself of a morning." Rosalyn looked up, a radiant, knowing smile on her beautiful face. "You'd have liked Cate. I suspect the two of you would have quite a bit in common." She nodded to herself and chuckled as she turned back to her work.

Quite pleasant for someone so obviously a complete mental case.

Rubbing her damp palms together, Ellie found her mind reeling with the absurdity of what she'd been told. According to this Rosalyn, Ellie had been hurled through time by Faerie magic—*Faeries, for God's sake!*—landing her here with these people.

Obviously that was ridiculous, which left Ellie desperately scrambling to figure out what could actually be happening. Reason assured her of the impossibility of all that Rosalyn had told her.

And yet that same reason didn't—couldn't—explain all she had seen here already.

Oh, it covered all the nonsense about time travel and the Faeries Rosalyn claimed were responsible for her being here. But she couldn't come close to explaining the clothing these people wore, the building she was in or, most disturbing of all, the weather.

You did not have freezing rain in July in central Texas. Ever. It simply did not happen.

Thinking of what she'd seen outside the wooden shutters earlier this morning, Ellie shivered and continued to shift her weight from one bare foot to the other in an attempt to limit contact with the cold stone floor.

"Here, lass, take this." Rosalyn held out a large mug.

Ellie grasped the offered cup with two hands, sniffing at the rising steam, redolent with the aroma of mint. "What is it?"

"It's a broth of herbs. I canna recall exactly the name Cate used, but I assure you, it's quite good. I have it myself of a morning now."

"Tea?" Ellie asked absently, her attention drawn to the room itself rather than the occupant.

They were in what Ellie would call a sitting room or a front parlor back home, though she had no idea if they were anywhere near the front of this place. She'd quickly lost her sense of direction as they'd walked through the long, dark hallways to this cozy room.

Rosalyn had called it her "solar." High walls, made of what appeared to be large stones, were hung with massive tapestries. It certainly looked like what she'd expect from authentic fourteenth century.

Ellie shivered again. It *felt* like what she'd expect from authentic fourteenth century, too.

There had to be some explanation for all this. Some explanation *other* than Rosalyn's absurd flight of fancy that the Fae had sent her here.

"That's it! Tea," Rosalyn murmured before taking a sip. "You'd be warmer, lass, if you'd but wear the stockings and slippers I offered you."

"I prefer my own boots, thank you. And my own clothes."

The costume she wore now was absolutely amazing. Layers of linen and woolen gowns. She had awoken this morning, her legs tangled in the heaviest, longest woolen nightgown she had ever seen and all of her clothes, except her underwear, gone.

She'd barely had time to worry about how she'd gotten into such a costume before Rosalyn had swept into the room, arms full of the things Ellie wore now.

The woman had also been full of the most unbelievable story Ellie had ever heard.

A story of the existence of Faeries. Faeries with their own plots and schemes. Faeries who, according to Rosalyn, were obviously responsible for Ellie being there.

Faeries indeed.

Fantastic story aside, Ellie had accepted the excuse of wet clothing and allowed herself to be cosseted into this bizarre costume, but she had refused to put on the footwear. At this moment, however, she admitted to herself that her stubbornness was very likely a case of what her mama used to call "cutting off her nose to spite her face." Still, it had seemed important to her at the time to be in control of something—even something so insignificant as what she wore on her feet.

Rosalyn arched an eyebrow, looking up at Ellie from the seat she'd taken by the fire. "Aye, well . . . you'll be waiting a goodly while for those things to dry. You were soaked to the skin last eve." She patted the seat next to hers. "For now, let's relax here by the fire with our tea and have ourselves a visit, shall we?"

Ellie arranged herself in the large chair, curling her feet up underneath her. She waited until her companion had taken a sip before speaking. Though begging was not something that had ever come easily to her, desperation was a great motivator.

"Please. Just tell me where I am and how I got here."

Rosalyn placed her hand on Ellie's arm, the small, sad smile she wore as frightening to Ellie as the words that accompanied it.

"We've been all through this. Yer at Dun Ard, in the

year of our Lord 1304. I ken this to be a shock to you, but it's how the Fae work. They've a reason for sending you here. We've only to discover what yer to do and we'll assist you in yer task in order to get you home to yer family again."

Enough!

Ellie jerked her arm from the woman's gentle touch, her tea sloshing as she jumped to her feet and backed away. "Are you completely nuts? Or do you think I am? I have no idea who you are, or why you're doing this to me, but I am not for one minute buying this load of bullshit about Faeries and freakin' time travel. There is no such thing!"

Rosalyn stared at her unblinking, finally setting her cup on the small table by her side before folding her hands in her lap. "How can you no believe in the Fae when clearly you descend from them?"

"I what?" Ellie took another step back, feeling as if Rosalyn's quiet words had been a physical assault.

"You bear their mark. You are a Daughter of the Fae. Their blood courses through yer body the same as it does mine."

"I have no idea what you're talking about." Ellie glanced around the room, her eyes lingering on the door. Would it be locked? If she ran for it right now, could she get there and out before this Amazon could catch her?

When she looked at Rosalyn again, the woman was standing, her back toward Ellie, pointing over her shoulder.

"Loosen my laces and I'll show you."

"Loosen your laces?" Ellie barely recognized the

squeak of her own voice as she inched toward the door.

The look Rosalyn bestowed upon her was irritated, to say the least.

"This is my favorite shift, lass, and I've no intention to ruin it just to prove my point. Now loosen the laces at my neck as I asked and be quick about it."

The command sounded so like something Ellie's grandmother might have said that she responded without thinking, doing exactly as she was told. With shaking fingers she untied the laces and stepped away, waiting for whatever came next.

The woman wiggled her arm, dropping her gown and shift off one shoulder, baring a portion of her back.

What Ellie saw took her breath away.

"Oh my God. How . . . ?" She couldn't finish.

There on Rosalyn's back was an identical match to the mysterious mark that had appeared on Ellie's breast.

"Aye. I suspect you ken what it is I'm talking about now, do you no?"

Rosalyn shrugged the dress back up into place and motioned to her laces. Ellie retied them, ending with a neat bow, though her actions were purely mechanical.

How could they have known about the mark? She'd shown it to no one other than the doctor.

Ellie sank to her seat, her hand hovering over the mark on her chest, which, oddly, tingled now. When she looked up, Rosalyn was seated as well, calmly sipping from her cup.

"Do you believe me now, lass?"

"I . . . I don't know what to believe."

The coincidence of the marks was too strange to have been contrived, and yet how could she accept a story like this? If she could only manage to get outside, to look for some familiar landmark, to find some way to escape back to her own life.

"It's not that I'm doubting your word, it's just . . . would you allow me to go outside, to look around and see for myself?" Ellie held her breath waiting for the answer.

"Of course you doubt my word. I dinna expect I'd do any less in yer place." Rosalyn smiled, patted her hand and rose from her chair. "I'll arrange for you to ride out to the village. Will that do?"

Ellie nodded weakly as the woman walked to the door. This was it. She was going to get her chance. Once outside, she'd find the perfect spot and make a break for it. Then she'd find her way into town and get help.

Rosalyn stopped in the doorway. "Though the rains have stopped, there's still quite a chill. Perhaps you'll want to wear the footing I brought you earlier? I'd no recommend yer riding about the countryside in this weather in yer bare feet." She walked out, but then popped her head back in. "I'd no even thought to ask. Do you ride, lass? Are you comfortable with horses?"

"Yes ma'am."

Ellie sat very still after the door closed, knowing she must be near hysteria.

For who but a hysterical woman would even consider asking the horses for help?

Six

Oh no—not the dog killer!

Standing on the bottom step of the great staircase leading down to the courtyard, Ellie watched with a sinking heart as the big man strode purposefully toward her, leading two horses in his wake. In the light of day he appeared even larger and more imposing than he had last night. With his plaid wrapped around his body and the hilt of his sword peeking up over his shoulder, he looked like some determined warrior straight off a Hollywood movie set, intent on destruction.

Hold on, maybe that was a slight overreaction.

In fairness, he hadn't killed the dog; he'd only *threatened* to kill the animal. At least, she didn't think he had. He'd promised he wouldn't.

She studied him as he approached.

His hair, waves of deep burnished copper, was neatly

pulled back and tied at his neck, though a couple of unruly curls had escaped their binding.

Her breath caught in her throat as he drew near and met her gaze. The liquid brown of his eyes immobilized her, holding her captive as if something in them beckoned to her, causing her to miss whatever it was he'd just said.

"Wha . . . what? What did you say?" She gave herself a mental shake. This was not like her.

Concern and doubt shone on his face. "I asked naught but if you were ready to go, *Elliedenton*. Are you sure yer up to traveling? That yer recovered enough to sit yer mount? If you canna even hold a simple conversation . . ." He left the thought hanging as he reached for her arm.

His words, softened by the deep, melodic burr of his brogue, caught at her, blanketed her senses, disoriented her.

No, this was not at all like her.

"Of course I am," she huffed, jerking away before he touched her. If the man could fluster her with a look and render her speechless with nothing more than the sound of his voice, she didn't want to find out what his touch might do.

He ducked his head and backed away a step, but not before she saw the smile that lit his eyes.

How dare he laugh at her? Wasn't it bad enough they were holding her prisoner here?

Okay. Stop. She was letting herself get carried away again.

After all, he *was* preparing to take her into town. Still, she saw no reason for his amusement. At least, no reason that wouldn't be completely humiliating.

"And my name isn't all one word like that. It's Ellie.

Short for Eleanora. It was my mama's name. Eleanora Ann. Denton. Just like you're . . ."

What the heck was his name anyway? She couldn't remember. And why she had rattled through that ridiculous explanation of her whole name and where it came from like some nervous teenager meeting the school's star football player was beyond her.

She huffed out an irritated breath. It was so hard to be haughty when she didn't have all her facts. And when she couldn't control her own words. Or her rapidly beating heart.

He straightened, the smile still there, and tilted his head in a little bow. "Caden. It's no short for anything. MacAlister. Son of Duncan. Next laird of the Mac-Kiernan." He stopped, a small frown wrinkling his brow as he abruptly turned to adjust the straps on his horse. "Yer ready, then?"

Ellie gritted her teeth. He was making fun of her! Stepping down off the last stair, she moved toward him, crossing both arms under her breasts.

"I told you I was ready. And where's that poor dog? Did you go ahead and murder him even though you promised me you wouldn't?"

Caden's smile had disappeared when he faced her this time. "There are many a thing I'm no in this life, but one thing I *am* is a man of my word. I've no broken any promises to you or to anyone else."

Though her goal hadn't been to anger him, Ellie's embarrassment spurred her to continue when she would have stopped.

"Oh really? If that's true, then just where is he?" She stumbled back a step at his glare.

"You doubt me? The damned beast is . . ."

Caden's words were cut short as he grabbed Ellie and swung her up off the ground, enclosing her in his arms and whirling about, just before a great shove knocked them forward.

"EllieEllieEllie!"

The excited voice echoing in her mind immediately alerted her to the source of the great shove.

The object of her concern had arrived. And only Caden's inserting himself between her and the great dog had kept her from being the main recipient of all that happiness and affection.

The four-legged beast was fine, but the look on the face of the two-legged beast told another story altogether.

An apology might be in order.

Quickly.

If Caden hadn't given his word to his mother, he would be on the far side of the MacKiernan lands by now. Alone.

Instead here he was, plodding along on horseback at the side of a daft Fae and a slobbering murderous beast.

"I don't understand. None of this is right," Ellie murmured for perhaps the hundredth time. As she had each time before, she brought her horse to a stop, scanning the countryside around her.

When his mother had come to him asking that he escort their unusual guest down to see the village, he could think of nothing but how the woman had felt in his arms last night.

No! his self-protective mind had roared. *Keep yer distance from the lass.* But his internal warning had been swept away by the traitorously meek "As you wish," he had uttered out loud.

He'd no more than begun to speak to her when he'd proven he should have listened to that inner voice, babbling about himself as if trying to impress her. It had taken all his will to simply stop his flow of words.

Since that initial embarrassment, he'd kept himself in check. Watching. Waiting to see what she would do. It didn't take long for him to reassess his plans.

Ellie's openmouthed reaction as they'd ridden out the gates of Dun Ard had given him cause to reconsider their destination before they'd hardly begun.

Instead of the village, he'd turned them toward Sithean Fardach. Though his family home had fallen into disrepair over the years, that in itself would ensure the place deserted, and he wouldn't have to deal with explaining this woman and her strange behavior to anyone.

He glanced back at her now, still motionless in the center of the trail, the great deerhound on guard at her side.

At this rate it would take all day for their short trip.

Still, he held his tongue.

When he'd seen her waiting on the steps this morning, she'd fair taken his breath away. Oh, there'd been no mistaking her womanly form when he'd gotten a good look at her last night. Or when he'd held her in his arms. But today, dressed as a proper lady, she was extraordinary. Her long dark curls, pulled back and tied low at her neck, only served to emphasize the green of her eyes.

She'd been flustered and then angry, each emotion racing across her face in quick succession, coloring her cheeks and lighting her eyes. Clearly she had no gift for artifice, no ability to conceal her feelings, for which he was grateful. That would be a rare find in a woman if it were genuine.

And now?

Now she looked bewildered. Frightened. Vulnerable.

She could be pretending. Trying to lure him in for some purpose all her own. Certainly his past experience with women had taught him to be wary of their plotting ways. Yet this Ellie didn't seem to be acting for his benefit. In fact, for most of the ride she'd hardly seemed aware of him at all.

It was for that reason more than any other he held his irritation in check and quietly asked the same question he'd been asking for the last couple of hours. "Do you want to go back now or do we continue on?"

She shook her head as if waking from a dream and lightly tapped her heels to her mount's sides, signaling him to forward movement.

"Let's go on, please," she responded quietly, as she had each time he'd asked the question.

He stole a quick glance her direction as she pulled even with him, catching her chewing on her bottom lip as she studied her surroundings. Not that he could blame her for her confusion. His mother had told him last night this woman had been sent by the Fae.

From the future.

Caden didn't for a minute doubt what Rosalyn claimed. He was all too familiar with his family's heritage, his own mother's gifts. And though it had been nine years, he remembered clearly watching the Fae magic take his cousin Mairi and her betrothed back to their own time.

The magic of the Fae was very real to Caden, as was his understanding that the Fae did nothing without motive. And certainly nothing without a price. The last time the Fae had touched their lives, the price had been dear, changing his whole world. He'd nearly lost his youngest brother and his sister in the incident. He had lost the woman he'd thought would be his wife and, along with her, the future he'd envisioned for himself.

If this woman had been sent here by the Fae, there was, as his mother had said, a reason for it. A reason he intended to discover before his family again had to pay such a price.

Onward they continued, riding side by side until at last they reached the top of the hill and entered the open gates of Sithean Fardach.

A wave of sadness washed over Caden as it always did when he entered the deserted, decaying courtyard. The smaller sheds where he had played as a child had fallen into disrepair, some of them no more than mounds of rubble.

"What is this place?"

Ellie's question drew him from his melancholy thoughts.

"Sithean Fardach. I was born here." Had his father lived, this, not Dun Ard, would have been his home. "Though this is the MacKiernan ancestral home, the last laird built Dun Ard and moved the family seat there. My mother is a MacKiernan by birth. When she married, she stayed here with her husband and raised her family until my father's death when we were but children. After that, the current laird of the MacKiernan, my cousin Blane, insisted we join him at Dun Ard so that he could see to our welfare and safety. That's been our home ever since."

Ellie slid down off her horse and approached the great stairs, pausing to run her hand over the wood of the railing before turning back to him.

"It's real, isn't it?" she asked in a shaky voice. "I don't know how, but all of this is real."

Caden dismounted and moved forward, keeping his focus on the woman in front of him. She sank to the stairs, sitting down like someone who'd had the air knocked from her.

Instinctively he reached out for her, his hand lighting on her shoulder before he'd even had time to consider the movement.

"I'm sorry. I ken this must be difficult for you."

"Difficult?" She lifted her head, her eyes the damp sparkling green of fields in summer. "You can't imagine. It's sheer madness. I don't have a clue as to where I am or how I got here. And I'm left with no alternative but to accept the idiotic ramblings of some insane woman."

Caden tried unsuccessfully to stop the smile her rant inspired, knowing she didn't find any of this amusing.

"I can only assume the *insane woman* you speak of is the lady Rosalyn, and that being the case, those *idiotic ramblings* must be what she's told you of the Fae."

A look of exasperation crossed Ellie's lovely face. "Exactly. The lady Rosalyn. She has this bizarre theory that I'm descended from Faeries, for God's sake. She apparently thinks that she is, too." Ellie shook her head incredulously, looking down at her feet. "That woman is a full-on nutcase."

"That woman is my mother." Caden paused, enjoying the effect his words had.

Ellie met his eyes slowly, the red of her embarrassment creeping up to color her face. "Your mother?"

"Aye. My mother. And if she says yer a Daughter of the Fae, then without a doubt, you are."

"I'm sorry." Ellie rose to her feet, ducking her shoulder to slip out from under his hand as she turned. "I didn't mean to be insulting about your mama." With that quick apology, she lifted her skirts and ran up the stairs.

"No insult taken," he called after her. Now that was more the behavior he expected from a woman. Run away rather than face up to what she'd said or done.

Ellie had made her way to the top landing before he thought of his last visit to the keep. "Mind yer step up there, lass. The wood in this staircase has weathered over many a generation of my family. It's no so sturdy these days. Best you come back down where it's safe."

He started up after her, scanning the steps for which ones carried the splintered cracks he had noticed the last time he'd been here.

She pushed open the great door but didn't enter. Instead she backed up to lean against the rail of the landing, tilting her head as if listening to something. Suddenly she whirled and yelled, "Don't come any closer!"

It wasn't her words that held him in place so much as the look of sheer panic on her face as the railing under her hands gave way.

* * *

Ellie pitched her body back toward the doorway, hitting the landing with a hard thump as she watched the railing she'd had under her hands only seconds before smash to the ground far below. She rolled to her hands and knees, scooting toward the edge of the landing to peer over.

Stop! Too big! Danger!

A high-pitched reedy voice echoed through her mind, as insistent in its message as it had been the moment before the rail collapsed. She had known instantly it wasn't the big deerhound. This voice was different, more commanding somehow. Besides, she could feel the big dog's presence at the bottom of the staircase, his worry transmitted freely to her.

Too big! Danger!

A cracking sound froze her to the spot, but the frustrated grunt that followed had her on her feet and moving. Five stairs below her, Caden's foot had gone through the rotted wood.

"Are you hurt? Didn't I tell you to not to come any closer? Now look at you."

Damn the man. He'd been coming up after her. She'd warned him, but of course he hadn't listened. She should have known he wouldn't. Just like every macho farmhand she'd ever known. Unless an order came from a man, it was ignored.

"I'm no hurt. My boot's absorbed the scrape. But you stay put. Dinna you move even a hair. I'll be right there to get you." Caden jerked at his foot, attempting to pull it from the wood.

The stairs wouldn't hold his weight. She knew from the feelings and pictures flowing through her mind. She couldn't allow him to come up after her. It was bad enough his foot had gone through the stairs. If she hadn't dashed way up here in the first place, none of this would have happened.

But she'd let her pride get the best of her. When she'd stuck her foot in her mouth and insulted his mama, right after he'd been so nice to her, well, the only thing she could think of was to put some distance between them.

So the next move was hers.

"I'm coming down."

No, no! Too big. Don't move!

The warning sounded too late as the board beneath Ellie's foot splintered, pain searing up her calf as her left leg plunged through the rotted wood.

"Damnation, woman! Dinna I tell you stay as you were?" Caden bellowed, wrenching his own foot free.

Ellie didn't think it would take much effort to pull out of the hole, but with even a tiny shift of her weight she could feel the board that held her giving way. She remained absolutely still, crouched on the step with one leg dangling through the hole as Caden slowly crawled up the stairs separating them.

Though he stopped two steps below her, their eyes were nearly level. She wondered at the determination she saw there, especially since all she felt at the moment was mind-numbing fear.

"Can you pull free?"

It might be unreasonable to think the sound of her own voice could shatter the wood and send her hurtling down, still, she only shook her head in response. The vision of that rail splintering as it crashed into the ground over a story below her was too fresh in her mind.

"Is yer limb wedged in tightly, then?" Caden reached out, his fingers grazing over and around her knee where it disappeared through the opening in the step. "It feels as though you've room," he murmured.

"Not wedged." She felt breathless and she could hear her own heart pounding. "But the wood seems to give way with every little movement."

He nodded thoughtfully, capturing her gaze with his own. "Dinna you fear, lass, I'll no allow you to fall. I swear it."

His voice curled about her, comforting her and somehow bolstering her courage. When his fingers tightened in a reassuring squeeze around her knee before he drew his hand away, she had to fight the gasp that threatened to escape. Surely it was only her desperate fear of falling that caused her heartbeat to speed up.

"When I lift you," he began.

"No! It won't hold your weight, too." What was he thinking? They'd both be lying down there with the smashed railing if he tried that.

A look of irritation swept across his handsome face as he leaned in closer.

"You'll be listening to me now, *Elliedenton*, with none of yer blether. You'll do as I say and I'll have you safely out of there, you ken?"

Her eyes locked on his and she nodded, meekly enough, she hoped. There would be plenty of time later to discuss that attitude of his. Right now she'd simply trust that he could do what he said.

"Verra well. When I lift you"—he paused briefly, as if testing whether or not she might interrupt again— "you'll push up with all yer strength. Ready?"

At her nod, he rose slowly to his feet. She ignored the cracking sounds around her, keeping her gaze focused on his face.

"That's it, lass. Yer doing fine," he murmured a second before he leaped past, grabbing her under her armpits and lifting up.

It felt almost like an amusement park ride as she flew up into his arms. He pushed off with his legs, sending them into the air as the wood that had been under her seconds before fractured and crashed to the ground below.

She hooked her arms around his neck as the force of his leap propelled them across the corner of the landing and through the old castle's dark, gaping doorway. They hit the stone floor with a mighty thud, knocking Ellie's breath from her lungs even though Caden had managed to cushion her fall, once again, with his own body.

A body she now lay gratefully huddled into, his powerful arms holding her tightly to him. A strong, solid, all-male body that made her feel small and feminine and fluttery and—

"By the Fates," Caden groaned. "I dinna believe I'd care to go through that again anytime soon."

His words drew her up short. What was wrong with her? She was having the most bizarre twenty-four hours of her life and yet she could lie here mooning over some guy just because he had a velvet voice and big biceps?

"Yeah. Exactly. Me either."

But she didn't lift her head from his shoulder and he made no move to dislodge her.

At least, not until he roared, "Rat!" and rolled her protectively under his body, curling around her, encasing her in his embrace.

With Caden's warm breath feathering over the top of her head, Ellie was almost tempted to change all her prior negative opinions about rats. How could anything be all bad if its mere presence resulted in this? Though with her nose jammed into the wall of muscle that passed for Caden's chest, she was finding that breathing had become a challenge.

She managed to shift her head just enough to find a spot where she could get some air, but the tiny opening she'd located was quickly filled with a small, furry head. A light, warm breath feathered over her face. Followed by a small, warm tongue.

"No rat. Big One stupid."

The deliverer of all the earlier warnings had arrived.

"It's not a rat." Ellie's muffled voice reached Caden's ears as her hands slid up his chest.

"Looked like a rat to me," he muttered, scanning the area around them in the musty gloom, hunting for any sign of the creature that had darted past his face as he tried to ignore the feeling of her hands moving over his body.

"Well, it's not, trust me."

The sigh that followed her words was deep, the heat of her breath penetrating his shirt, seeming to crawl inside his chest, sparking awareness of her throughout his body. The cushion of her hip fit perfectly under the leg he'd thrown over her, the soft, silky texture of her hair rubbed against his chin, and her small, delicate hands burned into his chest as she pushed harder. . . .

"Maybe you could get off me now? I'm suffocating here."

Sensibility returned in a rush and Caden jerked away from her. "My apologies. I d-dinna mean to . . ." He stuttered to a stop. "I was only thinking to protect you from the rat." He stood, straightening his plaid to busy his hands. What the devil was wrong with him?

"I already told you it's not a rat. And she doesn't appreciate your calling her that one little bit."

He looked down to find Ellie sitting up, cuddling some small, mangy, furry thing.

"She doesn't appreciate . . . What in the name of the Fae *is* that thing?"

"It's a dog, of course." Ellie shook her head. "Poor little thing is half starved, abandoned out here."

"Well, put the wee beastie down and come along." He walked to the door and gazed out over the landing and the fractured staircase beyond. There would be no going back that way.

"No can do, big fella. This little lady saved my neck out there. I'm bringing her with us."

"What nonsense is this?" The woman collected pathetic creatures like most women collected jewels.

Her only response was a groan that had him at her side in an instant. He very nearly groaned himself as she pulled her skirt above her knees, baring two very shapely legs.

"Now what are you . . ." he bit back any further comment when he saw the streak of deep red trailing down the back of one of those lovely appendages. "Yer bleeding."

"Yep. It's not bad, really. But I bet I'll have one beauty of a bruise there tomorrow."

She looked around as if hunting for something before using the tail of her dress to wipe along the cut. The long jagged tear oozed red once again, forming little drip lines.

A stomach-wrenching blow of guilt rolled through him. His fault.

Her beautiful skin was torn and bleeding and it was all his fault. He and Andrew had been to Sithean Fardach just last summer. He had seen the damage to the stairway then. Drew had even warned him there could be a danger. He should have done something then. He could have sent someone over from Dun Ard to replace the rotted timbers. He should have stopped her from running up the stairs.

Too late now.

He hadn't listened to his brother last summer just like he hadn't listened to him nine years ago about Alycie. He'd never learn. And now another woman had paid the price of his refusal to hear a warning.

"Let's get you back to Dun Ard. My mother will have salves to help with yer healing." He leaned over and swept her up into his arms. Carrying her seemed the least he could do.

She threw one arm around his neck, but held on to the ragged bundle in her lap with the other.

"Yer no going to leave the little vermin behind, are you?"

She shook her head, a smile lighting her eyes as she tightened her hold on the creature. "Nope. And she's not too fond of your calling her names, either."

Caden stepped over a pile of rubble as he made his way down the hallway toward the kitchen. "And I suppose you ken that because the hairy rat there told you, did she?"

"Exactly right," she responded, and then laughed.

The sound echoed off the high stone walls like music played by a traveling minstrel, stopping Caden in his tracks. It was the first time he'd heard her laugh, the first time he'd seen the beauty of happiness reflected in her face.

Laughter was the music of life to Caden. There had been a time when he sought its melody in everything he did. But that had all changed nine years ago.

Now he stood in the crumbling shell of his childhood home holding a woman in his arms whose laughter soothed that part of his soul he'd feared lost.

If his mother was correct and this woman was here to be wife to one of his brothers, all he could think was that one of them had damn well better lay claim to her quickly.

Seven

"You're afraid of rats!"

The idea hit Ellie like an epiphany as she rode by Caden's side back to Dun Ard. She blurted it out without thinking.

"I am no afraid of anything so small as that," he bristled.

She chuckled and instantly regretted doing so as he visibly stiffened.

"I wasn't trying to insult you. It's just that your being frightened by a rat is so out of character with that first impression I had of you. Honestly, I wasn't laughing at you. I was just surprised that you're not what I thought you were."

"I was no afraid," he muttered through gritted teeth, looking off to the distance, scanning the rough terrain ahead of them. "But they're dirty buggers at best and I dinna fancy the idea of one crawling upon you."

Ellie ducked her head, working hard to hold back a smile. Of course he wouldn't admit to being afraid of anything. And yet it was so endearing somehow. This huge, muscled man, who had risked his life to rescue her on the stairs, bothered by a little animal. It showed a soft side. A side she should have recognized from the way he carried her through the castle in spite of her protests. Or from the way he tore off a piece of his shirt to dab at the long scrape she'd received from her encounter with the rotted stair before gently wrapping the cloth around her leg from knee to ankle.

"What did you say?" she asked as he continued to mutter under his breath.

"Only that trying to keep you from dirty creatures is a wasted effort as long as you continue to collect them." He pointed to the small dog in her lap.

Obviously his feelings were still hurt by her accusation, so she only shrugged. No point being drawn into an argument over something she felt needed no apology. The warning she'd received from the bedraggled bundle of terrier in her lap had saved her from going over the side of the landing with that rail. She'd even told him as much. And though she was sure he didn't believe her, just admitting it out loud had made her feel wonderfully happy, like a confirmation to the world she wasn't going insane.

"Next thing, you'll be naming the beasts," he continued, as if warming to the subject.

"I already have."

He pulled his horse to a stop, turning to stare at her, his disbelief evident.

"The big boy here is Baby, because he truly is a pitiful

baby who's been badly treated. And this"—she stroked her hand down the matted fur of the little dog in her lap—"this is Missy, because she believes herself to be a fiery, dominant mistress of dogs. What do you think?" She intentionally flashed him her best smile.

"Baby and . . . I dinna even ken where to start with what I think. I've no ever met a woman with such a wild imagination as to—"

"Caden! Caden!"

Whatever else he might have said was lost as his attention was drawn to the rider who quickly closed the distance between them, yelling his name.

"Steafan! What are you doing out here?"

"Yer lady mother sent me to find you. Yer brother has returned home."

"Colin's home?" Caden straightened in his saddle.

"No, more's the pity, and still no word. It's Andrew who's come home. And he's brought yer sister and the whole of the MacPhersons with him, it seems."

"I see. We've been invaded, then."

"Invaded?" Ellie repeated, pulling her horse up even with Caden's. If this was indeed the fourteenth century as it certainly seemed to be, invasion was a horrible reality, with people you might have considered family taking over your home and lands.

No sooner had the thought entered her mind than it lodged in the back of her throat, thick and heavy, bringing with it the vision of Ray standing on her front porch, gloating.

The little dog in her lap growled and she cuddled the animal to her absently, lost for the moment in her memories. If her recent experience was any indicator, the threat of someone taking one's home and lands hadn't ended with the fourteenth century.

"Dinna fash yerself so, lass. It's no a need for concern. Only the MacPhersons come to call."

Ellie nodded, still unable to speak past the lump that formed at the memory of her troubles. Allowing her horse to drop back behind those of the men, she ignored their quiet conversation to pursue her own thoughts.

She no longer doubted that she wasn't in the twenty-first century any longer. That was pretty clear. There was nothing—nothing!—even remotely indicative of her century. No air traffic overhead, no wires or plumbing or pipes. Not a stray piece of plastic or a single aluminum can on the ground. Not so much as a cigarette butt. On her ranch back home, even acres from where anyone ever traveled except her, bits and pieces of modern man's debris would show up, blown there by the wind.

But not here.

And there was certainly no question about this not being Texas.

How something so absolutely impossible had come about was beyond her ability to imagine. Her only hope was to accept it. Trying to understand it would drive her crazy, so she wasn't going to go there. Just accept.

Until she could find her way home.

Caden rode next to Steafan, unable to concentrate on his friend's chatter, his attention drawn instead to the woman accompanying them. A glance back assured him she followed still, though she appeared immersed in her own thoughts, her expression troubled and far away.

With a shake of his head, he resisted the inclination to turn his mount and pull back to ride next to her.

This unusual need he felt to hover over her, to see what she would do, what she would say next, surprised him. It was so unlike him to have more than the most fleeting interest in any woman.

He'd learned his lesson with Alycie. Women were not to be trusted. After her betrayal, he'd decided then and there to pattern his life after his cousin Blane's. He would never marry. He had no need for a woman to be happy. He had Dun Ard and her people. That would be enough for him. He would choose one of his brothers' sons to be his heir, just as Blane had chosen him.

No, women were trouble best left to someone else.

So why did this particular woman weigh so heavily in his mind?

He turned his head to check on her once more.

Guilt, in all likelihood, drove his interest. He had failed in his responsibility to protect her today. He'd been lax in not recognizing a potential danger, and that sloppiness on his part had brought her injury. His choices had resulted in near tragedy for someone he was supposed to be protecting. He'd failed her. As he had failed others who'd depended on him in the past.

All the more reason he'd never marry.

"Are you no listening, Cade? I need yer answer."

Caden jerked his attention back to his friend. "What?"

Steafan sighed before answering. "Yer mind went wandering, did it?"

"My apologies, my friend."

In truth, Steafan Maxwell was more like a brother

than a friend. He'd been apprenticed to Dun Ard when both of them were but boys. And being of an age, they'd bonded immediately. Caden was eternally thankful that not even the problems with Alycie, Steafan's sister, had ruined their friendship, for he couldn't imagine the future at Dun Ard without Steafan at his right hand.

"I'm no surprised. No with all you've had to fash yerself over. I dinna want to add to yer problems, Cade, and I ken I've only just returned from Inverness, but I've a need to fetch my mother to Dun Ard. I dinna want to think of her waiting on the farm all alone for word of Dair and Colin."

Caden nodded. He should have considered that himself. "When do you plan to leave?"

"I've sent word to my mother to be ready. I'd like to leave the end of the week." Steafan's eyes shifted away and then back. "If I have yer permission, that is."

Caden nodded,

"Of course you have it."

No mother should wait alone for word of her son's death.

Shaking off her gloomy thoughts, Ellie realized she'd ridden the whole distance back to Dun Ard without speaking. Though Caden had been quiet for most of their earlier trip, she had felt somehow connected to him, as if he maintained the silence to give her time to sort through her situation.

The ride back was different. Once Caden's friend had joined them, the two of them had ignored her completely.

But that was just fine, she reminded herself irritably. It didn't matter at all that Caden would choose his friend's company over hers. Besides, she'd needed the time to adjust before facing whatever was to come.

As they approached the gate, Steafan kicked his mount, racing ahead, while Caden slowed his pace, allowing Ellie time to draw even with him.

Glancing up at his face, she was surprised to find he appeared more tense and withdrawn than he had for the entire day they'd spent together.

And considering their day, that was saying something.

They rode through the long tunnel in the wall that Caden referred to as a gate, coming out into a flurry of activity in the courtyard. When they'd left here earlier, there had been only a few people around. Now there were horses and men everywhere.

Caden drew his mount close to hers, guiding them toward the great stairs. She didn't miss the fact that he maneuvered them so that he was a barrier between her and the bulk of the activity.

The man waiting at the foot of the stairs for them had to be the brother Steafan had mentioned. He leaned against the great stone wall, one foot propped up on the stairs, looking far more relaxed than Caden had since she'd known him. Still, the resemblance between the two men was striking.

Caden dismounted and reached his hand up to Ellie. She assumed he meant to help her down, but instead he swept her into his arms, carrying her as if she weighed nothing at all.

He stopped briefly at the foot of the stairs, meeting the smiling gaze of his brother. "No word of Colin?"

The smile disappeared as the other man shook his

head. "But it's no been so verra long, Caden. Dinna be thinking the worst yet. Give Blane time."

"I suppose yer right. Where's Mother?"

"Fussing after Sallie in her rooms, I'd guess." The dazzling smile returned. "And this must be our guest? Can she no walk under her own power? Or have you another reason for carrying her about?"

"She's hurt," Caden growled, pushing past his brother and marching up the stairs.

"It's not all that bad," Ellie protested, though no one seemed the least bit interested in what she had to say.

The great door opened just before they reached the landing and the man standing there scrambled out of their way as Caden barged through.

"Lady Rosalyn!" he yelled, heading down the hall and starting up the next set of stairs.

"No, seriously, I hardly feel it now."

"Yer cold, yer tired and yer hurt. It'd be no surprise that you'd lose feeling in the leg. We'll have it taken care of in a moment. Quiet yerself now." He reached the top of the stairs and strode down the long hallway. "Mother!" he roared, even louder than before.

Rosalyn appeared in a doorway at the end of the hall. "What in the name of the Fates are you carrying on about?" Her eyes widened when she saw Ellie in his arms.

"What's happened?"

Caden followed his mother down the hall to Ellie's room, gently depositing his charge in the middle of her bed while his mother hurried off to collect her healing basket.

Rosalyn had been quite clear as to what was expected of him today. Take the girl down to the village. Let her see it to help her accept where she was. But had he been content to do that simple task as it was given him? Oh no. Not him.

He didn't trust the lass. Didn't want to be embarrassed by her or have to explain who she was if they came upon someone. So what had he done? He'd taken her to the decrepit remains of his childhood home and exposed her to serious injury.

Now look at the poor wee thing, sitting in the bed, hurt, waiting bravely for her wound to be tended.

His plan when he'd entered her room had been to make a quick escape, but she'd grasped his hand as he put her down and hadn't let go.

With her other hand she still held tightly to the filthy bundle of dog she'd carried all the way from Sithean Fardach.

He'd never seen a woman so concerned with the welfare of all the creatures she touched. Someone with that kind of compassion couldn't possibly be a threat to his family.

And yet . . . she was a woman, and he'd learned all too well not to assume he knew what was going on in a female's mind based upon her behavior.

Besides, she'd been sent there by the Fae, who always had their own reasons for what they did. He wouldn't forget that, wouldn't be caught unawares this time.

A high-pitched screech from the doorway jerked him from his thoughts.

Anabella MacPherson, the mother of his sister's husband, stood dramatically poised to enter the room, one hand over her heart, the other pointing at their wounded guest.

"What *is* that?" Anabella advanced on the bed, her eyes narrowing as she neared. "A nasty wee beastie? What are you thinking to bring that vile creature in here?"

"I . . . I rescued her." Ellie's grasp on his hand tightened as she looked up at him, confusion bright in her eyes.

From the dog's whimper, Caden assumed her hold on it had tightened as well.

"Leave her alone, Anabella." His sister entered the room, her swollen stomach and rolling walk reminding him of one of the ducks that waddled around their pond in the spring.

"But look there, Sallie. She's a dirty creature in her lap. I'll be having no filthy animals in the keep where my own grandchild will at any moment be making his appearance in the world." The woman nodded her head vigorously.

"*Her* appearance," Sallie corrected, herding the woman from the room. "And I'll be sure yer given plenty of notice as to when *she* will be putting in an appearance, but it's no going to be in the next few minutes. Now come along." She rolled her eyes as she disappeared through the doorway.

"My sister. The great round one, that is," he explained for Ellie's benefit since she still watched him. "No the old one. That's her husband Ranald's mother." He wrinkled his nose in distaste, feeling a need to put Ellie at ease.

How Sallie had put up with Anabella all these years was beyond him. They argued constantly, yet seemed the best of friends. It baffled him.

Ellie's nervous stare turned to a grin, but that was wiped away at the sound of a scream, followed by Anabella's voice shrilling down the hallway.

"We're surrounded by filthy beasts!"

Ellie tilted her head to the side as if listening before turning an apologetic smile his way. "It's Baby. He's looking for me because he's worried."

"Mother says this great beast is hunting for you." Andrew entered the room, Baby at his heels.

"Where is Lady Rosalyn?" This was taking forever. Who knew what kind of pain the lass endured while people paraded in and out.

"Here I am." Rosalyn hurried into the room, her healing basket on her arm. "Move," she ordered the huge dog, giving him a shove as she moved toward her patient.

He ambled around to the opposite side of the bed, laying his head on the mattress, staring at Ellie, a forlorn expression on his huge face.

"Now," Rosalyn began, sitting down beside Ellie, "let's see what kind of damage we have."

"I don't think it's all that bad. And Caden bandaged it really well before we left the old castle." Ellie let go of his hand and the dog in her lap to grasp her skirts and lift them up to midthigh, unself-consciously baring the injured calf.

And a bit more.

Caden's breath caught, as it had at Sithean Fardach when she'd done the same to allow him to bind her wound. The smooth expanse of soft white skin mesmerized him, called to him so that he had to grip the post on the bed to keep himself from reaching out to stroke it.

"Aye. Quite a thorough bandaging, I'd say." Drew's eyes sparkled with mischief before they returned to Ellie's uncovered legs.

"Andrew. Out!" Caden had no intention of allowing his brother to stand about ogling the woman. It might well be that she was Andrew's intended but she could just as easily be here for Colin. No, it was best to keep his brother in his proper place for now.

"I've no a need for either of you. Both of you, out." Rosalyn dismissed them with a wave of her hand.

"You'll be fine now," Caden assured Ellie as he hesitated at her bedside, oddly reluctant to leave her.

"I know. I am fine." She nodded and smiled at him as she reached over to scratch Baby's head. "Really. You don't need to worry about me."

Worry? He wasn't worried about her. It was simply his responsibility to see to it that she was tended. After all, it was his fault she was injured in the first place.

"Go," his mother ordered, leaving him no alternative.

He and Drew eyed one another in the hallway before his brother grinned and threw an arm around his shoulder.

"Come on. What say we go down to Cousin Blane's solar and inspect the laird's ale in his absence?"

"No, Drew," Caden countered. "It's been a torturous day. I say we inspect his whisky instead."

He could use a good stiff draught.

"It's no so bad." Rosalyn looked up from examining the wound on Ellie's leg. "Though I'd expect it to be tender for the next few days."

Ellie nodded her agreement. "That's what I thought. Mostly just scraped it up when I went through the stairs."

"Was it worth it? Are you convinced of where you are?"

Ellie studied the top of Rosalyn's head bent over her work as she decided how to answer. These appeared to be good people, giving her no reason to doubt them.

"I guess so. I believe I'm where you say I am. But for the life of me, I don't know if I'll ever be able to accept how it happened or the who-did-it part."

Rosalyn's fingers stilled in their work and she glanced up thoughtfully. "It's more than likely that *you* are the one who did it. You've the power of the Fae in that mark on yer breast, lass."

That damn red mark again, creating havoc in her life since the morning she'd first found it.

She'd awoken drenched in perspiration after a fitful sleep, as she had for the whole week since Nora's accident. Only on this particular morning, her breast, right over her heart, felt so odd—warm and tingly, like tiny feathers dusted across it without cease.

Pressing against the spot with her hand had no effect as she stumbled to the bathroom and tugged her T-shirt off over her head to stare in the mirror at the most frightening thing she'd ever seen.

The beginnings of the mark were already there and continuing to pop out on her skin as if some invisible hand drew it as she watched. There was no pain, more like feeling tiny butterfly wings brushing over her skin. The tingle traveled up to her head, to the very roots of her hair and out to the tips of her fingers, growing, pulsing, heating her skin. The sensations overwhelmed her, continuing to build and swirl around and through her.

She had grabbed on to the edge of the sink to steady herself and she felt the sensations center in her chest, where the mark continued to grow, burning and expanding until, with one final burst of power, there was nothing.

When it finished, a deep red imprint stained her breast, looking so much like a rose she'd stood breathless, exhilarated, weak, wondering for a moment if in her grief she'd lost her mind.

I grant you all you ask. And more.

The words, musical and masculine, had echoed through her mind, reinforcing her fear.

"Would you tell me about the mark. Please?"

Rosalyn stopped her ministrations and, shifting her position on the bed, tilted her head. "You've honestly no idea what it is, do you?"

Ellie shook her head and shrugged. "I woke up a month ago and there it was. At first I thought I was crazy. Then I thought it was some horrible disease that was going to be the death of me."

The older woman smiled and patted Ellie's thigh reassuringly. "It's more likely to be the life of you."

"How could I have done this? I mean, I know you say I have power in this mark, but how?"

Rosalyn went back to work on Ellie's leg, smoothing a salve over the wound. "Tell me the last thing you remember before you found yerself here. What you were doing, anything you might have said."

"Well, I was sitting under a tree, down by the river

that runs through our back pasture. I was . . ." Ellie hesitated, not wanting to spread out all her problems for this woman. "I was thinking about some things I needed to deal with, watching a storm on the horizon. Then lightning hit me. That's pretty much all there was."

"Was it now? There would have been words you spoke, I'm thinking. I'll need to hear them to help you find yer way home again."

"Words?" Ellie felt a flush heat her face as she remembered what she'd said aloud just before the lightning hit her. "I was . . . this is going to sound so stupid. I was just sort of wishing to find a man." How humiliating.

"Any man or one in particular? The exact words will make a difference in what we need to do."

Ellie took a deep breath and blew it out. What the heck? As embarrassing as it felt, Rosalyn didn't seem to be making any judgments, just seeking facts.

"I wished to find the one man who's meant for me, wherever he is." She knew she mumbled the words, but sharing something so private made her feel like she was a small child caught with her hand in her grandmama's bear-shaped cookie jar.

"Ah-ha!" Rosalyn looked up, a twinkle in her eye. "Now we have something to work with, lass. There you are, all tidied up." She patted Ellie's knee and stood, gathering all her bandages and pots, putting them back in the large basket sitting beside the bed. "You've had quite the day. I'd think it best for you to rest now. I'll send one of the lasses up with some nice herb tea and a bite for you and yer beasties to eat. Would you like that?"

"But what does it all mean? What do I have to do to get home?" She'd humiliated herself by giving the woman the exact words. The words that made her sound like some pathetic, love-starved teenager. The least she deserved was some answers.

Rosalyn paused, her hand on the door. "It's verra simple, lass. You've come to find yer true love. Once you do, you'll be able to go home." She smiled and walked out the door.

"Wait!"

The older woman poked her head back in the door. "Aye?"

"That's it? I just find this *true love* and then that's it, I go home? I don't actually get to keep him? I mean, if it's my true love or whatever, shouldn't I be spending the rest of my life with him?" How wrong would that be? Not that she really, actually wanted a man of her own.

"Did you ask to spend the rest of yer life with him? Or just to find him? Power lies in the words. What words you speak determines the outcome."

"Okay, then, when I find him, I'll just ask to keep him." She grinned at her hostess. How hard could this Faerie stuff be?

"I'm sorry, lass. The power disna work that way. You set the terms when you invoked the magic." Rosalyn shut the door behind her.

It wasn't bad enough she'd apparently wished herself into some other time to find the one man meant for her. Oh no. In true Ellie Denton style, she'd set it up so she'd just get to meet the man. Just see what she'd be missing out on her whole life. And then *poof*, gone.

Ellie turned on her side and cuddled the warm little

dog in her arms, ignoring the tears rolling down her cheeks.

Classic. Just get to see your heart's desire. Just get to touch it and then it's gone. Well, if that wasn't just the story of her whole life.

Crap.

"Mother?"

Rosalyn halted her steps toward the back of the keep, turning at the sound of her oldest son's voice.

"Aye?"

"Ellie, is she . . ." Caden stopped and rubbed a hand over his face. "Will the wound leave a scar?"

"No. You should have listened to the lass. It's no a bad injury at all."

Caden sighed and straightened his shoulders, looking as if a great weight had been removed from them. "Good. That's good."

Rosalyn patted her son's arm and turned to go, stopping as another thought occurred to her.

"I was right, by the way. About why she's here."

"Yer sure, then? She's to wed Colin or Andrew? Can you say which?"

"Och, Caden." Rosalyn clicked her tongue and smiled as she closed the distance between them, tugging at her tall son's shoulder to place a kiss on his cheek. "You of all people should ken the ways of the magic better than that. No even a full-blood Fae would be able to answer that question. I can only say she's been sent to find her true love, and my heart tells me that man is a MacAlister."

He shrugged and nodded, almost as if to himself.

"Either way, it's good news. They both deserve their happiness."

"But Caden MacAlister deserves none of his own, is that the right of it?"

In response his jaw tightened, the muscles clenching in the stubborn sign so familiar to her. There would be no discussing anything with him now.

"We've no secrets between us, Mother. You ken as well as I why I've made the choices I have. It's for the good of the family, the good of Dun Ard. I've no a single doubt it's what fate intended for me."

"You canna carry the weight of the world on yer shoulders forever, lad." They'd had this same argument so many times.

"It's no the world, Mother, only my own wee piece of it." He kissed the top of her head and disappeared back into Blane's solar.

Poor Caden. He wrapped his burden of guilt around himself like the plaid he wore. In truth, that burden should be hers, not her son's. After Duncan's death she should have been stronger, but she hadn't been. She'd placed too much responsibility on the shoulders of her eldest child. A lad of ten should be carefree, not burdened with a mother consumed by grief.

The betrothal to Alycie was her doing, too. And though Caden blamed himself for not recognizing Alycie's unhappiness, she was the one in day-to-day contact with the girl. She more than her son should bear the responsibility for not having seen the girl's desperation and all that came after.

"What's done is done. There's no good to come of dwelling on the past."

Shaking her head, she turned and headed down the hall. Of all her sons, Caden was most like his father. He held himself responsible for everyone. And though he believed in the magic of the Fae, he saw only the risks, not the rewards, of his heritage.

Perhaps the future would alter that perception.

Rosalyn slipped out the door of the keep and into the dark, her feet sure in their destination.

In spite of her troubles, a chuckle bubbled to her lips as she strolled through the evening into her garden. She pulled her plaid tightly about her shoulders to ward off the chill and made her way to her favorite little wooden bench. The one she had brought with her from the garden at Sithean Fardach when she had moved here all those years ago.

Sitting down, she followed her normal ritual, running her fingers over the smooth letters carved into the underside of the wood. She had no need to see them; she knew them by heart.

For my beloved.

The seat Duncan had built for her with his own two hands.

"Have you been watching, my love?" she whispered to the stars. "I kenned she was the one from the first moment I laid eyes upon her. And I was right."

She closed her eyes and imagined her beloved Duncan by her side as she did each night, confiding in him as she always had. A short talk each evening, sharing the problems and joys of the day. Lately there had been so many worries to share. Now, at last, something good.

"They're yer sons for a fact, Duncan MacAlister, refusing to love, needing to be pushed into it, each and every one of them. And they're fair testing my patience and my promise to you not to interfere in their lives with my magic." She rose to her feet, brushing her fingertips to her lips and sending a kiss to the heavens. "I remember. A promise is a promise. Good night for now, my love."

She walked a few steps toward the keep and stopped, once again turning her face up to the stars. "But they're my sons, too, with the blood of the Fae running through their bodies. And a true Fae deserves true love."

And thanks to the bonnie dark-haired lass upstairs, one of them would have it. Best of all, *she* hadn't had to break her promise to Duncan by touching her own gift of magic to make it happen.

Now if the Fae could only see their way clear to bringing the missing men of her family home safely, she would be one very thankful woman indeed.

Eight

"*I* demand to see my cousin at once."

Blane MacKiernan straightened to his full height as he spoke, rubbing the wrists that had only now been cut free of their binding by the guards who stood on either side of him. He wouldn't allow his enemies to see him as weak, regardless of his position.

The men behind the table on the dais laughed and banged their tankards against the wood, quieting only when one rose to his feet. He was a tall, lanky man, dressed in the fine clothing of a lord. His expression of contempt was as visible as the graying beard he wore trimmed to a point. This would be the man who held Colin hostage awaiting payment of the ransom.

Austyn Wodeford.

As they had neared Wode Castle, Blane and the three men who traveled with him had been surrounded by a party of twenty armed warriors. He had held his men in check under the assumption they would be escorted to this man, where they would hand over the ransom and collect Colin.

They'd been escorted, all right. After having their weapons taken and their hands bound behind them. Blane hadn't seen his men since they'd entered the bailey.

"I dinna believe yer in any position to be making demands, MacKiernan. If I were you—"

"If you were me," Blane interrupted, "you'd no have been dragged into the great hall of my home with yer hands bound. It's a gentlemen's agreement I'm here to settle."

Wodeford laughed and the others joined in, once again quieting when he picked up his tankard and loudly banged it to the massive table.

"There's nothing gentlemanly about our meeting, MacKiernan. The king has given us the right to hold for ransom any who fought against him in lieu of taking their lives. It's purely business to me."

"Business, is it? I've come to pay yer damned ransom in exchange for my cousin's freedom. And yet you take the men who ride with me. Bind me to bring me to yer hall. Is this the way you conduct business at Wode Castle? You and yer *king*."

Wodeford grabbed up a small sack that lay on the table in front of him. A sack Blane recognized.

The silver he had brought to pay for Colin's release.

"Is it this you refer to as a ransom?" Wodeford asked as he moved close. "This paltry bit of silver you carried with you? I'm doubting King Edward would consider this sufficient to release a man who had taken the lives of his own soldiers."

"It's exactly what you asked for." Blane stared into the eyes of his captor. He knew he walked a fine line.

"Aye, so it is. But that was before the Laird of the MacKiernan himself came down from the hills to deliver it. I'm thinking yer return to yer family is worth easily twice as much."

Blane reined in his instincts to strike out. It would do his cousin no good.

"Has yer *king* approved kidnapping as well, you greedy bastard?"

In answer Wodeford swung, the full strength of his hand and the weight of the coins he held connecting to the side of Blane's head.

The blow sent Blane reeling and he stumbled to one knee, his head bowed with the pain shooting through his entire face. He would not fall to the ground, would not lose consciousness, would not give his adversary the satisfaction.

Through the ringing in his ears, he clearly heard a gasp, and an instant later, a soft cloth wiped across his face. He looked up to find himself staring into the most beautiful brown eyes he had ever imagined.

"Catriona! What do you think yer doing? You've no business in the hall. Get out of here." Though Wodeford's voice did not rise, there was no mistaking the menace there.

"You've hurt him, Austyn. There's no a need for that. The man's the MacKiernan laird. You've no a right to treat him so."

Catriona knelt next to him, one delicate hand lying

on the back of his neck. He watched her—a woman, not a girl—her soft brown hair liberally laced with gray. Beauty in her spirit as well as in her face.

"Right?" Wodeford ground out between clenched teeth. "Dinna forget yer place, Sister, or you'll be feeling the back of my hand as well. Now get out of my hall!" He grabbed her arm and jerked her to her feet, shoving her away from them as he spoke.

She stumbled, stopping as if she might say something else.

"Go!" he thundered, and she ran, disappearing through the entryway.

"I demand to see my cousin," Blane insisted again, though this time the words sounded garbled as they passed over his already swelling lips.

"And so you shall," Wodeford answered quietly before breaking into laughter.

Nine

*W*ake up!

The urgent voice in Ellie's head dragged her from her dream to the waking world. A magnificent dream it had been, too.

She stretched and scratched the back of her neck. Not that she could remember the exact details of the dream, but she had that warm, fuzzy-world feeling that was left when she was hauled from a really good dream.

Ellie searched her memory as she rolled over and pulled the covers tighter around her, letting go long enough to scratch the top of her head absently. There had been a man, and he'd held her close. She remembered that much. And he had smelled so good. Like leather and lavender and—

Forget Big One. Open door.

"I was not dreaming of *him*," she denied. Why she even bothered to argue with the voices in her mind was beyond her. She pulled the covers over her head, blocking out the early morning light.

But not the voice.

Now!

If the urgency of the command hadn't gotten her to open her eyes, the whimper that accompanied it would have.

Both dogs sat at the closed door, staring back at her. *Hurry!*

"Oh, crap! I bet you need out." She jumped from the bed and threw open the door.

The dogs raced off down the hallway, and only after they'd disappeared down the stairs did it strike her that the big entryway door would be closed as well. After last night's scene with that old woman and the dogs, Ellie didn't even want to contemplate what might happen if they did their business right at the front door.

The heavy woolen nightgown she wore tangled around her legs as she started after them, causing her to stumble and bang her shoulder into the hard stone wall.

Damn long skirts.

She lifted the gown above her knees and hooked the tail over her arm, freeing herself to run after the animals.

Sprinting down the curve of the stairs, she was quite proud of herself that she managed not to slip on the narrow stone steps. Gaining speed as she ran, she jumped from the next-to-the-bottom stair and smashed into what felt like a wall.

A hard, warm wall of chest that barely moved in response to her slamming into it.

"Hold on, lass. What's got after you to have you leaping from the stairs?" Andrew grasped her upper arms to keep her from falling.

"Sorry about that. I have to get the front door open." She attempted to pull away but he wasn't letting go.

"And why would you need to do that so early in the morn? Yer no thinking of leaving us, are you?" Andrew's brow wrinkled, his confusion evident.

"I wasn't trying to leave. Baby and Missy have to *go*." Surely he didn't need *that* explained.

"What in the name of the Fae is going on here?"

Caden's roar echoed down the hallway, causing Ellie to jump.

"Who are Baby and Missy?"

Andrew's question barely registered as Ellie's attention centered on Caden's approach. He looked angry. And the look was aimed squarely at her.

"That's what she calls the herd of beasts she's collecting," Caden answered as he reached them. "The ones that tried to knock us down as we came in the doorway."

"Oh good. They're out." What a relief she didn't have to worry about that little problem right now.

"Drew! Unhand the woman and quit yer gawking," Caden ordered.

Her arm freed, Ellie stepped back, relieved to have Caden's ire directed at his brother rather than her.

The relief didn't last long.

"And what do you think yer doing? Did you no show enough of yerself to all in the keep last eve? Where else might you be planning to go like that?" Caden pointed toward the floor at her feet, but his eyes didn't leave hers.

"Like what? Oh." Ellie unwound the tail of her nightgown from around her arm, allowing it to curtain down to the floor. "Sorry." So her legs were showing. So what? Lord, but this guy was easily offended.

"What were you thinking, walking around like that?"

Obviously she hadn't been thinking, but she wasn't about to admit that. Not to him anyway. "I said I was sorry. I needed to get the dogs out and I couldn't run without breaking my neck with this stupid thing wrapping around my legs." She waved her hand in the general direction of the bottom of her nightgown.

Good grief. The man was getting all bent out of shape about her flashing a little leg. She shoved her sleeve up, scratching at her arm. "I don't see what the big deal is."

"The big deal?" Caden sputtered. "You'll no go about exposing yerself like that again. Do you hear me? And what are you doing there?" He wiggled his finger her direction, pointing once again.

"First of all, you don't get to tell me what to do. Second of all . . ."

"Looks to be bites," Andrew interrupted calmly. "Fleas would be my guess."

Caden grabbed her arm, inspecting the spot she had scratched.

"Fleas?" For an instant, her brain refused to comprehend the obvious.

Oh, Lord, no! Sure enough, there were three little red bumps on her arm, itching like crazy. More on the back of her neck. Her legs itched, too. In fact, it suddenly seemed as if there was no part of her body where she couldn't feel the irritating movement of tiny, disgusting little insects.

"I'd say yer Baby and Missy brought guests along." Andrew's broad grin made it clear he saw no need to hide his amusement at her predicament.

Caden shook his head, tightening his hold on her arm. "I'd best show you to the bathhouse."

She stilled. "Bathhouse?"

Now *that* sounded promising enough to ignore Drew's laughter as Caden led her down the hallway toward the back of the keep, dragging her behind him like an errant child.

Not bad.

Ellie sank into the wooden tub and submerged her sore shoulder under the hot water.

Caden had left her here earlier, after filling the tub for her and pointing out how the bathhouse worked.

The whole thing was actually pretty ingenious. Part of the building was nothing more than a roof and walls over a small stream. It reminded Ellie of the New England covered bridges she'd seen in photos, only with a grate replacing the bridge part.

The other side of the bathhouse was a simple room divided into two areas by a rock wall that stood at least as tall as Ellie. On either side of the rock partition sat a large wooden bathing tub.

The building itself was set up off the ground with wooden slats for the floor. Water could be drained out of the tubs onto the rocks below and flow down the side of the mountain.

A massive stone fireplace was centered between the

two areas, allowing water from the stream to be easily dipped into the huge cauldrons hanging over the fire and heated for the bathing tubs. The fire also provided some heat to the bathing area.

The tubs themselves, although wooden, were easily as large as the old claw-footed tub in her bathroom back home, though deeper.

Not bad at all.

Other than the idea that more than one person at a time might be in here bathing.

She dunked her head under the water once more, wiping at her eyes as she broke the surface.

"You'll do better with some of this soap."

Ellie jerked forward, sloshing water over the edges of the tub as she pulled her body up against the edge.

The old woman standing in the doorway put her hand to her mouth to cover a smile. "My apologies, milady. I dinna mean to startle you."

Apparently the "kitchen lass" Caden had mentioned he would send out had arrived, though she was by no means a girl.

"Soap?" Ellie held out one hand, continuing to lean her body up against the side of the tub. She didn't consider herself a prude, but she wasn't particularly comfortable having this strange woman see her completely naked.

"Aye. It's a special blend the lady Rosalyn makes to help rid us of the wee vermin." The woman ignored Ellie's hand as she approached, rounding to the back side of the tub. "Come this direction and let Bridey help you with yer lovely hair."

"I don't want to be a bother, ma'am. I can just . . ."

"Yer no a bother to Bridey." The maid lifted Ellie's hair and began to rub the soap into it. "It's a fact I'd rather do this than feed the fires for the ovens." She chuckled to herself as she continued to massage the soap into Ellie's hair.

"You're Bridey?"

"That I am, good lady. Cook to the house of Mac-Kiernan these last twenty-odd years, I am. But when Master Caden comes a-stormin' into my kitchen and tells me he needs a helper to go down to the lady he's given up his morning bath for, I says to meself, I'm no sending one of the wee lasses up to do this. No, Bridey's coming out to see to this lady for herself."

"What do you mean Caden gave up his bath for me?"

"Each morning, fresh after his training in the lists, Master Caden comes straight out here before anything else—regular as the seasons, he is. It's been a ritual for the lad since the day he finished this bathhouse."

"Caden built this? By himself?"

"Aye, that he did. With his own two hands to channel his energies away from his grief." Bridey clucked her tongue as she continued to scrub Ellie's head. "I should no be telling stories on the family, you ken? But that poor lad, you'd no believe what he's been through. What with all the trouble with his betrothed and her ending up on Iona. Fair broke his heart, she did, the wretched lass. And her all the time puttin' on airs as to what a good, church-loving soul she was. So his mother, God love her, put him to work out here. Dunk." With only the one word of warning, she pushed Ellie's head under the water.

Ellie surfaced, sputtering, to find Bridey on her feet, unfolding a large sheet of cloth.

"Here you go. We'll dry you off and get you back into the keep. Where are yer things?"

"Things?" Ellie stood, quickly wrapping the drying sheet around her. The cloth was much larger than a bath towel, but thinner.

"Yer shift and yer overdress, lass. Where are they?"

"In my room?" At the old woman's raised eyebrows, Ellie hurried to continue. "I was in my nightgown when I came out here."

The eyebrows climbed higher.

"I could put my nightgown back on, I guess," she finished lamely. That nasty, flea-infested blanket of a nightgown. The very idea made her shudder.

"You'll do nothing of the sort. Wait here. I'll go fetch something for you and send one of the lassies down with it." The old woman started out, stopping to pick up the nightgown. She held it away from her body, by the tips of her thumb and first finger. "And this will go directly into the washing kettle." Shaking her head, Bridey hurried out the door, leaving Ellie to wait.

"How long can she possibly freakin' take?"

Ellie shivered as she peered around the corner of the bathhouse door one more time. It had to have been at least twenty minutes since Bridey left to get her clothes.

The slatted floor that allowed the easy dumping of bathwater also allowed for easy gusts of wind and the thin drying cloth was little to no protection against that.

She tiptoed back to the fireplace, turning to warm her backside for a moment before returning to the door.

Another glance outside. Nobody in sight.

"Well, this is just stupid."

She'd go get her own clothes.

"The wind has a warmth to it." Caden lifted his nose, scenting the air. Old Kenneth had taught him this skill of determining the weather. Or given him the gift of the knowing. Caden wasn't sure which. "The snows are over. We'd best begin moving the sheep from winter pastures."

"Verra well," Steafan answered. "I'll put together a party to ride out at first light."

"It's done, then," Andrew agreed. "If only all our challenges were so easily met."

Caden nodded his approval, halting as something brushed past his leg.

Ellie's rat dog.

The creature pranced—there was no other way to describe it—across the yard. The little dog sat down next to the larger beast Ellie had rescued and stared back at him, her ears perked straight up on her head. If he didn't know better, he'd think she'd been trying to get his notice.

Ridiculous.

And yet the uncomfortable feeling lingered as his attention fixed on the animals. In unison their heads turned away from him toward the back of the keep. After a moment, again at the same time, their gaze returned to him.

He couldn't remember having seen the like of it.

After the second repeat of their unusual action, he glanced in the direction their attention was drawn, immediately spotting what they saw.

Ellie. Clad only in a drying cloth.

"By all the Fae of the Glen," Caden growled. It hadn't been more than two hours since he'd warned her about covering her body properly.

"You'll need to put a stop to that behavior," Steafan cautioned. "Even if she is a guest of Lady Rosalyn's."

As if he needed his friend to tell him that. "The woman's determined to drive me mad."

"At this rate, she may drive us all mad," Drew chuckled. "Ah, but, Cade, what a way to go, eh? She's a rare treat for the eyes."

"Damn yer eyes," Caden ground out, already stalking across the distance that separated him from Ellie, Drew's laughter ringing in his ears.

She'd seen him. Frozen in her tracks as he neared, her eyes open wide like a doe caught in the sites of his bow. Her head bobbed back and forth as she looked from the bathhouse to the keep, like she thought to escape him.

When he reached her, she held up one hand as if to stop him, the other clasping the top of the drying cloth, keeping it from slipping any lower than it already had.

"I can explain." Her words tumbled out breathlessly.

"Truly? The bathhouse disna appear to be on fire, and I canna think of any other acceptable reason for you to be parading about, yer body exposed as it is." He kept his voice quiet, controlling his urge to yell. The last thing he wanted was to draw a crowd of men to this spot. Having Steafan and Drew gawk at her was bad enough. "Did I no give you very specific orders, this very morning, to keep yerself properly covered? I canna imagine what explanation you might have."

"Orders?" Her hand dropped to join the other, clutching the drying cloth at her breasts. "You know what? I don't have to explain anything to you." She twirled, giving him her backside as she started toward the keep.

And a very nice backside it was, clearly outlined with only the thin drying cloth as covering. As Drew had said, she was quite a treat to watch.

He started to turn away, to allow her to make her own way back to her room wearing nothing more than that wisp of cloth, in spite of her having ignored all he'd told her. But then she stepped on something.

"Dammit!" Ellie halted, balancing on one foot.

The cloth she still held with one hand parted as she lifted her other foot to examine her sole, slowly revealing more and more smooth white skin. Her calf, her knee, her thigh . . .

Steafan's strangled cough from somewhere behind him snapped him out of what felt like a trance.

"Enough!" he roared, only vaguely recognizing the unusually possessive nature of his anger.

Not unusual, he quickly rationalized. After all, while she was at Dun Ard, she was his responsibility. One of his people. He expected his people to do as he told them, especially when it was for their own good, and she was no exception. He would not have his orders ignored.

Swooping in, he scooped her up and threw her over his shoulder, one arm behind her knees and his other hand firmly on the backside he'd just been admiring.

Before she had presented ever so much more for him, and everyone else who happened by, to admire.

He would not have her exposing herself to the drooling gaze of every man at Dun Ard lest he be forced to fight them all to save her honor, such as it was.

"Put me down," she demanded, her voice coming from somewhere in the region of his left shoulder blade. "Right this minute."

"I dinna think so." He stalked across the open area and into the gardens, headed to the nearest door of the keep.

"Now!" she yelled, pounding her fist on his back as she tried to kick free, like a spoiled bairn in full tantrum.

Apparently he'd been too subtle in his dealings with their stubborn guest.

One sharp smack to the lovely backside under his hand and she instantly stilled, a surprised gasp her initial response.

"You have absolutely no right to do that," she hissed. "When you put me down, I'm going to . . ."

"Yer going to get properly dressed when I put you down," he interrupted, feeling much more in control now. "And I'll no see you about Dun Ard half naked again, else I'll turn you over my knee and have at yer lovely arse with another whack. Do you ken my meaning?" If treating her like a willful child was what it took to get her attention, so be it.

They were inside the keep now, heading up the stairs.

He was keenly aware that he still held his hand firmly against the arse he'd just threatened. And he had no intention of moving it. Perhaps she'd take it for a lesson as to what happened to women who flaunted their bodies in public.

"Where I come from . . ." she started, but he cut her off again.

"But yer no there, are you now?"

When her body stiffened, he knew he'd hit his mark.

"So you'll do well to behave according to where you are. It's no safe in this time to be caught out as you were today. Many's the man who'd take nasty advantage of the situation."

He kicked open her door and strode into the room. Dumping her unceremoniously into the center of her bed, he turned and headed back out, but not before both lovely thighs came into view as she scrambled to hold the drying cloth closed.

For just an instant he sorely regretted her success, but he forced himself to walk away.

He paused at the door, speaking without turning to look at her.

"Dinna forget what I've told you. I'll no look kindly on yer disobeying me again." He closed the door behind him as he left but waited outside, listening to her tirade through the door.

"Disobey? You . . . you fourteenth-century chauvinist! Like you think I have any intention of doing what *you* tell me?" she yelled after him. "No man tells me what to do! Besides, there's nothing wrong with the human body. It's a beautiful thing. You're just . . . just . . . medieval!"

Mede-what?

He shook his head and smiled to himself. She might be angry, but she would think twice before she behaved in such a manner again. There were too many men about at Dun Ard these days he didn't know well. Too many troubles in the land to take unnecessary chances.

Something heavy smashed against the door as he walked away.

With the lass having a temper like that, one of his brothers would have his work cut out for him.

The feel of Ellie's firm round bottom floated through his mind and he clenched his fingers into a fist.

At this moment, though, he couldn't for the life of him feel anything even approaching pity for that brother.

Ten

$\mathcal{E}$llie stood next to her bed, looking for something else to throw. Granted, the overbearing sheepherder would be too far away to hear it, but hurling that metal basin across the room had felt wonderful. She'd had nothing but frustration lately and felt herself long overdue for a good venting.

Whether he truly deserved it or not, Caden MacAlister had been the proverbial straw that broke the camel's back.

That man's attitude was just absolutely . . . Ellie started her pacing again, searching for the appropriate adjective to fit the object of her ire.

"Male!" she fumed, halting in the middle of the room.

And like all the other men she'd dealt with in her life, this one irritated the living daylights out of her.

"Him with his big ol' shoulders and his silky voice,

rolling those *r*'s every time he talks. Doesn't give him the right to . . ."

Her words trailed off as a shiver ran down her spine at the memory of his hand possessively clamped on her rear end as he'd carried her to her room. His touch made her feel . . .

"Pissed!" she yelled at the closed door, stamping her foot for good measure.

Pissed. Angry. Not all hot and bothered, not needy and certainly not like she wanted those massive arms around her again. Not at all like she wanted to be flattened up against that wall of muscled chest with his breath feathering over her face.

Ellie shook her head to clear those pictures.

"Oh, this is so not good."

What she needed was to get her act together and find her way home. She needed out of here and away from that infuriating man. Besides, if she didn't get back soon, Ray would have settled himself in to the ranch and there'd be no getting rid of him. Ever.

Her stomach lurched at the thought of Ray living in her home. He'd be scarring up her mama's furniture with his dirty old boots, dropping his cigarette ashes all over the rugs, trashing the home she loved. The very idea had her anger flaring anew.

A quiet knock interrupted her mental rant. She stormed across the room and jerked open the heavy door, more than ready to give Caden a piece of her mind.

"S-sorry, milady." The young girl at the doorway hastily stepped back.

She should have known. Caden would never have rapped on the door so timidly.

"What?"

The sharp word had barely left Ellie's mouth before guilt washed over her. This poor child cringing away from her hadn't done anything to warrant such treatment. Ellie huffed out her breath, letting go of her hold on the anger.

"Let's try that again." She smiled down at the girl. "You haven't done anything wrong so you don't need to apologize. That was totally rude of me to snap at you like that and I am sorry."

The girl's face paled and she shook her head, her blue eyes so large they seemed to take up her whole little face.

"No, milady, I do deserve yer wrath. Cook sent me to get yer dress and to bring it to you at the bathhouse." Her chin started to quiver and she blinked rapidly but continued on, her words gathering momentum, rushing out one after the other. "But Angus—my brother, that is—he found a bird's egg and I wanted to help him hunt for the nest where it belonged and then I forgot all about the dress until I heard the fuss in the garden and saw himself carting you up here and now I dinna ken what I can do to make it up to you and cook is going to be so verra angry with me."

As if the torrent of words had taken everything the child had to give, she hung her head, her eyes firmly fixed on the floor.

The big tears rolling down the girl's cheeks only made Ellie feel worse. Now what was she supposed to do?

What you do to make pup cry?

Missy padded through the doorway, slowing to rub

against the girl's leg before crossing the room to lie down in front of the fireplace. Once there, she fixed Ellie with an accusatory stare.

Just what Ellie needed. Guilt from a dog.

A dirty, flea-ridden dog at that.

Ellie felt a smile growing as another thought struck her. Perhaps she could solve two problems at the same time.

"What's your name?" she asked, reaching out to tuck one of the child's wild red curls back under the scarf from which it had escaped.

"Anna," the girl sniffled without looking up, her hands worrying about each other.

"Well, Anna, cheer up. I think I know something you can do to help me that will more than make up for what you didn't do. And don't you worry. Cook will never even have to know about the whole dress thing. It'll be our little secret. How does that sound?"

Anna's head snapped up. "Truly? I'll do anything you like, milady. Just tell me what you want of me."

"First we'll need to drag one of those big wooden tubs out into the garden." Ellie glanced across the room to where Missy lay. "You ever give a dog a bath before?"

Missy stopped in midscratch, her ears perking up. *Bath? Don't need bath.*

"That's what you think," Ellie muttered.

"Not a bad day's work if I do say so myself." Ellie grasped the wet hem of her skirt and wrung the water from it as she surveyed the muddy mess around her.

With Anna's help she had changed all her bedding and then set about the day-long task of rounding up a large wooden tub and two suddenly elusive dogs for bathing. The crowd of giggling children they had drawn quickly made it apparent to her that dog bathing was a previously unknown form of entertainment in this time.

With the help of Anna's friends they had at last managed to wrestle first Missy and then Baby into the large tub to wash them down with the same soap Ellie had used to rid her own body of the fleas this morning.

Was that only this morning?

Ellie stretched her aching back and wiped a hand across her face, feeling the mud encrusted there. The whole dog-washing operation had worn her out, but it had been well worth it.

"Looks like yer the one who needs a dousing now." Anna's eyes sparkled with merriment.

"Looks like," Ellie agreed as she unrolled her sleeves. It had done no good to put them up. They were soaked. Just like the rest of her. Wet and muddy.

"You've likely missed the evening meal, mi . . ." The girl stopped and ducked her head shyly. "Ellie. Would you like me to bring something up to yer room for you to eat?"

Ellie smiled down at her little helper. It had taken the better part of the day to get the ten-year-old to use her name.

"That would be great, Anna, thank you. It's just as well I missed eating with everyone. I don't think I have the energy left to carry on a decent conversation. Oh!" She paused and wrinkled her nose as the memory of an earlier meal struck her. "None of that wine stuff."

Anna laughed and shook her head. "You got some

from the barrel gone bad, eh? No worry. I'll make sure you get a better serving tonight." With that, Anna turned and raced off toward the kitchens.

Ellie followed more slowly, opting to take a side entrance from the gardens that led into the hallway rather than going through the bustle of the kitchen.

When she reached her room, she found Missy and Baby waiting patiently in the hallway. Ellie could almost swear they were smiling at her.

"I see you're none the worse for your afternoon." She reached down and scooped Missy up in her arms before opening the door.

Don't need carried.

Though the protest rolled through her mind, Ellie noticed the little dog made no effort to get away as she scratched behind Missy's ears. She plopped the animal on her bed and grinned when Baby hopped up next to the little dog, the two of them almost completely filling the bed.

"And where do you think I'm sleeping tonight?"

Missy looked innocently toward the fireplace and back again.

"Don't even think it."

You dirty.

Ellie looked down at her soggy dress. The dog had a point. As tempting as it was to simply peel out of her dress and fall into bed, she'd worked too hard at cleaning everything just to dirty it all up so quickly.

With a deep sigh of resignation, she gathered a clean shift and overdress and headed back to the bathhouse in time to see the sun setting behind the horizon.

Once there, she chose the tub behind the rock wall

farthest from the door and filled it as Caden had showed her earlier. When the tub was ready, she undressed and tossed everything into a pile on the floor next to the bench where she'd laid out her drying cloth and change of clothing.

She stepped behind the wall and into the bath and sat down, enjoying the caress of the hot water on her sore muscles. After a quick wash, she leaned her head back against the wooden tub and relaxed her whole body, letting her mind run free while the warm water lapped around her.

What an amazing turn her life had taken. Here she sat, hundreds of years from home, her closest confidante a bossy little terrier.

She had to smile in spite of herself. To think she'd fought the whole psychic talking-animal thing for weeks. Now, after only two days of allowing them to flood her mind with their thoughts and pictures, it felt as natural as having a conversation with a person.

"Weird," she murmured into the silent room.

It was so quiet out here, the crackle of the fireplace and the gentle noises of the little stream the only sounds other than the gentle slosh of water when she moved.

"I'll just soak here for a minute more," she murmured as her eyes drifted shut.

"Rider at the gate!"

The yell from high atop the wall walk shattered the evening silence.

Caden dropped the bundle he carried and raced across the inner bailey and up the stairs leading to the

wall walk. As he burst through the doorway, the guards-
man on duty stopped him with a shake of his head.

"Sorry, Caden. It's only one of the shepherds coming in. I heard his mount but couldna see him until he
reached the light of our torches."

Caden nodded, steeling his face as he held his emotions in check.

It had been more than a fortnight since the lone rider
had approached that very same gate bringing news of
Colin's capture and the ransom demanded for his release. More than a fortnight since Blane and his small
party of men rode out those same gates to pay the ransom and bring Colin and Alasdair home. More than a
fortnight with nary a single word about either his cousin
the laird or his youngest brother and the friend who'd
been taken with him.

Caden stooped to retrieve the bundle of clothing he
had dropped before continuing on his original path toward the bathhouse.

He'd missed his morning soak. After all these years,
he realized he rather enjoyed the practice and felt his
day was incomplete without it.

Though he'd given up his chance this morning for
a good cause. He felt a grudging smile grow as he remembered the look on Ellie's face when she realized
fleas from her beastie herd had infested her as well.

Then he thought of her as she'd looked outside, the
thin drying towel falling away to reveal more and more.
Thought of how she'd felt under his hands, warm and
firm.

Oh yes, he needed that bath. But he wouldn't need to

spend much time heating the water. In fact, the colder the better.

Ducking his head as he walked through the doorway, Caden entered the bathhouse. He dropped his bundle by the nearest tub and pulled his shirt off over his head, dropping it at his feet. Only when he sat down on the bench to remove his boots did he notice the clothing already lying there. And the dirty pile on the floor.

That's fair odd.

There weren't a large number of regular bathers here at Dun Ard. His family had all acquired the habit, but the majority of the people who worked and lived there hadn't.

Reaching a tentative hand down to the garment on the floor, he fingered the cloth, recognizing the mud-spattered overdress. He'd seen Ellie wearing it as she'd comically chased those damn beasties of hers around this afternoon, a whole gaggle of laughing children following in her footsteps.

Why would she leave her soiled clothing out here? And more important, why was her clean clothing laid out here as well?

Caden cocked his head to the side, listening intently. At first he heard only the crackle of the fire and the bubbling of the stream that passed through the bathhouse. Concentrating harder, he picked it up.

The slow, quiet rhythm of breathing.

He stood and walked over to the fire, glancing around the wall separating the bathing tubs as he passed.

Ellie lay in the tub. He could just see her face resting on the edge and one lovely arm draping over the side.

By all the Fates!

The confounding woman was asleep!

He picked up a water bucket and swung, smacking it into the side of the great black cauldron with a resounding thud.

Ellie awoke with a start, jolted by a loud noise from her pleasant dream into a place that was cold and uncomfortable. It took an instant to remember where she was.

How could she have fallen asleep in this stupid tub?

Every part of her body felt stiff and cold as she sat up, the chilled water sloshing around her. She lifted her hand up to rub her neck but froze when she heard someone clear his throat behind her.

Slowly she turned, pulling her body snug up against the tub as she looked that direction, the dread in the pit of her stomach telling her who she would see before she looked.

"Have you decided now to make this yer new bed?"

Caden.

He stood by the fire, a large bucket in his hand. But it wasn't what he held that riveted her attention. He was dressed in nothing more than the plaid wrapped around him. The flickering light of the fireplace danced off his bare chest. Surely it was just an optical illusion that made him look so large. So muscular. So appealing.

Why, why, why? It felt as if she'd saved up every stupid mistake throughout her whole life just so she could commit each and every one of them in front of this man. She swallowed hard, stalling, trying to gather her thoughts, feeling at a distinct disadvantage.

"I guess I fell asleep. I was really tired when I came out here." She steeled herself for the lecture she knew would be coming.

Instead he turned from her and dipped his bucket into the huge steaming cauldron before carrying it past her to the other side of the wall, splashing the water into the other tub.

"What are you doing?"

He barely spared her a glance as he made a second trip to and from the cauldron, once again emptying his bucket. "I missed my morning bath because of you. I dinna intend to forgo this one."

She shivered as she watched him lift the steaming bucket, the muscles in his back rippling with minimal effort.

She had to get out of here.

Unfortunately all her things, her drying cloth and her clothing, lay on the bench in the room. Out past the divider wall.

Crap.

There was no discreet way to get to them.

"Um . . . would you mind tossing that drying cloth over here?"

Caden put the bucket back on its hook and crossed his arms over his chest, looking at her from across the room as if considering what she asked. "No. I think not."

He crossed to the other side of the partition and she heard the splashing of water.

Oh. My. God. It sounded like the man was getting into his bath. The sudden visual she had of all those rippling muscles climbing into a tub less than six feet away from her—buck naked, no less—tore another shuddering breath from her.

"No?" she squeaked. "All you have to do is toss it over here."

"You can get it yerself. You did tell me this morning that you were responsible for yer own self, did you no?"

More splashing.

The water she sat in felt like ice now and her teeth were beginning to chatter. Pride or no pride, she really couldn't hold out much longer.

"But I can't get to my things without walking in front of you."

"That should no be a problem for you. After all, yer the one who told me there's nothing wrong with the human body. I wouldna want to be thought *mede-val*."

She could actually hear the smirk in his voice. "Medieval," she corrected absently, wishing she could take back everything she had said earlier. Her grandmama used to have a saying about using care with your words in case you had to eat them later.

Crap. She'd really let her mouth—and her temper—get her in a fix this time.

"Okay. Maybe I was a little hasty this morning. I was angry with you treating me like I'm stupid all the time." She paused, waiting for some response. When all she heard was more splashing, she began to feel desperate. "I'm really cold over here, Caden. Please."

Just great. Now she sounded like some whiney, begging little girl.

"Verra well." His arm appeared at the end of the partition, the drying cloth clasped in his hand. A little toss and it landed only a foot from her tub.

Shivering, she climbed out and clumsily wrapped the cloth around herself, her fingers so cold it was difficult to tuck everything properly.

"Are you decent now? As decent as *you* get, that is."

"Yes."

She barely had the word out before he appeared around the partition, a scowl on his face. Grasping her shoulders, he shuffled her toward the fire.

"I never thought you stupid, Ellie. And I dinna intend to treat you as such. But you dinna seem to realize that you need to think before you act. I'm only concerned about yer welfare. It's an unsettled time in our land. We've men working here who are little more than strangers. I canna vouch for all of them being trustworthy."

He stood behind her, his hands rubbing rapidly up and down her arms as she faced the fire. "You've no a bit of warmth left to you, lass. What were you thinking to stay in the water so long?"

She shook her head, unable to think of any good answer. The fact that what he said made sense didn't help at all.

Allowing him to turn her around so the fire could warm her backside, she realized he was still dressed in his plaid and completely dry. "I thought I heard you get in your bath."

He shrugged and resumed vigorously rubbing her arms. "A bit of deception on my part."

She didn't even care right now. The heat radiated off his body and she leaned into him, resting her cold cheek against his warm, bare chest. He stilled for only an instant before his arms came up around her, enfolding her into an embrace.

She lifted her hands to his chest and the wall of muscle jumped under her touch. She probably should feel guilty, but she just couldn't. It felt wonderful here in his arms. She looked up, intending to apologize for what must have felt like two ice cubes she'd pressed against his body, but his expression stopped her words before they formed.

He was going to kiss her. She was sure of it. And, to her surprise, she wanted him to. He dipped his head toward her and she closed her eyes, eagerly anticipating what was to come.

"Caden!" Steafan's voice echoed from somewhere out beyond the door. "Caden! Are you out here?"

Caden pushed her away and over to the partition. "Stay here and be quiet. It would no do at all for us to be found out here together. When I've left, I want you back in the keep. Will you do that?" He waited for her to nod her agreement before he scooped up her clothes and shoved them at her. Then he strode toward the door.

"Aye," he called out. "I'm here."

Ellie backed into the shadows clutching her bundle.

"There's a problem in the pastures. One of the shepherds has come to fetch you. They need you up there."

The men's voices grew faint as they left the bathhouse.

Ellie quickly slipped on her shift and overdress, giving Caden more time to draw Steafan away. She waited until she could hear nothing at all before starting back to the house, knowing that the shivers going through her body now had nothing to do with the cold and everything to do with what she had just experienced.

How could one man make her feel so angry one minute and so exceedingly far from angry the next?

A shiver raced up her body, leaving a trail of goose bumps raised on her skin.

She really had to figure out what she needed to do to get home and do it. Fast.

Eleven

"I do so hate this part." Plopping down in the chair next to Ellie, Sallie lifted her feet to the small stool nearest the fire. "I feel like an overripe fruit, ready to burst."

"I think you look great for someone who's expecting a baby any day."

Ellie meant her words. Sallie was a lovely woman. Her fiery red hair picked up glints from the sun shining through the open shutters. And even though her petite body was very obviously pregnant, she carried the baby like an enormous basketball right in front of her.

"Well, I dinna *feel* so great. This wee lassie of mine is poking her arms and legs about searching for more room than I have to give." Sallie sighed and laid her head against the high-backed chair in which she sat. "Distract me with some lively conversation, Ellie. Help me take my mind off this great swollen lump of a body."

"Why are you so certain this one's a girl?" Every time Ellie had heard Sallie speak of the baby it was in terms of *she*.

"It's the way of many Faerie descendants. Three boys and a girl. At least, in our line it seems to be the case. And I already have my three boys." She closed her eyes and propped her hands on her distended stomach. "Dinna talk of the babe. We need a discussion to take my mind away from this entirely."

What on earth did she have to discuss with Sallie? She barely knew the woman. The only thing that came to mind, embarrassingly enough, was Caden.

"Tell me about your brother. Why is he always so bossy and irritable."

"Bossy and irritable? That canna be a description for Drew so it must be Caden yer asking after." Though Sallie's eyes were closed, a soft smile lifted the corners of her mouth. "Surprised I am that none of the help has taken it upon themselves to tell you already."

Guiltily, Ellie thought of Bridey and her confidences about Caden's past. There must be something more. She dropped the needlework to her lap and leaned forward. It wasn't as if she were making much headway on the piece Rosalyn had given her earlier this morning anyway.

"As the oldest, Caden has always been bossy. But right now he's feeling the pressure of managing Dun Ard in our cousin's absence." Again without opening her eyes, Sallie shook her head. "No, that's not true. Caden has spent his whole life preparing to manage Dun Ard. He loves it. No, it's the circumstances of it now that are bearing down on him."

"What circumstances?" Considering she had no idea how long she would be stuck here, Ellie really wanted to try to understand what was happening around her.

Sallie's eyes opened, bright and piercing in their gaze. "You ken that Scotland fights for her freedom, do you no?"

Only when Ellie nodded her response did the other woman relax again.

"We're fair insulated here at Dun Ard as well as at the MacPherson keep, but the troubles managed to touch us all the same. My youngest brother, Colin, fights in the name of Scotland. He and Alasdair Maxwell were taken in battle and are now held for ransom. Our cousin Blane, the MacKiernan, has gone after him. But the time since he left grows long and we've no word of any of them. Caden fears for their safety, though he willna say so. He disna have to. We all hold that same fear. It's one of the reasons Ran brought me home to Dun Ard to wait for the birth of this babe. I needed to be here, with my family."

"How awful. You must be so worried. I had no idea men captured in battle were held for ransom." Everything she'd ever read about this century had led her to believe they were simply killed. Probably best not to add that little tidbit, considering everything.

"We've King Edward to thank for the ransom demand. He's encouraged the requiring of ransom for the release of what he calls the traitors." Sallie shook her head again and sighed. "And now Caden has this nasty sheep business to deal with on top of everything else."

Ellie's ears perked up. "Sheep business?"

"Aye. Apparently there's an animal showing signs of

sickness. Now Caden's worried he'll lose them all. He and Steafan rode up to check the flocks this morning early. Oh!" Sallie sat up, her hands splayed on either side of her stomach, her eyes open wide. "I hate it most of all when it tightens like this. I've no a choice but to hunt the nearest garderobe."

Ellie jumped up and helped Sallie to her feet, watching as the other woman waddled from the room.

The clear-cut picture she'd formed of Caden as a demanding, unhappy, controlling, medieval chauvinist was starting to fog over. Oh, he certainly was all those things, but perhaps there were underlying motivators for his behavior.

And for reasons that were not at all clear to her—she absolutely refused to even consider it might have anything to do with that little scene in the bathhouse last night—she suddenly found she wanted to do something to alleviate some of the pressures he faced.

Granted, there wasn't much she could do around here to help her hosts, certainly nothing to lessen Caden's worries over his brother and his cousin.

But sheep? Ellie knew sheep. She'd raised them herself and worked with the local vet back home, tending sheep as well as other farm animals. She'd taken classes preparing herself for veterinary school. All that plus her ability to understand animals? This was one task that was right up her alley.

Twelve

⁓

"Have you gone completely daft, woman?" Caden stared down into the confused eyes of their beautiful guest.

"I . . . I don't understand. I thought you'd be pleased," Ellie stammered, disappointment evident in her voice.

Pleased? He'd have to be the one gone daft for that. His ability to control events around him was slipping away faster than spring thaw down the mountainside and she expected *pleased*?

When he and Steafan had ridden through the gates into the bailey, she'd been waiting, sitting on the bottom stair with that ratty little dog curled up at her feet. For some reason beyond his understanding, his heart had begun to beat faster the moment he'd spotted her.

He'd barely had time to dismount before she'd run up to him, placing her soft little hand on his arm. His fool imagination had only begun to skip into a fantasy about her having missed him when she'd gone to yammering about the ridiculous notion he should take her up to the sheep pastures.

"I can help you." The confusion was gone, her eyes clear and determined.

"There's naught you can do, lass. Now away with you. I've hours in the saddle and I'm tired and hungry." Tired, hungry and at a complete loss as to how he'd save their animals. The new sheep was diseased. Within the next few weeks, more would fall prey to the crippling affliction. If they lost the flocks, it would mean hard, desperate times for Dun Ard and their people.

He had enough to worry about without adding on Ellie's look of disappointment when he'd declined her help. He refused to accept responsibility for failing to meet the expectations of yet another woman and he turned his back, heading for the stairway to the keep. At this moment he only wanted to escape her and her reproachful gaze.

"You hold it right there, cowboy." Ellie caught up with him and grabbed a handful of his sleeve, jerking his arm back. "Don't you walk away from what I'm offering you without even thinking about it."

Cowboy? Again with the names he didn't understand.

"I can help you." She repeated the words, slowly, distinctly, as if she thought he hadn't understood. She leaned in closer to him and lowered her voice. "This is something I have some experience with, Caden. I worked with a vet back home."

A vet? He didn't have the time or the energy for trying to figure out what she was talking about this time.

He glanced pointedly at her hand before untangling

her fingers and pulling his sleeve from her grasp. "Verra well, *Elliedenton*. I've thought about yer offer, and now I'm declining it. Go find someone else to harass."

Again he turned from her, and made it all the way to the first stair before she called out after him.

"Don't you make me go tell your mama how stupid you're being."

Caden's back stiffened, his foot on the second stair before he turned, his face a dark scowl. "Are you threatening me?"

Uh-oh.

If that look meant anything, the man was angry. One big, strong, gorgeous highlander, pissed as hell, and headed right for her.

Ellie swallowed hard but held her ground. She wasn't backing down on this one. He needed her help and he was going to get it whether he wanted it or not.

"Not threatening. Promising." She smiled up at him, but had to work at keeping the smile in place as he stalked toward her.

He moved in close, invading her personal space, towering over her, and she fought the urge to lift a hand to his chest to push him away. Or to wrap her fingers in the cloth of his shirt and pull him the extra couple of inches it would take to bring those full lips down to where she could . . .

Stop it! The reedy voice floated into her thoughts, jerking her back to reality. *No time for dream pictures. Big One angry.*

At her feet, Missy growled menacingly.

The dog was right. She needed to stay focused.

"I'll no have you bothering Lady Rosalyn, do you ken? She's enough worries on her as it is." His eyes narrowed as he spoke, his dark lashes sweeping down over them.

"Then don't you go giving her more to worry about. I know sheep, Caden. I've lived my whole life on a sheep ranch. Please. Trust me on this. If your sheep are sick, there's a good chance I can help you figure out how to get them better."

She clenched her muscles to resist the need to fidget under the strength of his glare until finally he sighed and looked up to the sky.

"I canna believe I'm going to say this. Give me time to gather something to eat on the trail and then I'll take you up to see the sheep. But yer beasties stay here. I'm no dragging that menace along to badger my poor animals." He pointed down at Missy and shook his head. "I'm sure I'm going to regret this."

"No. You won't, Caden. I promise." She threw her arms around his neck and gave him a quick hug, letting go instantly when she felt him stiffen. "You go get our horses ready and I'll go grab some lunch for you."

Running toward the keep with Missy at her heels, she glanced back to find Caden still staring after her. "Go on!" she yelled.

As she entered the keep it occurred to her that maybe Rosalyn had been wrong. Maybe she hadn't been sent here to find her true love at all. Maybe the reason she was here was to do this exact thing—help these people save their livelihood. And once she completed the task, she could get home and deal with the mess waiting for her there.

That had to be it.

Regardless, she fully intended to see to it that not only would Caden not regret what he was about to do, but one day he would count taking her out to see his sheep among the smartest things he'd ever done.

"It's bad, is it no?" Caden stared at her over the wiggling body of the ewe lying on the damp ground between them, his dark eyes serious.

She nodded her agreement, her mind racing for what she could do to prevent the catastrophe he feared. The animal under her hands had made its pain clear to her in no uncertain terms the moment they had arrived. She had known immediately to check the ewe's front hooves.

Other sheep milled about them, one particularly friendly old ewe pressing her runny nose to Ellie's shoulder. But she wasn't getting anything from their minds, no thoughts, no pictures, nothing that would indicate they suffered any pain, so perhaps all wasn't lost.

Still, this wasn't good. If she were at home, she could run into town and pick up what she needed to treat them. But here? There would be no vaccines, no prepackaged bags of zinc sulfate for sterilizing footbaths. If she could just remember what old Doc Lambert had said when he'd rambled on about the ancient history of treatment for sheep.

Caden released his hold on the animal and the ewe scrambled to her feet, limping away.

"Have you seen the like of this before?" He remained on his knees beside Ellie, his hands stroking another of the sheep that had wandered to his side.

"Yeah, I have. I won't lie to you, Caden. It's a serious problem. We call it foot rot in my time, and if we were there I'd call the vet to come out and treat these animals."

"Vet?" His eyes crinkled at the corners in the most adorable look of confusion.

She struggled to focus on the task at hand. Not on him.

"Veterinarian. A person who treats animal diseases. I was studying to be one myself." Ellie felt her heart skip a beat at the look of approval Caden cast her way.

"Well, we've no *vets* here." He rolled the word on his tongue as if tasting it. "Any ideas?"

"As a matter of fact, I do have a couple. It's a real good thing you keep the animals all broken into smaller flocks. It'll make it easier to contain this outbreak. First off, we have to keep all the others away from this place and these sheep. Once we figure out a way to treat them, we'll want to wait a good two weeks or so before we allow other animals near this pasture."

Caden nodded, giving her his full attention. "Two weeks?"

"Yep. At least fourteen days. Maybe a bit longer for safety's sake. You're sure this particular ewe is new to the flock?" Perhaps it wasn't too late.

Again he nodded his response. "Steafan and Gilberd were in Inverness for supplies. Gilberd got himself into a game of chance and came away winner. And there stands his winnings." Caden pointed at the infected animal.

"We need to check every hoof in this whole group, one at a time." Ellie rose to her knees to attempt a head count.

"Twelve. We've twelve more here but it's growing late. We're likely to lose the sunlight before we finish."

Ellie pushed up to her feet and reached a hand down to Caden. "Okay, then, we better get up and get a move on if you're going to wrestle us twelve sheep before sundown."

It felt like they'd been at this for hours, especially now that the wind had picked up.

"I sure hope your mama doesn't mind that I've ruined this dress." Ellie tore one last strip of cloth from her skirt and handed it to Caden as he held another sheep to the ground.

"Dinna fash yerself over the damage to yer shift, lass. It was a good idea you had to mark the animals so we could tell which one's we'd already checked." She had amazed him all afternoon, pitching in and helping, proving she actually knew of what she spoke.

Working together, they tied the strip of cloth around the animal's front right leg and then checked her hooves. By the time they finished, a splattering rain had begun to fall.

"Well, crap. Isn't *this* just what we needed?" Ellie rose, her hand above her eyes to deflect the fat raindrops.

The first jagged bolt of lightning split through the evening sky followed by a small rumble in the clouds.

They couldn't stay out in this.

Caden grabbed Ellie's arm, pulling her along with him to the cramped shelter of a rocky overhang. "We'll wait out the storm here. I've no a problem riding home in the rain, even in the dark, but I've no fancy to be caught by the lightning."

A most unladylike snort escaped from Ellie as she edged next to him. "Yeah. You especially want to watch out for the green kind."

A shiver ran through her body and he pulled her closer, lifting the plaid from his shoulder and wrapping it around her as he did so.

"Thanks," she mumbled.

"Are you warm enough? Yer legs are shaking a bit."

"No, I mean, yes," she stammered. "I'm warm enough. I'm just tired."

He should have thought of that. She'd worked hard for the last several hours, chasing down the sheep, helping to wrestle them to the ground and inspecting their hooves for any signs of the *infection*, as she'd called it.

"It doesn't look to be letting up anytime soon, so why don't we sit to wait. There's room if we press back against the rock."

They rearranged themselves and he once again wrapped the end of his plaid, and his arm, around her shoulders. The heat from her seeped into his body where her face lay cushioned against his chest, and he involuntarily tightened his embrace until the full warmth of her body pressed up against the side of his own. Only to protect her from the cold, nothing more.

He wondered how she kept from covering her ears to block the infernal thumping outside their shelter until he realized the pounding that assaulted his hearing didn't come from outside. Instead it was the sound of his own blood drumming against his ears, keeping time with his racing heart.

Could she hear it? He cleared his throat, anything to make noise, just in case. At the sound she jumped, lifting her head and jerking her hand from his chest where it had rested.

"I . . . I hope somebody lets the dogs inside. Missy doesn't like storms. They frighten her."

Dogs? Inside? His mind scrambled to catch up.

"And how would you be knowing that?"

She fidgeted next to him and he tightened his arm around her, again drawing her close against him.

"I just do," she murmured at last.

"When we visited the old castle, you told me the wee beastie spoke to you. Was that the truth?" He paused for her response, but when none came he asked the question he'd wondered about earlier today. "Was it that which led you straight to the afflicted animal when we arrived here? I'd told you nothing to help you pick her out and yet you found her out of all the others. Straight to her and her one damaged hoof at that."

Ellie sighed and nodded, a small, jerky movement, barely perceptible, but she wouldn't look at him. "Animals are sensitive to our thoughts and emotions. I know it sounds crazy, but somehow I pick up on theirs, too. I see pictures and hear words so that it's like they're talking to me inside my head."

He placed a finger under her chin and turned her face so he could look into her eyes. In what was left of the fading light they looked like large, frightened gems of green floating in the pale sea of her soft white face.

"You've no reason to deny the gifts of yer Fae heritage. No here. No with me."

She smiled then—only a tiny uplifting of the corners of her mouth, but a smile nonetheless.

"Thank you, Caden. You can't imagine what it means

to me to have someone know about this and . . . and just accept it. Like it's normal or something." She lifted her hand to his face, the chill of her fingers cooling against the heat of his skin. "And I want you to know, I *will* think of something we can do to keep you from losing all these animals. I swear it."

As if possessed by a force he couldn't deny, he lowered his head until his lips touched hers. A soft gentle touch that, he told himself, was only meant to comfort, to reassure. But when her eyes fluttered shut and the hand on his cheek slid around the back of his neck, her fingers twining in his hair, the kiss deepened, as if the moment had taken on a life of its own.

The soft lips meeting his parted and his tongue, against his will, darted inside, tasting the sweetness that was the woman in his arms.

She moaned and pressed against him, her tongue swirling around his own, and he felt himself drowning in visions of taking her. Here. Now. Visions of her under him, wanting him as much as he wanted . . .

Caden grabbed her hand and pulled it from his neck, lifting his head and breaking the kiss.

Outside their shelter the rain had died off, the storm passed over.

Inside, he felt the storm rage on, the only sound that of their heavy breathing.

"We should go."

"Right. Right," she answered, scrambling away from him and out into the night.

By the Fates, what she must think of him! The woman was to be family, as soon as one of his brain-dead brothers claimed her, and here he'd been sprawled upon her, thinking thoughts he never should about another man's betrothed. Especially the betrothed of his own kin.

What was wrong with him? Hadn't he taken enough from his brothers already? And if that didn't stop him, the memory of what had happened with Alycie should. His blind acceptance of her had very nearly cost the lives of those dear to him.

All because he was so centered on himself, on what he expected, what he had taken for granted, that he'd failed to recognize what was actually in the hearts of those around him.

There were good reasons he'd chosen to devote his life to Dun Ard, forsaking all emotional entanglements. Unfortunately, around this particular woman, he seemed to have difficulty remembering what they were.

Bringing Ellie out here alone had to be the stupidest thing he'd ever done.

Thirteen

So much for those earlier altruistic thoughts of being sent here to save some stupid sheep. So much for denying her desires for any man.

Ellie tightened her grip on the reins, grateful for the dark of the cloudy night they rode through on their way back to Dun Ard. Thank goodness Caden couldn't see her flaming face.

Wasn't she just a fool from here to Sunday, kissing him like that? If he hadn't stopped things when he did, who knows what might have happened next?

Ellie had a pretty good idea.

She shook her head, trying to push away the memories of that kiss and the raw desire still rumbling around inside her body.

You don't suppose he could be the one?

No, no, no. She wouldn't let herself even consider the possibility. If she actually were here to find her one true love, he certainly would *not* end up being some overbearing, medieval macho sheepherder. She'd had her fill of those back home.

"Damn straight," she muttered out loud, needing to reassure herself.

"Pardon?" Caden reined his horse closer to hers. "Did you say something?"

Crap.

"Just . . . um . . . thinking. About the sheep. Yeah. About the sheep and what we can do for them." That's what she needed to do. Focus on something important. Something *not* Caden MacAlister.

"And?"

He expected an answer now? A response when he rode so close his leg actually brushed against hers?

Think, think, think.

"Well, we need something to kill the infection. To sterilize their feet. I know there's something. I remember Doc Lambert, the vet I worked with, talking about it. Just give me some time. It'll come to me."

If she could concentrate on the problem and not on him, that is. She pulled on her reins, giving herself a little distance from him.

She so had to get home.

"Riders at the gate!"

The cry echoed faintly ahead of them, their journey almost at an end as they drew near the gaping black opening in the wall of Dun Ard.

A head appeared over the side of the great wall above them. "Open the gates!" The words rang out as they waited while the massive grates were drawn up, allowing them access to the courtyard.

They came to a halt when they reached the stairs and Caden dismounted. Within the blink of an eye, he was at her side, his large hands fastened around her waist, lifting her down to the ground.

At his touch, Ellie's breath caught and the feelings she had pushed away came rushing back. She had to force herself to step away from him.

This wasn't good. Perhaps she was simply tired.

A young boy, looking as though he'd just tumbled out of a sound sleep, appeared out of the dark and led their horses away while she and Caden trudged up the stairs.

Caden pushed open the massive door and she edged past him, careful to avoid allowing her body to touch his, not sure she could endure that touch without embarrassing herself. Again.

Across the torch-lit entry toward the stairs she hurried, her only thought to escape to her room.

But escape wasn't in the cards for the moment.

A sleep-rumpled Andrew stepped down onto the bottom stair, blocking her path. Wearing only his hastily wrapped plaid, his bare chest glinted in the flickering of the torches.

Ellie gasped and stepped back into Caden, unsure if she was more unsettled by the look of anger on the man's face or the silvery scar, jaggedly cutting a path that began at Andrew's shoulder and disappeared beneath the waist of his plaid.

"And where the hell have you two been?"

At Ellie's gasp, Drew's body stiffened and his eyes grew shuttered, a look Caden had come to know. It was that damned scar and everything it represented to his brother.

"Step aside, Drew. We've worked long and hard and we're both ready to retire for the night."

Rather than moving away, Drew leaned against the opening to the stairs, completely blocking access, his arms insolently crossed over his chest.

"At this late hour, I've no a doubt you've worn yerselves out." The younger man tilted his head and arched an eyebrow.

"And what do you mean by that, little brother?" Caden stepped in front of Ellie, pushing her behind him. He didn't like the insinuation, particularly not in light of how close he had come to allowing exactly that to happen.

"I think you ken my meaning well enough. It's no matter to me what you've been up to with the lass, Caden, but have you no a care for the worry you've caused our mother this day? Is it no enough for her to fash herself over one missing son, but you have to give the woman cause to worry over two?"

"And how is my spending the day in the high pasture searching for a way to save our flocks more worrisome than the times you disappear for weeks on end to Inverness or Edinburgh?" He would not be lectured by Drew, not considering his younger brother's irresponsible ways.

"This is no about me." Drew stepped from the stair, pausing to catch his balance as his left leg gave way. Pain reflected in his expression before he quickly closed himself off again.

Caden resisted the urge to reach out to help his

brother. He knew from experience it would only worsen the situation to acknowledge the weakness in any way.

Ellie was another matter. A tiny, breathy "Oh!" at his side and she started forward. He grabbed her arm and pulled her back behind him again, hoping Drew had missed her movement.

He hadn't.

"I may no be the man you are, Caden, but I've no trouble imagining what you spent yer day doing." Drew's hand slid to the outside of his left thigh, kneading the muscle as if his fingers had a mind of their own.

Caden took a deep breath, swallowing the anger that bubbled to the surface. His brother was exhausted. He had to be or he'd never acknowledge the pain he experienced, not even with an unconscious movement like the rubbing of his hand.

The mark on Drew's chest was nothing in comparison to the one scarring his leg. Or the scar in his mind. And since Caden felt partly responsible for both of his brother's injuries, he wouldn't allow himself to vent his anger on Drew now. Instead he forced himself to speak quietly, calmly.

"We spent our day checking sheep's hooves, looking for more signs of the rot the new animal carries."

Drew's hand froze. "So it's true? Steafan allowed Gilberd to bring home a diseased ewe?"

"It's no as if Steafan did it on purpose," Caden defended. "It was Gilberd's prize."

Drew shrugged. "Gilberd is hardly more than a lad. The fact remains that Steafan dinna check the animal and now we've the disease to contend with, aye? For someone so concerned with securing his place as yer future overseer, I'd say Steafan's shown a serious lapse in judgment."

Caden nodded his reply, not trusting himself to speak the words out loud. As if he hadn't enough trouble, now Drew's jealousy of Steafan reared its ugly head.

It had been this way since the injury to Drew's leg in the battle with the Nuadian Fae nine years earlier. Caden had always been close to Steafan, but with Drew off his feet for so long, he'd grown ever more dependent on his friend.

He knew Drew blamed Steafan's sister for the whole incident and, by association, Steafan himself. That had to be the reason Drew constantly found fault in the motives for everything Steafan did.

Caden hadn't the time to fash himself over Drew's petty jealousies now. He had to center all his efforts on the threat to the flocks. If they lost all the animals to this plague . . .

"Copper sulfate!" Ellie announced as if she'd just found a bag of silver pennies on the floor. "I knew I'd remember sooner or later. It's not as good as the zinc, but it'll work and it should be available in this time."

"What in the name of the Fae is she blethering on about?"

Drew's look of confusion must mirror his own.

"Ellie?"

"We get it from a copper-bearing rock. Mixed with water, it makes a solution we can use to treat the foot rot." The woman smiled at them both, obviously pleased with herself.

"A copper-bearing rock?" Drew echoed. "And we would find that where?"

Ellie's smile faded. "Wherever you'd go to get stuff like this. Wait. I think it's called . . . oh, crap." She closed her eyes and her forehead wrinkled. "Blue vitriol! That's it. Don't you have apothecaries or something?"

"Blue vitriol." Caden rolled the words in his mind. It had a familiar sound.

"Bluestone?" Drew asked. "Yer talking about bluestone, aye?"

"Yes, yes!" Ellie's excitement was almost contagious. "Do you know where we can get some?"

Drew's expression hardened. "What say you, Brother? Do you believe this farfetched idea could help save the flocks?"

Caden wavered. True, the woman had proven her knowledge of sheep this day, but how could a simple rock save them? It made no sense. While he wanted to believe her, trust her, the doubt still lingered. She was a woman, and she had, after all, been sent here by the Fae. And the Fae he'd met weren't particularly trustworthy.

Apparently his indecision showed.

"As I thought." Drew shook his head.

"Wait." Ellie stepped in front of Caden, her hand on his forearm. "You aren't even going to try this? It'll work, I know it will. If you have any idea where we can get our hands on this stuff . . ." Her words died off as she searched his face, hurt and disbelief shining in her eyes.

Caden tore his gaze from hers to find his brother limping toward the stairs.

"Since you've no a need for me, I'm returning to my bed. If there's news of Colin and Blane, you'll fetch me, aye?"

"I will. Get yer rest. We need to be ready no matter what word comes." If anything had happened to his youngest brother or his cousin . . .

Drew snorted, again shaking his head. "I dinna need to be rested to wait behind with the women and wring my hands. And since that's all I'm good for, I'd no be too concerned with my rest if I were you."

Caden could only watch his brother disappear up the stairs. It would do no good to argue. It would do no good to point out that Drew was an excellent swordsman, that he demonstrated his skill daily in their practices together. Drew would only see what he believed. That he practiced to keep his damaged leg from becoming completely useless. That the one accident in the lists last year proved his unworthiness. The one accident for which Caden was responsible.

Rosalyn told him Ellie had been sent for one of his brothers and he trusted his mother's word in the matter beyond question. But how could he ever have considered Drew an appropriate husband for Ellie? His brother spent too much time grieving for what he was not instead of concentrating on what he could be.

No, Ellie deserved better than that in a husband.

It was obvious to him now that she must have been sent to wed Colin.

Now if he could only get Colin home safely for Ellie to wed.

Fourteen

"A few more days and you'll no even smell the stench."
Colin MacAlister closed his eyes and rolled from his
back to his side facing the wall.

Blane seriously doubted that.

Thank the Fates the sun was finally up. Perhaps it
would get warmer in here now. Though with the throb-
bing in his head, he was grateful for the muted light.
Morning was visible only from a dim shaft showing
under the ill-fitting heavy wooden door and through
the one opening in the back wall. The combination
cast a gray glow within the confined space where he
sat.

The cell the two men shared was a small, hastily con-
structed rock building, not even tall enough to allow his
cousin to stand fully erect.

Not that Colin needed to be standing. The beating
Wodeford's men had given him had seen to that. Blane

was just thankful the younger man appeared to be on the mend.

Blane shifted on the damp earthen floor, pulling the edge of his heavy woolen plaid up over his nose. He leaned his head back against the rock wall and listened to the sound of Colin's breathing, once again slow and steady with sleep.

Last night, he had been hauled from his audience with Wodeford and tossed into this place. His only consolation had been in finding his cell already occupied by the cousin he had come to rescue.

Some rescue.

"I should no have allowed myself to be taken," Colin had confided as they sat huddled together in the dark. "But they held Dair with a sword to his throat and I couldna risk what they might do to him."

"So you surrendered your weapon." It wasn't a question. Blane knew what his cousin would do under such circumstances. The same as he would have done. The young man's sense of responsibility for his friend would have prevented any other action.

"Aye. They separated us as soon as we reached Wode Castle and I've no seen him since."

"No word from any of the guards on his condition or whereabouts?"

Colin had laughed grimly. "They willna speak even a single word to me, though I've listened in on the conversations they have with one another. Even so, I've learned nothing of Dair. It's no likely they thought they could collect a ransom for one such as him, so I fear . . ." Colin had stopped as if speaking his fears out loud might bring them to pass.

Blane's stomach rumbled, bringing him back to the present, and he huddled deeper into his plaid. Colin had warned him they brought food only once, each evening, so he knew he had a long wait.

Glancing once more at his cousin, he wished he could join the younger man in slumber. Sleep would be a welcome visitor to distract his mind from the cold, the hunger, and the worries about the fates of Alasdair Maxwell and his own men.

"*Psst!*"

Blane sat upright and looked around the room. The noise hadn't come from Colin. He still lay curled on his side, his even breathing changed to light snores.

"Psst! Laird MacKiernan?"

A woman's voice?

Blane followed the sound to the rough window in the back wall. The opening, no larger than his own two hands, was level with his face as he looked out.

"Who's there?" In the silence of the early morning, his words sounded unnaturally loud to his own ears.

"*Shh!* We've a need to speak quietly, good sir."

A woman stood under the roughly hewn window, too short to peer directly inside. She lowered the hood of her cloak and looked up at him, her large brown eyes soft with concern.

It was the same woman who had come to his defense in the hall last evening, Wodeford's sister.

"Catriona?" The name slipped off his tongue without thought.

She stood very still, clutching a bundle to her chest. "I'm honored, Laird MacKiernan, that you'd remember my name."

"I could no forget the lovely lady who spoke up for me. But why are you here?"

She appeared flustered but didn't look away. "I've brought you food. It's no much. Only a few rolls and some cheese." She opened the bundle and handed the food up to him.

After having gone so long without, he saw it as a veritable feast.

"And this," she added, reaching out with what looked like a palm-sized pillow. "It's a poultice. For yer face. Where my brother struck you. It should help the pain and swelling."

"How can I thank you for . . . ?" he began, but she cut him off.

"There's no a need for that, good sir. Just eat it quickly and say nothing to anyone." She folded the cloth she'd had wrapped around the food and pulled her cloak back over her head. "I'll try to bring more later."

With a shy smile, she turned and ran around the corner out of his sight, leaving Blane to stare after her as he rubbed the fragrant little pillow between his fingers.

Fifteen

❦

"You have to trust me on this. I know what I'm talking about." Ellie leaned over Caden's shoulder, watching as he worked to repair the piece of equipment lying in front of him. "We just need to walk the animals through the copper sulfate mixture. It honestly wouldn't be that hard to do."

Why couldn't she just shut up? Every time she'd seen Caden for the last few days, she'd babbled on like this, like some kind of deranged magpie. But she couldn't seem to stop, even though she knew he had no faith in her idea of how to treat the foot rot.

She couldn't seem to make herself move away from him, either.

"Aye, so you've told me, lass. Several times." Caden spoke patiently, not looking up from his task, not even when her hair fell across her shoulder and dangled down onto his.

She should really straighten up and back off. Just move away from the man.

But no.

"What could it hurt to at least try? We'd just need to get the rock and make the solution and then walk the animals through it."

She could only babble on and move closer. Close enough she could feel the heat from his back on her legs. Close enough to admire the way his auburn hair just brushed the top of his shoulders, soft curls caressing his strong neck. Close enough she could almost count the individual gold flecks in his deep brown eyes when he turned his face up to her.

"So you've told me many a time now." He lifted the tool he was working on. "Do you want to do this repair yerself? Because I canna finish with yer hanging over me like a bird of prey."

"Oh. Right. Sorry. I was just trying to . . ." She let the explanation die away as she straightened and he returned to his task.

It was the babbling. If she could just manage to shut her mouth for one minute she wouldn't be so annoying and perhaps she'd be able to convince him. But it was so hard. If he would only believe her. Instead he greeted her with silence.

So she babbled, because the silences were too uncomfortable to bear.

For in the silence, in the moments she didn't fill with inane chatter, her thoughts drifted back to the day they'd gone out to check on the sheep. To that rock overhang with the storm raging outside and his lips warm against hers, his arms holding her tightly, his hands . . .

"Are you no listening at all, woman?"

Startled from her thoughts, Ellie jumped and stepped away, her foot landing on the tools Caden had neatly stacked on the floor. The metal under her slipper rolled and her feet flew out from under her, pitching her backward. Before she could hit the ground, Caden was there, arms outstretched for her to fall into.

Or rather onto.

He'd twisted around to grab her, pulling her forward onto him. When she landed, it was on his solid body instead of the hard ground.

The *oof* sound underneath her sent her scrambling to get to her feet but to no avail. His arms held her securely atop him, face to face, staring into the depths of those eyes.

Brown like warm molasses. Sprinkled with gold.

She stilled and placed her forearms on his chest to balance herself as she pushed up to give herself some distance. That close she couldn't get her voice to work, couldn't even think.

"Are you unhurt?" The words rumbled in his chest, vibrating against her body.

"I'm okay. Just embarrassed. Again." She shook her head, hating the heat that flooded her face. "I swear, Caden. It feels like I've saved up every stupid, klutzy thing I could possibly ever do just so I could repeatedly make a fool of myself in front of you."

He grinned at her and the breath caught in her lungs.

"You do seem to have a talent for the blunder." His hands slid from her waist up the sides of her back. "But I dinna think you a fool, *Elliedenton*. Completely immodest and inappropriate in every way for a lady, but no a fool."

She could hardly deny those charges, straddled across his body with her dress bunched up to her thighs. But she didn't have to listen to them.

Instead she lowered her face to his and kissed that wonderful, firm mouth. Feathered the tip of her tongue over his lips until they parted. Sucked his full lower lip into her mouth.

He rolled, and she found herself under him, his body snuggly fit to hers as he took charge of the kiss she had begun.

One hand cradled her head as he left her mouth and trailed the fire of his lips down her neck onto her shoulder, nudging the gathers of her shift out of his way as he went.

His finger traced the neckline of her garment, followed by his tongue, pushing the material lower until his hot breath caressed her breast.

When his hand covered that same breast, she lifted her hips, locking her legs behind his back.

This felt so right.

The fire consumed him as it did each time he was close to her.

Ellie's skin tasted like honey and he hungered for her as a starving man for crumbs.

The breast under his fingers molded to his hand as if it had been made for him. He ran his thumb over the nipple still hidden under her shift, emboldened when he felt it harden under his touch.

He grasped the strings that held the shift in place and

pulled, loosening her neckline, granting him the access he wanted.

Her little moans drove him wild.

He pushed the cloth from her breast and froze at what greeted him.

A deep, dark red rose adorned her breast.

Her Faerie mark.

The Fae. She'd been sent by the Fae. Sent through time to find her man. His brother. She belonged to his brother.

He looked to Ellie's face to find her staring at him, her eyes the dark inviting green of the deep forest.

Her hands fluttered up and her thumbs brushed against his cheeks. "How can this be possible? It can't be you I was sent here to . . ."

"No!"

It had come out so much more harshly than he'd intended. The hurt and shock on her face cut him to the quick. "No," he said more gently, pulling her shift back up to hide the beauty he'd exposed. It couldn't be him. He'd had his one chance at love. And learned his lesson painfully well. Love was not for him.

From the time he was a child he'd known Alycie Maxwell was to be his wife. Both his mother and hers, Grizel Maxwell, had approved the marriage, encouraged it for as long as he could remember. He'd taken for granted their lives together without ever a single thought to the girl herself.

Had he loved her?

He had no idea what love was. All he knew was that he'd been unable to hold her, unable to forge a bond such as he'd seen between his parents. Though he'd always prided himself on his ability to understand those around him, he'd been oblivious to Alycie's true desires.

In her desperation to be rid of him, she had betrayed his family. He'd driven her to it.

And since then, following his heart had brought nothing but ill to those dear to him. So much for the value of his love.

Dedication and duty—those he understood. Loyalty. Sacrifice. Responsibility. All were the tenets he held dear. The ones to which he'd devoted his life.

But *love*? That word was not part of his destiny in any sense other than his love for Dun Ard, his family, his people. Beyond that, it was nothing to him. A useless emotion meant for others, not him.

Besides, those dear to him were all better off when he kept his mind to business and his emotions tightly reined. When he didn't, when he allowed his emotions to lead him, it caused only grief.

Hadn't he been the one who had insisted Drew come along that day they'd faced off against the Fae warriors and their men? It was his fault Drew had been injured, that he carried the pain and scars on his leg.

When Colin had come home from battle, hadn't he been the one who had insisted Drew continue to practice in the lists with Colin?

It was his fault Colin's sword had left that horrible scar down Drew's chest, stealing whatever confidence Drew had left. His fault Colin bore the guilt for the accident.

His fault Colin had gone off to fight in every battle he could find, that his youngest brother considered himself unfit for anything but death and destruction. The instant Colin's sword had sliced down Drew's chest, Caden had seen it in his eyes.

He'd stolen Colin's honor.

And now he thought to ruin the woman who had been sent for Colin? The one woman who might restore to his brother what he had taken away?

"No," he repeated as he pushed himself away from her. "I'm no the one, lass. I had my chance with a woman I loved and she rejected me. I'll no put anyone through that ever again." Not him, not his family.

How like the Fae to send so great a gift for his brother with such potential for pain attached.

What was he to do? He couldn't seem to keep his hands off this woman. This woman the Faeries had destined for his brother.

He turned his back and started for the door of the workshop.

"In the future, you're no to come to me unaccompanied, do you ken? I'll no be left alone with you again."

That should solve the problem. He wouldn't allow himself the opportunity to be tempted.

He strode from the work shed across the bailey toward the keep, only now noticing the activity there.

Riders!

He picked up his pace, fighting not to break into a run.

How could he have missed the call of the guards?

Foolish question. He knew exactly how he'd missed the cry of "Riders at the gate!"

His steps slowed as he recognized the men who even now dismounted.

Steafan had returned with his mother. He had brought Grizel Maxwell to Dun Ard to await word of her son's fate.

But who was the woman at Grizel's side? The one who even now dropped the hood of her cloak, looked up and caught his gaze.

"Holy Mother of God."

Alycie Maxwell had returned to Dun Ard.

What an idiot!

Ellie slowly got to her feet and walked to the door of the work shed, using a hand against the doorframe to steady her balance. Somehow her legs felt too weak to hold her up properly.

She'd thrown herself at the guy. She'd done everything but rip his clothes off, and given a few more minutes, she might have done that, too. Right out in public where God and everybody could just walk in the door and catch them.

She watched him stride away, and when he halted halfway across the courtyard, straightening his back as if he felt her presence, she quickly ducked behind the doorway.

Never, never had she embarrassed herself so badly.

She waited a couple more minutes before bolting out the opening of the little work shed and around the back, headed for the garden behind the keep. There she should be able to find some peace and quiet.

She hadn't made it through the gate before her hopes were crushed.

You upset. What Big One do?

Missy and Baby trailed silently behind her. Baby's

neck hair bristled as he swung his big head back and forth between her and the direction from which they'd come.

"Not now, guys. I need some alone time." She spoke aloud as much to calm herself as to answer Missy.

We keep Big One away.

Ellie snorted her disbelief, not caring about the unladylike sound. As if Caden would be coming anywhere near her ever again.

"Big One didn't do anything. It was me. I screwed up big-time."

Ellie had reached the center of the garden, where a lovely bench stood under what would be a wonderfully shady tree not long from now. She sat down and dropped her head into her hands.

What on earth had possessed her? As if it wasn't bad enough that he already didn't trust what she told him about treating the sheep, now she'd gone and completely ruined whatever credibility she might have had. Whatever would have made her think Caden had any interest in her?

Well, of course he had an *interest*. That much was pretty darn clear. Any guy would be interested in a woman who threw herself at him. Human nature didn't change just because you were thrown off a few centuries.

But she could have sworn she felt more than just a physical attraction when she was with him. A connection.

"I'm a total freakin' idiot," she muttered. That didn't begin to cover it.

As if ignoring her continued nagging to try her sheep

solution hadn't been clue enough what he thought of her, he certainly hadn't minced words this time. He'd told her exactly what he thought of her, of how inappropriate her behavior was. He'd had enough. He didn't want to be around her anymore. He'd made that clear.

And to top it all off, apparently he still mooned over some woman who'd dumped him. The perfect woman who obviously hadn't had any problems with being immodest or acting inappropriately.

"She may be all that, but she certainly wasn't very smart," Ellie confided to the dogs as she sat up straight. "Can you imagine anyone turning down a guy like him? I mean, how perfect could she be if she didn't even have the good sense to hang on to a guy like that?"

Both animals stared at her, eyes wide and unblinking.

"I could compete with her. If I wanted to," Ellie mumbled, scrubbing her face with her hands.

But Big One's angry.

There was that minor detail. Caden was angry. And she'd made a complete and total fool of herself.

The embarrassment she'd held at bay flooded back. How was she ever going to show her face in front of that man again? She just wanted to curl up in a ball. Wanted to escape. Wanted to turn back time and have another chance at the last hour of her life.

"But those damn Faerie things wouldn't do that, would they? Oh no, they'll dump me here, hundreds of years out of my element. And then I'm totally on my own without a single do-over in sight."

You would do different? Don't think so. Missy's words echoed through her mind as both dogs continued to stare.

And there was the frustration of this whole mess.

The damn dog was right. She wouldn't do anything differently. If she were thrown back into the same spot, her body straddled over Caden MacAlister's, she'd react exactly the same way. And she couldn't even come up with a good reason why other than it just felt right.

He was an overbearing, stubborn, controlling sheepherder but none of that seemed to matter one damn bit when she was around him.

"Well, crap." She reached down and pulled the little dog to her, cuddling the creature in her lap. "You already know me too well, don't you?"

"Who are you talking to?"

Ellie looked up in surprise at the words. Her new little friend, Anna, stood only a few feet down the path from her.

"Thanks for the warning, guys," she muttered before smiling her welcome at the child. "Only myself, Anna. Just hiding out here talking to myself."

"I come to hide here, too. Do you mind if I sit with you?"

Ellie patted the bench beside her in invitation. "And what are you hiding from?"

The child shook her mass of red curls, rolling her eyes as she did so. "Cook's in a fair frightful mood. Says the family is in for it now and she's no happy about it in the least. And when Bridey MacInnis is no happy, the whole of the kitchen suffers, believe me."

"What's happened?"

Though she asked calmly, her stomach churned with nerves. She would absolutely die of embarrassment if anyone knew how she'd behaved. Caden had been awfully upset with her, but surely he wouldn't go say anything.

"Guests have arrived, and one of them"—the girl lowered her voice and looked around conspiratorially— "is the lady who was to have married Master Caden all those years ago. Cook is fit to be tied that the woman would show her face here even if her brother is missing with Master Colin."

The woman Caden still loved was here? Now? How horrible was that. If he were the one, her only way home, how was she supposed to find out with the woman of his dreams showing up?

The little dog in Ellie's lap growled. *Challenge her. It's your pack now.*

Ellie scratched at Missy's head absently.

Maybe the dog had a good idea.

Sixteen

That was, without a doubt, the stupidest idea she'd ever had. But what could she expect when she was taking advice from a dog?

Ellie prodded at the food on her trencher and stole another glance to where Alycie Maxwell sat right next to her.

She couldn't compete with that woman. Alycie was, as far as Ellie could see, perfect.

Though she looked to be a few years older than Ellie, she was a tiny little thing, barely reaching Ellie's shoulder. She wore her shiny brown hair in a braid that reached well below her thighs. Her light brown eyes smiled at everyone they lit upon. And every single word that came out of her perfect little pink mouth was kind and gentle.

Alycie Maxwell was truly gag-me-with-a-spoon nice and Ellie hated her. Or she would if she weren't having such a hard time trying to find something to dislike about the woman.

When Ellie had finally tried to sneak into the keep, Rosalyn had spotted her and taken her to the ladies' solar, where she'd been introduced to Alycie and her mother, Grizel.

Alycie had been warm and kind from the first moment, offering to help when the stitching Rosalyn had given Ellie to work on had become tangled. She'd patiently unknotted the mess Ellie had made and then showed her an easier way to work with the cloth.

Granted Alycie might have been stupid years ago when she dumped Caden, but she sure didn't seem stupid now. And she was, after all, back.

And now, as if sitting right next to Miss Perfect wasn't bad enough, at any moment Caden would enter the hall and she'd have to face him. With both of them knowing how she had behaved this morning. And how he'd rejected her.

Ellie downed her second cup of spiced wine and held it up to the serving girl for a refill.

She lifted her newly filled cup to her lips and glanced over the rim to see Caden stride into the hall.

His hair was loosed from the tie he normally wore and she almost swore she could see the individual strands picking up the glint of the candlelight. He paused just inside the doorway, his eyes scanning the table until he spied her.

Though he quickly looked away, she could feel the burn move up to her cheeks. Or maybe that was just the wine. She watched, unable to tear her eyes away as he entered and took a seat at the center of the table, well away from her.

Well, no wonder. Not only did he have today's little incident as a reminder of what he didn't like about her, but here she sat, right next to the woman he actually loved. What better contrast could she possibly provide? Great big ol' immodest, inappropriate her, side by side with sweet little Miss Perfect.

She felt physically ill.

"Finished, milady?" Anna stood at her shoulder with her hand outstretched.

"Finished?" Ellie gulped down the last of her wine and handed the cup to the girl.

"Yer trencher, Ellie," the girl whispered. "Are you done with that? It's time to change the courses."

"Take it." Who could eat? Her nerves had her stomach dancing like crazy. Food wouldn't go well at all with that mix.

Anna whisked the food away, leaving Ellie to stare at her hands, fingers splayed out on the bare wood of the table. She wouldn't look up again. She certainly wouldn't risk looking down the table to see if he might be looking back.

"As if," she muttered. Well, he might be looking her direction, but it wouldn't be at her. It would be right past her. One seat past her, to be exact.

"Are you feeling unwell?" Alycie leaned close, trailing the scent of roses and spice along with her as she touched her hand to Ellie's forehead. "Yer skin is quite flushed. Would you care to retire to yer room?"

"Fine. Feeling just fine." So now Miss Perfect was

trying to get rid of her. But wait. Wasn't that what she wanted? This could be exactly the excuse she needed to escape. "You know what? I think maybe you're right."

Ellie pushed back her chair and stood, immediately wishing she hadn't as the room began to spin around her.

"Steafan!"

Alycie's hiss seemed to come from all directions at once as Ellie clamped her hand on the back of the chair to keep from falling.

Lord, how strong was that wine?

And then she was moving, someone's arm around her, directing her forward, down the side of the huge crowded room and toward the hallway.

"Need some air." She managed at last to form the words that jumbled around in her head.

"Perhaps your room would be best, milady."

Steafan. It was Steafan who held her on her feet. Steafan was Caden's friend. And guys always talked to their friends. Did he know how she'd behaved with Caden? Was that why he wanted to take her to her room?

"No. Outside. Fresh air."

She had to get her head clear so she could deal with this guy.

The next thing she knew they were in the open moonlight, cool, fresh air caressing her heated skin. "Oh yeah. Much better." She stood at the far corner of the balcony, her cheek pressed against the cold stone wall, her hands draped over the railing. Just a minute or two of this and she'd feel better.

"While we have time alone, milady, I feel it only fair to give you warning."

"About what?" Ellie didn't open her eyes. Sight would only make the spinning start up again.

"Keep yer distance from Caden MacAlister. He'll bring naught but trouble for you. Do you hear me?"

Ellie nodded once, but stopped as the darkness behind her eyes began to swirl. "I hear you, but I don't have any idea what the heck you're talking about." Humiliation swept over her in a wave even as she feigned ignorance. He knew! Caden had told him everything and he was warning her away to protect his friend.

"I dinna ken the reason for yer being here, but if it's to find yerself a husband, Caden is no the one for you to set yer mind on. Yer no to have anything to do with him."

Is that what Caden thought? That she was out to find a husband? Had he said those things to his friend? "No, that's all wrong."

Rough hands clamped down on her already heavy shoulders and her head snapped forward and back as Steafan shook her.

"Open yer eyes and look at me! Do you hear what I say? Caden is to wed my sister. Yer to keep yer distance from him. He's no for the likes of you. Will you remember this?" Another shake and everything shattered around her with the movement, nausea rising to overtake her.

"She may not remember, but I certainly will."

The shaking stopped and Ellie put her hands to either side of her head to stop the uncomfortable rotation, trying to focus on that deep voice as she opened her eyes.

Drew strode across the balcony directly toward her,

an angry scowl on his face. He moved in closer, stepping in front of her, blocking her view of Steafan.

"I only spoke the truth."

"As you see it, perhaps." The world spun out of control as Drew lifted Ellie from her feet. "We'll talk about this another time, you and I."

And then she was moving again, out of the fresh cool air and into the confines of the keep.

"Wine got the best of you, did it?" Drew's chuckle rumbled in his chest. "Yer no a drinker, that's a fact."

Her mouth felt too slow to form an answer so she started to nod, but stopped immediately when the world began to move in the opposite direction. She closed her eyes again, trying to stay very, very still as he carried her up the stairs and down the hallway to her room. Everything had grown fuzzy by the time she heard Alycie's gentle voice behind them.

"Allow me to help you."

Drew's hold on Ellie tightened. "We dinna need any of yer help, Alycie Maxwell."

"I disagree, Andrew. In spite of how you may feel about me, you canna undress the lass and put her to bed as I can. Now lay her down and be on yer way. I'll care for her."

The air stirred around Ellie once again before the dark closed in and she remembered nothing more until she awoke sometime later, snuggled in her bed, a cool cloth draped over her forehead. A soft voice murmured at her side.

"Alycie?" Was that Latin the woman spoke?

"Go back to sleep, dear one. The rest will heal yer body as the scriptures soothe yer soul."

Oh, wasn't this just perfect? Alcyie was nursing her through the night, praying over her.

Now she'd never be able to hate the horrible woman.

"What are you fidgeting for, Son? Be at peace and eat yer meal." Rosalyn patted Caden's hand before turning back to her conversation with her friend, Gizel Maxwell.

Be at peace? He could hardly manage that. Not since he'd seen Ellie rise from her place down the table and leave the room with Steafan's arm about her shoulder.

When he'd entered the hall tonight, he'd spotted her immediately. Her long black curls shining in the flickering light of the hall and her eyes! He'd caught her gaze and felt drawn to her like a moth to a flame. Only his pledge to keep his distance from her had kept him from making his way to her side and likely making a fool of himself.

His pledge and the fact that she was seated next to Alycie.

The shock of seeing Alycie here at Dun Ard had quickly passed, much to his surprise. He'd been so sure that seeing her again would bring back some rush of emotion, but after that initial shock he'd felt amazingly little.

No desire, no anguish of love lost, not even the bitterness he was so sure he still harbored. In fact, the only emotion he was aware of was happiness at the joy he saw reflected on Steafan's face at having his sister here.

Throughout the meal his eyes had wandered their direction, the contrast between the two women striking. Alycie was subdued and plain as always, while Ellie seemed to glow with the fire of her emotions.

He'd waited, trying to decide if he should make his way down the table, if he should speak to either of them.

And then Ellie was gone. She and Steafan.

That made no sense, unless . . . Surely she couldn't have been sent here for Steafan. Hadn't his mother assured him the Fae intended her for one of his brothers? Or had that simply been what his mother wanted to believe?

The only thing that kept him in his seat was seeing Drew follow after them a few moments later.

Caden took a deep breath and picked at the food in front of him until he noticed Alycie leave the table and follow the path the others had taken.

He could stand it no longer.

Rising quietly from his seat, he followed her progress to the balcony, slipping into the shadows, where he could hear without being seen by holding the door open a small crack.

Unfortunately his hiding place gave him no view of the terrace.

"What have you done with her, Steafan?"

Caden's heart skipped a beat. Was it Ellie she spoke of?

"Drew has taken her to her room."

"Ah," Alycie sighed. "Andrew. I tried to speak to him earlier. He's still no forgiven me, no even after all these years."

"Forgiven you?" Steafan laughed, the sound disbelieving. "There's no a need for that. If anything, it should be you holding the grudge. But yer here now and things can be set to rights."

"There's naught I can do to make up for my actions in the past, Brother. I'm only here now to give comfort to Mother as we wait to hear news of Dair."

"Aye, of course you are. And when our brother returns safely, we can have the banns read and put everything right again."

Banns?

Caden didn't have long to consider the question before he heard footsteps approaching the door he held cracked open. He let the door slide silently shut and stepped away, wedging himself against the great cabinet just as the door opened again.

"I've seen yer life in that nunnery. I'd no put that hardship on any woman."

"You've a good heart, Steafan. Any woman should consider herself lucky to have you." Alycie smiled at her brother before heading up the main staircase.

Steafan stared after her for a moment more before he strode to the great entry door and let himself out, leaving Caden alone with his thoughts.

The conversation he'd overheard rattled him. Had Alycie decided to leave the nunnery and wed? Or was it Steafan they discussed? Either way, he was shaken his best friend hadn't come to confide in him.

Whose banns had Steafan meant?

Only one way he could think of to find out, even if it did mean he'd have to admit eavesdropping on his friend.

Caden had just stepped through the huge entry door onto the great landing when he heard the cry from the top of the guard wall.

"Rider at the gate!"

Seventeen

"Do we even have the silver to meet Wodeford's demands?"

Drew stood apart from the others in the room, voicing the question no one else dared to ask.

"Aye, we do. But it will take everything we have." Caden drummed his fingers on the desk in the laird's solar, where all those closest to him were gathered. He scanned the faces of his family, noting their concern, their trust.

"It's no choice at all the man's given you. You'll have to do as he demands and take the silver to him yerself. I'll travel with you."

Steafan gave voice to Caden's own thoughts. He had no real choice, only problems.

From her seat across the desk, his mother made no sound, but her eyes spoke for her as she reached out to clasp hands with Sallie.

The life of her youngest son depended on Caden's decision.

Alasdair Maxwell had returned to Dun Ard last night, battered, bloodied, weakened, and bearing the news that his captor now demanded twice the original ransom to spare the lives of their laird, Blane MacKiernan, and Caden's youngest brother, Colin.

"The end of our reserves." Drew approached his mother, placing a hand on her shoulder, as if to steady her for what he was about to say. "And if the sheep fail? If this rot takes them and we've no silver left? What would befall us then?"

Caden stilled, hating that his brother had hit on the very point that tormented him as he considered his decision. And yet his family deserved his honesty.

"A foul, bitter season where many of Dun Ard's people would face starvation."

"I say we combine the forces of the MacKiernan and the MacPherson and march on Wode Castle." Sallie's husband rose from his chair to pace back and forth. "I wager they'd hand over our kinsmen then. We've no need to—" Ranald Macpherson would have continued, but his words were cut short.

"No!" Steafan apparently realized his outburst had startled everyone. When he continued, it was in a much quieter voice. "No. You canna do such a thing. It'd be the death of our laird for sure." He rose from his chair and moved to Caden's side. "And the end of yer brother as well."

"It's no yer call. This is a family decision." Drew's anger sparked through the room.

"Steafan *is* family. Today's decisions affect him as

much as any in this room. Though it's no a family decision. It's mine to make."

Caden looked to his mother and sister sitting across from him. Neither spoke as he met their eyes, but their thoughts were clear to him.

As Blane's heir and surrogate, it was indeed his decision and they trusted him to make it.

The fate of all he loved lay in his hands. He couldn't afford to take rash chances. His choice lay between certain death for his laird and brother or the possible deaths of many of his people.

"Steafan is right. Wodeford hides under the banner of the English king. We'd no make it past Loch Ness before they'd be down on our heads. And the march would leave both Dun Ard and Castle MacPherson unprotected."

If only he could think of some way to improve his odds.

"What of Ellie's stones, Caden? Is it possible they could work?" Drew's words echoed in the silence of the room.

"Ellie's stones? What do you speak of?" Rosalyn looked from one of her sons to the other.

"She seems to think she can use bluestone to cure the sheep," Drew answered. "Is there any possibility she could be right?"

Steafan snorted his contempt. "Stones to cure such an illness? It's no more than a woman's fancy. A waste of time and silver."

Caden searched the hopeful faces all looking to him, waiting for his opinion. His friend was right. The idea seemed preposterous. Soaking a stone in water and walking the animals through it? He'd resisted even thinking on it until now. Purchasing the bluestone would require silver they could ill afford to spend, assuming they could even find the stuff. Silver necessary to save the lives of Blane and Colin.

And if the fool plan didn't work? Ellie would bear the brunt of that failure and he found himself loathe to place such a burden on her. It was his responsibility.

Still, if there were even the smallest chance it would work, he owed it to the people of Dun Ard to try. What choice did he have?

None. No more choice in this than in delivering what silver they had to free his kinsmen.

He rose from his chair, motioning to his brother as he headed toward the door.

"Let's go see."

If she lay very, very still, the pain in her head was almost bearable. But the weight of the huge dog across her legs was not.

Ellie pulled her feet out from underneath Baby and slowly scooted up in her bed until she was able to prop herself in a sitting position. The waves of nausea passed more quickly this time. Maybe she wasn't going to die after all, in spite of how she felt.

She could only remember feeling like this once in her whole life, when she'd first gone away to college and she and a bunch of girls from her dorm had driven into Austin to that cowboy bar. She'd only had a few of those longneck beers, but it had been enough. She didn't remember any of the drive back to campus, but she did remember the aftermath.

She tossed back the covers, not feeling the least bit guilty when Missy crawled away, twitching her ears in irritation.

"If you don't like it," she started, but stopped when the sound of her own voice sat her head to vibrating. *There's always the blankets I put on the floor for you,* she finished silently.

In response the little terrier stood, stretched and curled up next to Baby, promptly going back to sleep.

"Fine then," Ellie whispered, slowly swinging her feet to the cold stone floor. "Just let me get through today, and I swear, I'll never, ever drink that much again."

Slowly, she shifted her weight to her feet and stood, one hand on the bed to maintain her balance.

If we all just stay really, really quiet, I think I can . . .

The thought hung in midair as her door crashed open and both dogs jumped up, barking. Caden filled the doorway, with Drew right behind him.

"Hush!" she hissed, covering her ears with both hands. No doubt about it. She was going to die. Her head was going to explode like an overfilled water balloon.

"I need you to tell me truthfully. Will the bluestone work to cure the sheep?" Caden demanded. Very, very loudly.

Ellie held up both hands to stop him. "Lower your voice."

"I need . . ." he started again.

"I need for you to lower your voice. Or get out." To hell with pleasant. She didn't have the strength for pleasant.

Drew shouldered past his brother, an obnoxious grin

on his face as he crossed to the fireplace. "Our lass here was in her cups last eve, Brother. You'd best speak gently if you want her help on this bright morn."

Caden's eyebrow rose, but when he opened his mouth again, he spoke more quietly. "Will it work? The bluestone?"

The sheep? He was here to question her about the damn sheep?

Drew was back, gently guiding her to a chair by the fire, pressing a mug of something hot into her hands.

"What's this?" It had the smell of herbs to it.

"It's a potion Lady Rosalyn left for you earlier. Drink it slowly. It will help."

Steam from the mug blanketed her face as she lifted it to her mouth. The first small sip slid down the back of her throat, warming, calming her riotous stomach.

"The bluestone?" Caden reminded.

"Yes. I believe it will work. I'm sure of it."

She took another soothing sip as the two men stared at one another until at last Caden broke the blessed silence.

"That's it, then. It's the best chance we have. Now we've only to find some of the stuff."

"I know a man in Inverness. He's a . . ." Drew paused, a sheepish look crossing his face. "He's an alchemist. If anyone would know where to lay hands on bluestone, it would be him." Drew turned from them, heading to the door.

"Where are you going?"

Drew answered without looking back at them. "To make preparations to leave for Inverness on the morn. I've had dealings with Argeneau for a long time. It's likely he'll be willing to let me have the bluestone with no more than my promise of payment. I'm no of any use here anyway. It's no like my sword would be of any value when you carry the silver to Wodeford. Besides, you've made it clear it's Steafan you've chosen to take along with you, so it only makes sense I should be the one to go for the stone."

"Drew—"

"My decision's made," Drew interrupted. "I leave at first light. As I'm sure the two of you will."

"What's he talking about? Where are you going?"

Caden had followed his brother to the door but stopped to answer her.

"To buy the life of my laird, and that of my brother as well. I only pray that yer bluestone can save the rest of Dun Ard."

He held her eyes for a moment longer, as if he had more to say, but then he was gone.

Ellie took another sip of the warm tea and a shiver ran the length of her body.

Something didn't feel right. Not right at all.

Eighteen

"There you are!" Caden looked up from adjusting his horse's bridle when Steafan entered the stable. "I was concerned when I couldna find you anywhere this morning." He'd wanted to go over details of their journey one more time.

They had agreed only Steafan would accompany him. Riding alone, the two of them could cover the distance to Wode Castle more quickly and with fewer provisions than a larger party would require. Besides, it was as Wodeford had insisted. The heir was to deliver the ransom unaccompanied.

"I rode up to the high pastures to check on the men there one last time before we left."

"All was well?" Another example of why Steafan was so invaluable to him. Even in the face of a hazardous journey, his friend's first concern was for Dun Ard and her people.

"Aye. Will Drew be joining us?"

"No. He was away at sunrise." He would have welcomed his brother's company on this journey, even if their paths would have to take different directions after a few hours. But perhaps it was better that Drew traveled separately.

Steafan led a fresh horse out of the stalls and began preparations of his own as Caden left the stable for the bailey.

"Caden!" Ellie hurried his direction, both of her mangy dogs following closely behind. "I was afraid I'd missed you."

He almost wished she had. It was easier when he didn't see her. Or so he tried to convince himself. Still, there were things he needed to tell her.

"It's good yer here. I've set William and Roger to work on the troughs you said you'd need for the footbath. If you have any problems, go directly to Bridey. They're her youngest boys and she can get them working for you."

"That's fine. I'm sure they'll do great." Her hands fluttered around nervously as she spoke. "Something doesn't feel right, Caden. I know we already talked about this, but do you really think this is such a smart thing for you to do? I mean, this Wodeford guy already has your brother and your cousin. You're the next in line to take over this place. What's to stop him from holding you, too?"

"What's to stop him? We're at the end of the Mac-Kiernan fortune, that's what. Once he learns there's no more silver to be had, he'll be happy enough to be rid of us."

At least, Caden sincerely hoped that was the case. He had no choice. The message Alasdair delivered was clear. The ransom was to be delivered by the MacKiernan heir. Alone.

He could risk taking along a contingent of men. He'd certainly considered it. But as Steafan had counseled, more riders would only slow them down, require more provisions and pull defenders from Dun Ard. Besides, if he were heading into a trap, he didn't want the lives of more men on his conscience. Or the lives of his brother and his cousin if he didn't follow Wodeford's instructions.

There was no point in going through his reasons again. He'd already had this discussion with Ellie and everyone in his family last night at their evening meal. He didn't intend to waste any more time justifying his actions yet again.

"When Drew brings back the stones, yer no to wait for my return. Go ahead with the treatment as soon as you can."

Ellie looked away, biting at her bottom lip. When she looked back, he feared himself in for another argument. "There's no way I can talk you into sending Steafan alone, is there?"

No point in answering.

"Okay, okay. I get it. Will you at least take Baby along? I'd feel better knowing he was there to help you."

The big dog at Ellie's side wagged his tail expectantly.

"I'm no dragging that great beast along on this journey. I've no the time to look after yer Baby for you."

What did the woman expect? It was enough he was going after the man she was to wed. Even if she didn't know it.

The man was so damned stubborn!

Ellie bit back the protests that bubbled to her lips as she watched Caden swing his leg across his mount and ride out through the gates with Steafan trailing behind like the obnoxious toady he was.

She might have been drunker than a skunk night before last, but she remembered Steafan's lecture clearly enough. Caden was off-limits to her. Apparently Steafan's sister, who had rejected Caden years before, had changed her mind and the wedding was back on.

Steafan sent one last angry scowl her direction before his mount disappeared into the gaping dark hole of the gate behind Caden.

Fine. Steafan could glare at her all he wanted, she didn't care. It wasn't like she was out here flirting with Caden. She had good reason to be speaking to him.

This whole thing felt wrong. She had every right to be here trying to talk Caden out of going on this ridiculously dangerous mission of his.

Even if he was going to marry Steafan's sister.

And where the heck was Miss Perfect anyway? Shouldn't she be the one out here trying to talk Caden out of going? Or at the very least seeing her intended off? But no. Alycie was nowhere to be seen.

Ellie fumed, staring at the empty gate, ignoring the voices vying for attention in her head until Baby's sharp bark drew her notice.

Baby can track Big One. Easy.

"Yeah, but Caden said he couldn't watch out for you." She reached out and scratched between the ears on the huge head of the animal staring into her eyes.

A sound, suspiciously like a snort, rolled through her mind. *Baby watch out for Big One. Baby want to. For you.*

The big dog looked at her expectantly, his ears perked, his tail wagging hard enough to create a small breeze.

"Could you keep up with those horses?"

Hu-mans. Missy's voice now, heavy with disgust. *Swift Death a hunter. Brings down deer. Can follow horse. Easy.*

"Swift Death?"

Baby like new name better.

"Yeah, well, I should hope so."

The whole name thing rattled Ellie a bit, though it certainly reinforced the animal's survival skills. The dog knew his limits. If he thought he could do this, who was she to argue? "Okay. Take off, Baby."

The dog swiped his big tongue along her chin and gave her a look she could have sworn was a grin before he raced out through the gates following after Caden and Steafan.

Wiping the doggie kiss from her face, Ellie caught Missy's gaze. "Do *you* have another name?"

"People may call me many things, but few are brave enough to do so to my face."

Sallie's voice so close caught Ellie off guard. "No, I was talking to . . . never mind." The woman wouldn't believe her anyway.

She was going to have to be more careful. She'd gotten so comfortable communicating with the animals, she sometimes forgot no one else could hear them. From Sallie's concerned expression, she suspected a quick change of subject would be wise.

"What are you doing out here?"

"Enjoying the fresh air." Sallie stretched, her hand bracing her lower back. "I found when I carried the lads, near my time it seemed to help if I moved about. Come walk with me." The woman looped her arm through Ellie's and pulled her forward.

Ellie paced her steps to accommodate the waddle of her companion as the women crossed the bailey and headed up a slight incline toward an overgrown rock wall enclosure with an archway leading inside.

When they reached it, Sallie released her hold and sat on one of the walls, pushing curls back from her pink face. "That wee hill was perhaps more than I'd bargained for. Do you mind if we rest here for a spell?"

"Not at all." Ellie joined her on the rock wall, peering over into the weeds. It looked as if this had been a whole building at one time or maybe even one that had never been finished. "What is this place?"

"We call it Mairi's Garden." Sallie propped her shoulder against the archway as she scooted her body more securely onto the low rock wall. "It's been sadly neglected, I'm afraid."

"That it has. It was meant to be a chapel."

Beside Ellie, Sallie's jaw tightened before she turned to acknowledge with the barest nod of her head the woman who had joined them.

"Alycie."

"I'm sorry to see it's no been finished in all these

years. Does that mean yer family still holds to their pagan ways?"

The rebuke in Alycie's question was undeniable, though her voice was as gentle and soft as ever.

"We've never had a need for a chapel at Dun Ard, no with the village so close we can easily ride there." Sallie pushed herself up to her feet. "Besides, leaving it unfinished seems a fitting way to remember our poor cousin, does it no? Surely you've no forgotten Mairi? No forgotten that she disappeared."

Alycie clasped her hands tightly at her waist and looked away, her eyes blinking rapidly. "I've no forgotten," she whispered.

"Good." Sallie reached out for Ellie's hand. "I believe I've had enough fresh air for now. Will you help me back to the keep?"

Ellie felt like she'd stepped into a theater in the middle of a movie. And though right now sure didn't appear to be the proper time to ask questions, it was clear there was a history between these two women. No doubt about it.

"We made good time today, did we no?" Steafan stretched out his leg, nudging the stones at the edge of the fire pit with the toe of his boot.

"Aye, we did," Caden agreed absently as he walked to the edge of their campsite and stared out into the black of the night.

Ellie and her damn dog might think him too stupid to realize the great beast had followed him all day, but they'd be wrong. The dog, her *Baby*, was out there somewhere in the inky blackness watching him even now.

It would serve them both right to let the creature fend for itself.

With a shake of his head, he tossed the remainder of the meat he'd had for dinner out beyond the light before returning to the roll of blanket that would be his bed under the stars this night.

Thinking of the deerhound, and the woman who had sent him, Caden smiled in spite of himself as he watched the clouds skitter across the night sky leaving a trail of bright stars in their wake.

There was yet one more detail he should address before he slept.

"Steafan? You were correct to suggest we bring none of the men with us. Thank you."

"Good. I'm glad you see the right of it at last."

Not that the extra men would help if Wodeford planned some nefarious action anyway. Blane had traveled with additional men and it certainly hadn't helped him. In fact, the safety of those men was just one more item on a long list of worries that plagued Caden tonight.

At last his eyes drifted shut. They'd ridden long and hard this day and would again for many more before they arrived at Wode Castle. He reached for the oblivion of sleep that danced just beyond his reach. So close.

"When we return to Dun Ard, will you have the banns read right away?"

The question jolted Caden fully awake, but he didn't open his eyes. He didn't want to face his friend.

His mother had said Ellie was to wed one of his brothers. After all these years, he felt as close to Steafan as if he actually were a brother. And yet, if Steafan thought to wed Ellie . . . He couldn't follow that line of reasoning to its conclusion. He should be happy for the friend who had been like another family member since childhood.

But for some strange reason he wasn't.

"Banns?" The word stuck in his mouth. "Whose banns?"

"Yers and Alycie's, of course. If yer to stop her from returning to Iona, you'll need to act quickly."

Caden rolled to his side, propping his head on his hand to stare at Steafan.

"What are you asking? Have we no had this discussion many a time before? And always to the same end. Her coming back to Dun Ard makes no difference. You have to give up on that idea. I'm no going to marry yer sister now or ever. I released her from her pledge long ago. She disna want me."

Steafan stood to pace back and forth on his side of the fire, squatting down at last on one knee, the reflection of the flames casting a crazed glow in his eyes. "She'll change her mind, Cade. You can make her do that. I know you can. We can make her change it together."

"I've no reason to do that."

"You damn well have!" Steafan yelled, rising again to his feet to pace. "You've no seen that hell hole of a nunnery you sent her to live in. I have. She works from sunrise to sunset with no rest but on her knees for prayer. Her hands are raw to cracking from scrubbing their floors. We have to get her out of there."

Caden rolled to his back and closed his eyes against the memories of what Alycie Maxwell had done to his family. What she had done to him. What she thought of them all.

She had led his sister and his cousin Mairi into a trap, handing them over to that evil Fae, Duke Servans, and his men. Mairi had escaped, but in the battle that followed Sallie was taken prisoner and Drew had nearly died.

All because Alycie so despised the idea of marrying into a family descended from the Fae. She'd done it for nothing more than the Duke's promise to take her to the convent on Iona.

The woman had gotten what she asked for.

"It's no more than what she wanted. Her choice, Steafan. All by her choice. No mine."

"That's it exactly. Now that she's come home, we can make her see how she chose wrongly. You can have what you want at last. You love her. You can make her love you."

Caden opened his eyes, staring up at the jeweled night sky. For the first time in nine years, he thought about the words. Heard them.

You love her. You can make her love you.

"No," he said slowly, his words and the realization coming together. "You canna make anyone love you."

Either love was there or it wasn't.

His Faerie ancestors had to be laughing hysterically on the other side of the curtain between the worlds that he was so dense it had taken him until now to figure out this simple fact.

"In truth, I never loved yer sister. I took for granted the fact that we would wed, but I dinna love her. I respected her. Until she betrayed my family. The day she led Sallie into that trap, risking my sister's life by delivering her over to be kidnapped and brutalized by the Duke—on that day I lost what respect I had."

"Alycie was but a frightened lass. You canna hold that against her."

"I can. If no for her actions, Sallie would no have suffered as she did. If no for her actions, Drew would still be whole. I canna forget those things, Steafan. I dinna want to."

"By all that's holy, man, Alycie has suffered for the last nine years for her mistake. She never intended to bring harm to yer family. She's meant to be a laird's wife and lady, no a servant to a passel of nuns."

Drew's accusations rang in his memory. "Is it your sister's place as wife of the laird you fash yerself over, or is it yer own future as the laird's overseer you seek to secure?"

The two men stared at one another across the fire for long minutes before Caden rolled over, turning his back to his friend. "Rest easy, Steafan. Yer future disna depend on yer sister wedding me. It never has. As for any thought of me taking Alycie to wife, it's no going to happen. That's the end of it. We'll no be having this discussion again. Ever."

"Verra well, Caden MacAlister. You've made yer own choice and now we'll all have to live with it."

So we will, Caden thought, tightly shutting his eyes against the memories that would rob him of this night's sleep.

Nineteen

～

Caden pulled his mount to a halt, cocking his head to listen. No unusual sounds. No sounds at all other than the river burbling beside him. That in itself was unusual.

Something just didn't feel right.

"Why do you stop?" Steafan circled back, bringing his horse next to Caden's. "We've no time to waste."

Caden started forward, picking up speed, matching his friend's pace as they rode.

Of course Steafan was right.

Already they traveled more slowly than Caden would like. The high peaks would be too dangerous to summit this time of year, so they'd been forced to add extra days in going around.

Since early morning they'd followed the banks of the River Dochart toward Killin, where they could finally cut south and make directly for Wode Castle.

The river grew more turbulent the farther they rode,

and the land more sloped. Ahead, Caden could see a narrowing of the path they followed as it turned once again from the river and this time forced them back into a densely wooded area.

Mirroring the waters he rode beside, his emotions grew more turbulent, an unease settling over him. Obviously his worries over his brother, his cousin and the fate of his people were playing tricks on his mind.

He had to let all that go. Ellie and Drew would treat the sheep. He would trust her bluestone concoction to save them. And he was on his way to pay the ransom demanded for Blane and Colin just as Wodeford had instructed. For now he needed to focus his energies on his task, to concentrate on the hazards of the trail.

Glancing back, he caught the flash of gray fur and smiled in spite of himself. The damned beast followed still, darting in and out of the trees. The deerhound was every bit as persistent as his mistress.

Ahead of him, Steafan pushed through the dense foliage where the trail cut into the forest and disappeared.

The thought of Ellie calmed him. The memory of her concern the morning he'd left warmed him. Imagine her trying to warn him something didn't feel right about his going, as if he would actually change his plans. As if he hadn't considered all of it carefully.

What she didn't understand was that he had no choice. The responsibility of too many lives lay in his hands. Too much depended on his actions.

Once again, he drew up on his reins, bringing his mount to a halt.

Was that where this sense of disquiet had originated? Or did her warning simply dovetail with his own feelings?

His decision now to act on those feelings surprised him. If there was no problem ahead of him, he'd feel foolish later and share a good laugh with Steafan at his own expense when he had to admit to what he was about to do.

And if trouble did lie on the other side of the dense canopy, he'd be grateful for his actions.

Caden directed his horse close to the river, turning the animal so its body served as a screen between the forest ahead and his actions.

He dismounted and pulled a small bag from his things tied to the saddle. Then he squatted down and lifted the animal's front left foot as if to inspect it for injury. As he did so, he tossed the bag into the shallow edge of the water.

The weight of the silver inside should lodge it there, holding it securely until his return.

Standing up, he patted his horse's neck and then re-mounted. He should feel utterly foolish for what he'd just done.

A look over his shoulder revealed Baby, standing in the middle of the trail, nose lifted, scenting, hackles raised.

No, foolish wasn't at all what he felt at the moment.

"Here now, milady! That's no safe at all!" The large guard pulled Ellie back from the edge of the wall walk, frowning down at her as he did so. "Just what do you think to be doing up here? It's no a place for a lady."

Ellie bit back the first caustic response that came to mind. As her grandmama had always said, you catch more flies with honey than vinegar. Unfortunately her honey supply was running low.

She'd grown increasingly irritable with the men at Dun Ard telling her what was and wasn't proper for her to be doing over the last few days. From the two young men building the sheep troughs right up to this guard who looked like someone's grandpa, they all seemed to feel they had the right to direct the activities of all women—and her in particular—as if they had some secret, God-given knowledge and authority women didn't have.

It shouldn't have surprised her, of course. Their behavior wasn't all that different from that of the farm-hands back home.

Ellie clenched her hands together in front of her, consciously mimicking the meek gesture Alycie always sported, and forced a timid smile to her lips.

"I was hoping for some news of Andrew's return." Or better yet, Caden's.

Granted, she hadn't seen any other women climb the narrow stairs to the wall walk, but it obviously was the best place to look out over the countryside. And while logic told her scanning the horizon wouldn't get either of them back any faster, logic wasn't her strongest ally right now.

Instead fear prodded at her. A vague unknown fear, like a premonition that something very bad was going to happen and she couldn't do anything to stop it.

Which was just stupid. After all, she might hear animals talking in her head, but she couldn't foresee the future.

It had to be the knowledge of what had already happened to the last person who went after Caden's brother that made her nervous. That must be it.

"I'm just being unreasonable," she muttered, half under her breath.

The big guard continued to frown at her, his hands

at the ready as if he expected her to throw herself over the wall.

"I agree, milady. And that's why you should take yerself back down to the keep. Perhaps you need to rest for a bit."

"I'd prefer to remain right here, if it's all the same to you. I'll make sure to stay out of your way."

"I fear I'll have to insist you go. It's no a good idea—"

A deep voice from behind Ellie interrupted the guard.

"Gregor, you old bear, leave the lady to her own devices. It's no like it's an extra burden on you."

The guard's frown morphed into a wide grin just before Ellie whipped around to discover who was taking her side in this discussion.

"Dair Maxwell, you young whelp! Still trying to tell me how to do my job?"

"What? You'll no use my title? You'd no address me as Sir Alasdair?" Ellie's defender lounged in the doorway, his shoulder propped against the wall, a lazy smile on his lips and a twinkle in his eyes.

"Ach," the old guard grunted, shaking his head. "Sir Whelp, mayhaps. The nobles may have named you a knight, but I remember no so long ago you and young Colin both snotty-nosed bairns chasing around at the laird's feet."

Dair crossed the space separating him from the old guard in three long strides, and threw his arms around the man as they exchanged hugs with much pounding on one another's backs.

So this was the man who'd brought the news that sent Caden racing off to rescue his brother. This was Alycie and Steafan's brother. Ellie studied him as he and

Gregor continued their greeting. He was tall and broad shouldered, with long brown hair pulled back and tied at the nape of his neck. Even the bruising and cuts on one side of his face didn't detract from his beauty. Somehow they only made him look more dangerous.

"It's good to have you home safe, lad," Gregor mumbled before he straightened, cleared his throat and aimed a glare at Ellie. "But the lady should no be on the wall walk. Master Caden would have my arse for it if she were to come to harm."

Dair grinned, slapping Gregor on the back before he turned to Ellie. "You leave Cade to me. I'll watch over the lady if it makes you feel better."

In one step he was in front of her, bowing over her hand. "Sir Alasdair Maxwell at yer service, milady."

She was about to ask if all this male-posturing meant she got to do what she wanted without further argument when she spied a rider in the distance. Her heart sped up and she ran the two steps to the wall, stretching up on tiptoes trying to get a better view.

Dair's hand gripped her arm as she pointed toward what she'd seen.

"Rider at the gate!" Gregor shouted.

"Is it . . . ?" She could feel the pulse pounding in her head.

"It's naught but one of the shepherds coming in," Gregor answered, sounding almost as disappointed as she felt.

Perhaps she'd been wrong. Standing up here watching, dealing with the frustration of each normal visitor, getting her hopes up just to have them dashed—that was more upsetting than waiting down below.

"You know, I think Gregor's right. I'm going back down."

"Thank you, milady," the old guard responded, relief evident in his voice.

Dair still gripped her arm. "I'll escort you."

She didn't argue. It was easier to allow him to guide her down the stairs than to point out she didn't need his help.

At the foot of the stairs he bowed over her hand again. "If there's anything you need, dinna forget, I'm pledged to yer service now."

His grin with its quick flash of dimple was so contagious she found herself smiling back before turning to hurry away, not sure exactly where she hurried to. Just away.

So that's a knight. The history classes she'd taken hadn't done them justice. He was no Caden, but he'd turn heads, that was for sure.

Where you go?

Ellie smiled as the little terrier's voice lilted through her mind.

"Exploring. Want to come along?"

Missy matched her step and they strolled past the lists toward the back of the property, wandering aimlessly. The whole of Dun Ard, which had been so endlessly fascinating to her only days ago, now seemed empty and uninteresting.

Now that Caden was gone.

Perhaps it was because he was the one person she had confided her secret to. The one person who knew she spoke to animals and understood when they spoke to her. The one person who at least pretended to believe her when she'd told him, without making fun of her for it.

She stopped and looked around before she hung her head, shaking it in irritation with herself.

No, it was more than that, and she might as well face the facts. She missed seeing him, talking to him, listening to him. Touching him.

She just plain missed Caden.

"How stupid is that?" she muttered.

No stupid. Lonely when pack mate gone. Normal.

"He's not my pack mate. He belongs to Alycie." The woman he was engaged to marry.

Wrong. You alpha female now. You must challenge.

Great. Now she was getting advice on her love life from a dog. Advice she planned to ignore, because as she recalled, the last time she'd taken Missy's advice she'd ended up with nothing more than a killer hangover.

"Come on, let's see what other secrets this place has to offer." She picked up her speed, hoping to distract the little dog as well as her own thoughts.

Rounding a low hill, they came upon a large circle of stacked stones, obviously man-made. Closer to it, Ellie realized it was a graveyard, probably the family plot.

No! rang out sharply in Ellie's mind as she stepped into the circle.

"What?" She turned to look at the little dog standing outside the stones. "What's wrong with you?"

Dead Hu-mans in that ground. Maybe spirits.

Missy's normally wagging tail was still, drooping down between her legs.

"That's ridiculous. Why would you think something like that?"

Hu-mans worry much. Not at peace when they die. Not like dogs.

Dogs were superstitious?

Ellie grinned at the little animal as a childhood memory of some scary movie fluttered though her mind. A creepy, dark graveyard, complete with lightning strikes and a big iron gate that opened with a long-drawn-out high-pitched squeal.

Missy flattened to the ground, whimpering.

"Oh my gosh, what's wrong?" Ellie rushed toward the dog, scooping her up and cuddling her close.

Bad noise hurt ears.

"Bad noise?" Ellie's hand froze in midstroke. Surely she couldn't have projected her memory that clearly. "This noise?" She ran over the scene again, lingering over the iron gate and its screech.

The dog in her arms whimpered and began to shake.

"Well, I'll be damned. Sorry, Missy. I'll be more careful." She hugged the little creature to her, scratching the terrier's head.

Just another thing to file away without really putting any thought into. She couldn't afford to think on any of it too much. If she did, she would be overwhelmed by how her life had roller-coastered completely out of control.

Back home, Ray probably had the ranch declared his by now, and here she was, stuck hundreds of years away, unable to do anything to stop him. No, all she could do was constantly find new and ever weirder "talents" she was developing, like projecting thoughts and sounds into the mind of a dog.

If only she had someone to talk to so she could try to sort through it all. But with that wish, the only face that shimmered in her mind was Caden's.

And thinking of Caden brought back the overwhelming apprehension she'd been fighting all morning. An emotion so strong it was almost as if it were coming at her from the outside. Almost as if she were picking up on someone else's feelings.

But that was impossible.

Caden pressed his heels to his horse's sides and the animal moved forward, pushing through the foliage into the gloom of the forest. He slapped at the low-hanging branches, fighting the urge to draw his sword.

It was the perfect place for an ambush.

And yet they were still days away from Wode Castle. Reason would dictate he should have nothing to worry about here.

"Reason be damned," he muttered.

Every instinct of warning he had rang out in his head. Something was not right.

The narrow path ahead was empty. Where was Steafan?

Caden stopped ignoring his strongest urge and reached to his back, drawing his sword.

Not a moment too soon.

Four men moved out of the trees, surrounding him, their swords drawn. Without thought, Caden defaulted to his years of training, feinting at the first attacker and swinging his sword at the second even as he tugged on the reins to turn his horse into the others, using the animal's body as a weapon. He could handle this. He was mounted and this ragged band of brigands were on foot.

His blade connected, sending a jolt up his arm to match the man's screams. Caden pulled hard, swinging his sword down and across, ready to strike the next man, only vaguely conscious of the first man's body falling to the ground.

He deflected the thrust of the second attacker with the side of his blade, the echoing ring of metal dulled by the carpet of newly budding green around them.

"Halt!"

Caden spared only a glance in the direction of the command even as he lifted his sword to deliver another blow.

Ahead, Steafan knelt on the ground with his head bent, one attacker on either side. The larger of the two men held a sword poised over Steafan's neck.

How had they managed to capture him with no sound?

"I said halt! Drop yer weapon, MacAlister, lest you fancy having yer companion's head separated from his body."

They knew his name!

Caden turned his horse to face the only one of their attackers who was himself mounted, the man who commanded, it appeared.

"For Christ's sake, Cade, do as he says!" Steafan pleaded.

On his own, he was confident he could have defeated these men. But they had Steafan and they looked desperate enough to do as they threatened. He had no choice. He would not risk the life of one who was like a brother to him.

With one last look at his friend, Caden tossed his sword to the ground.

"Now climb down off that fine animal of yers and hand over the silver you carry."

Thank the Fae he'd listened to his internal warning of danger.

Twenty

Blane paced back and forth across the small cell, his head bowed to allow for the low ceiling. The sun was near to rising this day. That meant soon she would come.

Each day just before the sun rose, Catriona appeared outside the little window, various tidbits of food hidden in her cloak.

He appreciated the victuals she brought, but in all honesty it was the woman herself he'd grown anxious to see each day, more so than the food she brought.

Colin slept, curled up for warmth, his face to the wall.

Perhaps it was his warrior's training, to grab his rest whenever and wherever he could. Blane wasn't sure. He knew only that his young cousin had mastered the talent.

"Laird MacKiernan?" The hushed whisper floated through the open window.

Blane reached the opening in an instant, smiling as the angel standing outside dropped the cloak from her head and looked up at him.

"Did I no ask you to call me by my given name?" His hand itched to touch her skin, to feel the warmth of her cheeks as they turned pink in response to his question.

"Aye, that you did. Blane," she added shyly as she lifted the little bundle she carried to him.

Their fingers touched in the exchange and he grasped her hand, not wanting to let go right away.

"Is something wrong?" she questioned, but made no attempt to remove her fingers from his grasp.

He wanted to laugh at the absurdity of her question. Everything was wrong, starting with his being inside this filthy cave of a room, locked away from the most interesting woman he'd ever had the pleasure of meeting.

And yet when he looked down into her gentle eyes, he could only return her smile and shake his head. "No, my lady. Nothing is wrong."

"Is your cousin healing? I was so frightened for his health when I saw him last."

"He is better now." Amazingly enough. Once again, the recuperative powers of their Fae ancestry played into Colin's recovery.

"Is there anything I can bring you on the morrow?" She asked the same question each day though they both knew she was limited in what she could slip to them.

"The key," Colin muttered from his spot in the corner. "Tell her the damned key to this cell would be a nice enough gift to bring."

Perhaps his young cousin had only mastered the art of *appearing* to sleep.

"I canna. . . . I'm so very sorry, Blane." Catriona clutched her hand to her heart. "I canna bring the key. Food, perhaps a blanket I could manage. But no the means to yer escape. Austyn would never forgive me."

And therein lay the problem.

Blane had already learned much about the lady. She'd been widowed at an early age and had spent the last twenty years living in her family's castle under her brother's authority. Though she seemed appalled by his actions, and fearful of the man himself, she also felt indebted to him.

She would never assist in their escape.

And he would never ask it of her.

He was about to tell her so when he heard the other voice outside.

"Lady Baxter? What are you doing out here?"

Blane drew back from the opening. If someone discovered Catriona communicating with the prisoners, there was no telling what might happen to her.

"I . . . I was simply out here to . . ." Her voice paused and Blane's stomach rolled.

The woman was unable to lie, even to save herself.

"I'm afraid I must insist you accompany me back inside now, Lady Baxter."

"You dinna understand, Sim. I couldna allow the laird and his cousin to starve. Please dinna tell Austyn."

"I'm sure he'll understand, Aunt. Now you'll come with me, aye? I've no wish to haul you in over my shoulder, but I will if you defy me. It's no safe for you to be out here."

"You were much more agreeable as a child, Simeon."

Blane pressed his back against the wall of his prison, rage and helplessness warring for control of his heart.

"Dinna fash yerself over this, Cousin. She'll be well." Colin sat in his corner staring over at him. "She is Wodeford's sister, after all. He'd no bring her to any harm over a few crumbs of food."

Blane nodded blindly. She'd best be well. Or any who brought her harm would have to answer to him.

Twenty-one

Caden awoke with a jerk, uncomfortably aware of the strain on his shoulders. He sat on the ground, slumped against a tree with his arms stretched around behind it, his wrists bound together.

He had to organize his thoughts to come up with a plan. If only he knew who these people were or could recall some snippet of conversation, some clue to help him.

That first night was still a blur.

After he'd been surrounded and dropped his weapon, he'd climbed down off his horse. The last thing about the capture Caden remembered was a blow to the back of his head. Right after he'd announced there was no silver.

He leaned his head against the tree and clenched his teeth against a groan as the rough bark bit into a tender spot. He closed his eyes, trying to ignore the pain in his body and the apprehension in his heart.

The physical was much easier to dismiss even though the worry set his head to pounding. Worry or lack of food. Or the blow to his skull. It didn't matter. His discomfort wasn't important.

Two days. The thought ate at him. He'd lost two days.

His captors huddled around a small fire, talking and laughing as they passed around a flask. Again tonight they'd placed him far enough away from their fire that its heat did nothing to dispel the night's chill.

The cold didn't matter. The pounding ache in his head and the raw burn in his hands were nothing compared to the nauseous fear in his stomach.

Fear not for himself but for his family.

They'd traveled two days' time, going back over ground he and Steafan had crossed on their journey to the banks of the River Dochart. Until late this afternoon, that is, when they'd turned up a trail and headed into the high mountains.

Still, they were afoot. Once he regained his horse, he could make up the time. He had to.

Two days headed the wrong way. Two days stolen from his quest to save his brother and cousin.

His mind raced, every thought coming back to the same harrowing conclusion. If he couldn't free himself and manage to get the ransom to Wodeford, Colin and Blane would die.

And Steafan. He was forced to add Steafan to his list of worries as well. He lifted his head and scanned the circle once more, hoping to find his friend.

He had to locate his horse and Steafan. Both had disappeared on that first night.

Just one more time when those who were most important to him would suffer because he hadn't been strong enough. Hadn't been smart enough. Hadn't paid attention to the signs in front of him. No one would even know what had happened until it was too late. He should have listened to his instincts, should have shared his concerns with Steafan, should have—

Enough!

He fought back his inner demons.

He'd had enough of the guilt. It served no purpose but to distract him. He needed to keep his mind sharp and alert. He focused on the pain in his body, bringing him back to the here and now.

Who were these people? They didn't appear to be Wodeford's men. They were too ragged, too ill-equipped. And yet how had common brigands known his name, known he carried silver?

He prayed that Steafan had escaped, though the prospect seemed unlikely. He couldn't count on that. He needed a plan.

A cold, wet touch to his hand brought him up short. The soft whimper that followed convinced him of the source.

Baby.

He scratched at the dog's muzzle with his fingers, feeling almost foolish that something as minor as the dog's presence could bring him a sense of relief.

Relief was the last thing he should be feeling. It wouldn't do to have these men discover Ellie's pet. If anything happened to the beast, Ellie would be heartbroken. He flicked his fingers at the creature to scare him off, but the dog obviously thought it a game and rubbed his head against Caden's bound hands.

"Go," he hissed, shaking his head at his own foolishness. As if the animal could understand his words.

The thought barely reached his conscious mind before his hand stilled.

Ellie had told him animals were sensitive to the thoughts of all people. It just so happened she was also sensitive to their thoughts.

If what she said was true . . .

Could he risk speaking to the dog? Would the beast have any idea what he was saying?

A large warm tongue licked across his fingers.

It was worth a try.

"Go to Ellie. Tell her what's happened. Get her to send help."

Even if the help came too late for him and Steafan, maybe they could still save Colin and Blane.

The climb up the narrow, rocky paths had taken Caden's last energy reserves. He slowed, catching his breath before they approached an even steeper climb. His guards paused as well, waiting for an approaching horseman headed their way.

Caden used the opportunity to study his surroundings, none of which were familiar to him. In the trees below he spied a flash of gray fur, and for an instant stared into the familiar eyes of Ellie's big dog.

Of course it had been too much to expect. Still, the disappointment knocked the wind from him. Until that moment he hadn't realized how much he had depended on the beast to carry his message.

So much for any hope for help.

The man behind Caden shoved him as they started

forward and he stumbled, falling to one knee. The horseman rode close, yelling out his orders to no one in particular.

"Get him up and into the hall. His lairdship awaits our guest."

The guard who held the lead rope attached to Caden's wrists laughed and yanked him forward, jerking him to his feet and back onto the path.

Rounding yet another turn, Caden spotted a neglected stone building jutting from a ledge above, one side of the keep a mass of crumbling stone. Although this once must have been someone's ancestral home, it certainly didn't appear as such now. It looked to be in much worse repair then even Sithean Fardach.

As they approached, he would have sworn this place abandoned if not for the men standing on what was left of the guard wall. Only the large gate appeared to be in decent repair as the heavy portcullis lifted with a loud grating screech.

Through the gate and across the weed-grown bailey they trudged until they reached the rock walls of the keep itself. With the main stairs rotted away, a long ladder served the purpose of providing access to the second-floor entry.

Caden wasn't sure he had the strength to climb the ladder or even the will to try any longer. Then he thought of those who depended on him and he reached down deep, demanding more of himself. He would survive. He would not fail his family again.

"You'll need the use of yer hands, MacAlister."

The guard's words gave him momentary hope of an opportunity to escape until a loop of rope dropped around his neck and tightened just before the man sliced through the binding at his wrists.

They led him up the ladder and into the hall bound about the neck like a beast. Each time he slowed, the rope tightened, threatening to cut off his air.

Caden stumbled into the dark hall gasping for air, choking on the stench of dirty men, sour ale, and smoke.

Directly in front of him, a large fire burned in the center of the hall. Apparently the fireplace had stood on the crumbled side of the building.

"What have you done with my silver, MacAlister?" a voice rasped somewhere ahead of him.

Caden kept his head bowed, his eyes squinted against the burn of smoke. He rubbed at his wrists, stalling for time, hoping his vision would adjust to the smoke-darkened room enough to allow him to identify his captor.

"Who are you?" he managed to choke out before the rope around his neck tightened again.

"Show the proper respect," the guard next to him growled and something hard hit him in the back, knocking him to his knees.

"You have the honor to speak with the Laird of the Menzies himself, Symund MacNab."

Caden looked up to find a short barrel of a man strutting toward him out of the shadows, a stout walking stick at his side. The "laird" was every bit as ragged and filthy as the men who followed him. At least, he had something of an answer. A misbegotten group of brigands, likely men who had been banished from their clans.

Working his fingers under the rope at his neck,

Caden loosened it enough to allow him a deep breath before answering.

"I've met Alexander Menzies. I traveled to his castle with my cousin. Yer no him. And this"—Caden looked into the decayed gloom around him—"this is certainly no the home of the Laird of the Menzies."

Caden felt more than saw the stick swinging toward his head. By reflex, he grabbed it and jerked it from MacNab's unsuspecting hands. They'd underestimated him and he intended to take full advantage of their mistake.

Pushing to his feet, he twirled the stick until he felt it make solid contact with one of his guards. The rope around his neck slacked and Caden swung his arm out the other direction, his fist connecting with the face of the second guard before the noose around his neck tightened, robbing him of air. A blow to the backs of his legs took him to the ground.

As the rope around his neck tightened, his vision tunneled, and little stars of light danced around the outside of the dark circle he felt himself gazing down. A kick to his stomach curled him into a ball and he readied himself for the end.

"No! You canna kill him! No yet. He's the only one who can tell us where the silver's hidden."

That voice!

Caden struggled to turn his head toward the sound but the rope held him firmly in place. He fought the darkness that hovered around the edges of his vision, putting his last efforts toward seeing who approached.

"Weel, my greedy friend, if MacAlister's the only one who can find my silver"—MacNab's foot jabbed into

Caden's shoulder, rolling him to his back—"then tell me, what further need do I have for you?"

"Here now, MacNab, we have a deal. We're to split the money and yer to make him suffer for what he's done to my family."

Caden fought to keep his eyes open as hurried footsteps neared. He knew that voice. It seemed impossible but he had to see for himself.

"Aye, that we did. But that was when you promised me the silver. Without it, our bargain's null." MacNab bent to retrieve his walking stick, swinging it as he stood, connecting with the head of the man who had spoken.

A body fell to the floor, sending a wash of air over Caden. Just before the darkness completely overtook him, he rolled his eyes to the side and stared into the bloody face of the man he'd considered a brother.

Steafan Maxwell.

Twenty-two

Ellie felt like a coyote caught in a trap, ready to chew off her own foot in order to escape. Trouble was, there wasn't anywhere to escape to and nothing to escape from as best she could tell.

She couldn't even explain to herself what was wrong. Just some massive foreboding anxiety, like waiting for a tornado to hit. She was simply antsy as hell and needed something to keep her hands and her mind busy. Right this minute.

All around her the kitchen bustled with activity, but each time she offered to help, she was refused.

"Water, water everywhere, nor any drop to drink..." she muttered. The line from one of the classics she'd studied in school popped into her memory, and for the first time she felt as though she completely related to it. It seemed as though everyone but she had something to do.

"What is it you say, lass?" The big cook swirled past her in a cloud of flour and cinnamon.

"How about the wash? I could help with the laundry." She'd seen how hard the women worked at that particular task, how very long it took.

Bridey laughed as she smacked her fist into a big lump of rising dough. "It's no wash day, milady, or I just might take you up on that offer. Now off with you. Yer underfoot here in my kitchen and I've baking to do."

"Can I help with—"

"No," Bridey interrupted. "Now go on. Be a good lass and find something else to do with yerself."

Ellie wandered into the great hall where Anna and some of the other girls were cleaning tables to prepare for the midday meal. She reached for one of the pails of soapy water, but Anna's hand over her own stopped her.

"Dinna even think to do that," the girl cautioned as she shook her wild mop of red curls. "Bridey would have my hide if she found you in here cleaning."

"Come on, Anna. I'm going absolutely nuts if I don't find something to do with myself!"

"I've something you both can do." Sallie leaned awkwardly against the door, her hands splayed across her huge stomach. "My daughter has decided it's time to meet the world. I need you to find my mother and Ran. Quickly."

One look at the expression on Sallie's face and Ellie started off at a run. "I'll find Ran. You get Rosalyn," she shouted over her shoulder as she hurried out across the hallway and through the big entry door.

Gathering her skirts up in one arm, she raced across the courtyard, slowing for a moment to yell up at the guards on the wall walk who stared down at her.

"The MacPherson! Where is he?"

The big guard lifted an arm, pointing. "The stables, milady."

She didn't need him to add that her exposed legs were improper. She could see judgment in his expression. He could glower until his face fell off for all Ellie cared. Right now she was a woman on a mission, and speed meant more to her than some ideal of modesty.

She ran for all she was worth, across the bailey, into the stable yard and through the open doors of the stable itself.

"Ranald MacPherson!" she yelled as she entered, stopping to bend from the waist and catch her breath for a moment.

From one of the stalls in the back came a muffled "Aye?"

"It's time! Hurry up. Sallie needs you."

She barely had the words out of her mouth before he stood in front of her, bare-chested and dirty, a wooden paddle-shaped shovel in one hand.

"It's my Sallie's time?" He threw down the tool without waiting for her answer and began to run.

Once again, Ellie hiked up her skirts and took off after him. Halfway across the courtyard she'd nearly caught up when a sound caught her attention.

A low, keening howl.

She paused, scanning the courtyard, listening intently. Nothing.

She shook her head at her own imagination. Must be the excitement of the moment getting to her after such a long, dull spell.

Hurrying, she entered the keep in time to see Ran

scoop his wife into his arms and bolt up the stairs with what looked like every female in the place following in his footsteps.

Except Bridey. The old cook stood at the bottom of the stairs, a silly grin on her face.

"That's what every woman should have. A husband who loves her so much, he'd gladly make the fool of himself."

"I didn't think men in this time were with their wives when the women delivered babies." Ellie caught herself and quickly amended her question when she saw the puzzled expression on the woman's face, "Here in Scotland, I mean."

Bridey nodded as if that made more sense to her. "It's the same everywhere, I'd fancy. I dinna ken any who do." The wide smile returned as she leaned close to confide, "Ah, but there would be the devil to pay with Lady Rosalyn if Ran dinna attend to Sallie. And after all these years, I suspect the lad wants to be with her. Did you no see the way he looked at her? It's so romantic."

Missy's sharp bark interrupted Bridey's confidences.

Ellie looked down to find the little dog fairly dancing around her feet.

Stop shutting us out! Hurry!

"What?"

Missy ran toward the entry door, her nails clicking on the smooth stones.

Baby needs you.

Excusing herself, Ellie followed more slowly, the whine she thought she'd heard earlier returning and growing stronger. As she realized the sound wasn't in her ears but in her mind, she picked up speed. In the courtyard she paused, unable to locate the source of the sound.

"Where is he?"

Outside the walls.

Up the stairs to the wall walk she raced, ignoring the shout of the big guard as she leaned over the edge to look down below. Sure enough, Baby lay just outside the gates, his whimper clear in her mind now.

"Open the gates," she instructed the startled guard.

"Sorry, milady. My orders are to open only for recognized riders. Seeing as there's no one there . . ." He let the thought dangle as he stared at her.

"My dog," she countered irritably. "My dog is down there. Now open the gates or I'll do it myself."

The guard crossed his arms, a grin spreading over his face. "No, milady, I dinna believe you'll be doing that anytime soon."

Ellie glared at the man, quickly realizing she wasn't getting anywhere. "I swear they must sprinkle the food with stubborn around here," she huffed, turning to go back down the stairs.

The muffled "There's a good lass" from behind her did nothing for her mood.

If that big goon thought she was going to simply give up, he could just think again.

She stood at the inner gate, staring through the grate down the long dark tunnel. There had to be a switch or a handle or something around here. How did they lift the massive gates? To her right she noticed a low doorway built into the wall.

Missy's frantic urging and Baby's pathetic whimpers

continued to grow louder, filling her head. How she'd managed to shut it out before was beyond her understanding.

"Quiet! I can't think," she hissed as she stepped into a small dark room.

"Pardon?" The guard inside, the same one she'd encountered once before on the wall walk, looked up in surprise from the floor where he sat rubbing a cloth up and down the length of a sword.

"My dog's caught outside the gates. I need you to open them."

He shook his head, a patronizing smile lighting his face before he returned his attention to the weapon in his lap. "I canna open the gates without the man on the wall gives me leave. It's orders."

"Look." She paused, searching her mind for the man's name. "Gregor. Please help me."

Again the old man shook his head stubbornly. "Without the order, I'll no open the gates. Now be a good lass and run along."

If one more person told Ellie to "be a good lass" today, she was going to scream. She clenched her teeth against the irritation she felt and looked around the little room. Mounted on the wall were a series of gears with a large chain looped around them leading to what looked like the steering wheel on a pirate ship. That had to be what she wanted.

Fine. They wouldn't help? She'd damn well do it herself.

Ellie threw herself at the wheel, pulling down with all her strength.

It didn't budge.

"Here now!" Gregor yelled, on his feet amazingly fast for such a large man.

Though he grabbed her around the waist and pulled, she held on for all she was worth.

"Open the damn gate!" she shouted over his rumblings to let go.

"What have we here?" Dair's huge shoulders filled the small doorway as he entered. "Unhand the lady, Gregor. What would yer missus be thinking of you now?"

"She's trying to raise the gates," the guard huffed, backing away.

Ellie kept her hands clenched on the wheel, watching the two men. "My dog is trapped outside the gates. He needs me. And these . . ." She floundered for something appropriately harsh to call the guards who frustrated her efforts. "These *men* won't listen to me."

Dair's lips rolled in as if he bit them to keep from smiling and he quickly looked down at the floor. When he lifted his head, his expression was blank. "Gregor, lift the portcullis for the lady."

"I canna. The MacPherson gave us strict orders after the shepherds reported Gilberd's disappearance. We're no to open the gates without . . ." The old guard sputtered.

"On my authority, Gregor. Lift the grates. Milady? May I escort you out to retrieve yer animal?" Dair lifted an elbow, offering his arm.

Ellie backed away from the wheel, watching as Gregor slapped a lever before easily turning the crank.

"Well, no wonder," she muttered as she took Dair's arm and tried to reclaim some modicum of dignity, grateful Caden wasn't around to see this latest demonstration of her inappropriate behavior.

Through the first gate, she let go of Dair's arm and ran to the far gate, bending to slip under as it opened.

Baby lifted his head, panting.

"You poor thing. You're exhausted. She dropped to her knees and cuddled the dog's head in her lap. He shouldn't be here. He was supposed to be watching over Caden. The realization sent a lurch through her stomach even before she asked the obvious question.

"What's wrong, Baby? What's happened to Caden?"

"I willna allow it." Dair crossed his arms in front of him. "It's no proper for a lady."

Ellie clasped her hands in her lap, counting to ten to keep her temper in check for at least the hundredth time since she'd walked into this room. She had to remember the mind-set of the men in this day and age. Alasdair Maxwell couldn't help acting like a medieval macho knuckle-dragger. It's what he was.

"Mayhap you can follow the animal, Dair. Just to see if it's even the truth." Alycie spoke from her seat against the wall.

Rosalyn sat across the desk from Ellie, her own hands clenched tightly enough her fingers had lost their color. She looked up and captured Ellie's gaze, as if she desperately searched for some solution to their troubles. Some solution that could only come from Ellie.

"Well, crap," Ellie muttered rising from her chair and taking a deep breath. The knuckle-dragger was just going to have to get over himself. "It is the truth. Don't bother asking how I know. You're simply going to have to trust me on this one. And no, you can't just follow the dog. I'm going."

She'd made up her mind. For all she knew, this was what she'd been sent to do. And she certainly didn't intend to blow the opportunity to get home if it was. More important, Caden needed help and he was going to get it. From her. He believed in her enough to have sent the dog with a message asking for help and she wasn't going to let him down.

"It's no proper . . ." Dair began his litany again.

Her counting and clenching were at an end. The anger she'd contained so "properly" bubbled over. "What happened to you being pledged to my service?"

She waited only a moment, glaring at the silent knight. "Yeah, I thought as much. Listen to me, soldier boy. I don't give a rat's ass about 'proper.' I'm going after Caden if it hairlips every cow in the state of Texas, and you can either come with me or not. Your choice."

Behind her, Rosalyn rose from her seat to come around the desk and stand beside Ellie. "The lass speaks the truth. She must go. Will you no, as a personal favor to me, protect her on her journey?"

"I'll come along with you, Dair," Alycie stood and walked to her brother's side. "With me to chaperone, you'll no have to fear for her reputation, aye?"

Dair's glower lit on each woman in turn. "I canna fight the lot of you, can I?" He sighed and threw his arms into the air. "Verra well. It is decided. I canna allow you to go alone, so I go as yer protection, milady."

Ellie didn't mistake his bow for anything other than the sarcasm he intended, but it didn't matter. It didn't even matter that Miss Perfect was coming along.

Caden believed her. He'd trusted in her enough to send Baby with his message and she was going to save

Caden. Then he and his beloved could get married and have lots of perfect, proper little children.

And she could go home.

"I really do have to get going." Ellie stroked a finger over the downy soft forehead of the baby in Sallie's arms. Such a tiny little creature with such serious blue eyes.

Sallie shifted, obviously trying to find a comfortable spot in the bed where she sat and instantly her husband was at her side, helping to adjust her pillows. She smiled as he paused to stroke a big finger over his daughter's forehead just as Ellie had done.

"I ken yer need to be off, but I want to give you something to take along. Ran?"

Her husband moved to the end of the bed and opened the lid of a large chest, pulling out what looked to Ellie like a simple bundle of cloth. He laid it on the foot of the bed and unwrapped it carefully, revealing two belts and two small daggers, which he placed beside his wife before taking their daughter from her arms.

"Several years ago I learned the hard way of the need to protect myself. I've worn these ever since. I would feel so much better if you would take them along with you." Sallie moved the weapons to her lap.

"I don't think I could . . ." Ellie began, but Sallie was hearing none of it.

"You can. Many women in our time wear a belted dagger at their waist. Many claim it's for household use, but I ken the truth of it. Our men willna be there always when we need them. We have to take responsibility for our own protection."

Ellie stifled a grin. Apparently she'd been way off base

in believing all the women here were meek and subservi-
ent. This one, at least, was clearly as serious about self-
defense as anyone Ellie had met in her own time.

She reached out and took the smaller dagger and
belt from Sallie and fastened it around her own waist.
With its pretty jeweled handle, it looked almost like
jewelry.

"There. Now if I can just manage to wear this without stabbing my leg, I should be in fine shape defending
myself."

Sallie shook her head, a look of irritation settling on
her face. "Dinna be thinking like a fool-headed woman.
Do you no realize if yer taken, they'll see that weapon
and remove it? You'll no be able to stop them. We canna
be as strong as the men who seek to harm us, so we must
be smarter." She lifted the second dagger, longer than
the first and very thin. "While many a lady wears something like what you have at yer waist, no so many have
one of these. Here. You hide this one. I strap it to the
inside of my leg. Here." She slapped the inside of her
thigh before holding the weapon and strap out.

Ellie had misjudged her. Sallie was way more serious
about self-defense than Ellie had ever thought of being.

"Thank you." Ellie accepted the knife and leaned in
to give Sallie a hug. "I'll wear it, I promise. I really have
to go. They're waiting for me."

Hurrying down the hallway, Ellie considered the
lethal-looking weapon. Sallie might appear to be a
petite, helpless woman, but Ellie could learn a thing
or two from her. Somehow she couldn't imagine Sallie
allowing anyone to move into her family home and take
it over like Ray had done to her.

She entered her room and started to strap the knife to her inner thigh.

No, that might work for someone like Sallie, but Ellie had proven herself less than graceful on too many occasions since she'd been here to try that. She'd likely end up cutting a slice off her horse or severing her own artery at the rate she'd been going. The leg strap wouldn't work for her.

She leaned over the chest at the foot of her bed and lifted the lid, digging through the clothing she'd worn since she'd been here. There, at the very bottom, she found what she sought. Her bra and panties, tucked in the corner where she'd placed them that first day.

She unlaced her overdress and tugged off her shift before stabbing the dagger through the elastic back of the bra. She slipped her arms into the lacy straps and snapped the little fastener closed between her breasts before pulling up her shift and overdress.

Satisfied she was ready, she headed for the courtyard, where Dair and his sister waited, conscious of the feel of the little garment she'd once taken so for granted. Though the elastic now felt restrictive and uncomfortable, the cold blade had warmed against the skin of her back and hardly felt out of place at all.

She could get used to this. And though she didn't expect she'd ever be a major ass kicker, she was beginning to believe that just maybe she could be a force to be reckoned with. It gave her a rare sense of control over her destiny and made her feel for a brief moment like a heroine out of those books she loved so much.

Confidently Ellie pushed through the great entry door to begin her journey.

Twenty-three

"When we were but wee bairns, our father would build a huge fire in front of our home and we would sing along while he played a tune on his pipe." Alycie rested her head against the large boulder she sat next to. "It was all quite lovely."

"Yer memories and mine are fair different, Sister. My recollection is that the fire was to keep us from freezing outside when Mother had some poor farm woman in our home delivering a babe. And the pipe and singing were to cover the screams of pain coming from the childbed." Dair poked the campfire with a stick, sending a shower of flickering embers rising up into the night sky.

Ellie stretched her back and shoulders before kneeling down to warm her hands over the fire. They'd ridden hard all day, following in the direction Baby had led them. It felt like the longest day of her life, knowing Caden was held captive in that horrible place.

Must hurry. Smells of death, Baby had told her.

"Well, of course it does," she'd reasoned. "If it's as old as you say, I'm sure there have been many wars and battles fought there."

No. Fresh death.

A shiver ran through Ellie's body as she remembered the conversation.

Soon. She'd be there soon to free Caden.

Two moons, Baby had told her. Tonight was the first.

If only she could stop thinking of Caden suffering. Desperate, hungry, hurt.

It wasn't just her imagination running wild with her fear. When she'd first reached Baby outside Dun Ard, asking what had happened to Caden, he had flooded her mind with the pictures and sensations from his memory, each so real it was as if she'd been there herself.

Pictures of Caden's wrists raw and bleeding, bound around a tree trunk. She could feel his fingers, cold from exposure and lack of circulation when they'd stroked Baby's muzzle, as if they had touched her.

She'd heard his voice as he'd sent Baby to find her.

She'd seen him with a rope knotted around his neck, a look of utter desolation on his face. And when he'd turned, struggling to climb a horrible, rickety ladder, pulled forward by that awful rope, she could clearly see blood matting the back of his hair.

She would save him. She would. If only she could come up with some plan to actually get him out of there.

"And what of you, Ellie? Have you family awaiting your return home?" Alycie watched her expectantly.

Her companions had no idea just how far away "home" actually was for her and she had no intention of enlightening them, in spite of Alycie's subtle attempt to learn more about her.

"No. No family," she responded honestly.

Nothing waited for her but a no-account, sorry excuse for a stepfather squatting on her property against her wishes. A wave of frustration rolled over her. She couldn't do any more about Ray than she could about what was happening to Caden at this very minute. It was as if everything important was beyond her control, weighing so heavily on her mind it threatened to bury her.

If she could keep her companions talking, she wouldn't have to think. Not about the ranch, not about Ray and most especially not about Caden.

"So which of you is older?"

"She is." Dair grinned, pointing at his sister. "By several minutes."

"Minutes?" His response surprised her. "Are you twins?"

"Hard to believe when you look at Dair and me together, is it no?" Alycie smiled fondly at her brother.

It did seem hard to believe. Dair was so large and Alycie so tiny. But as Ellie studied them in the firelight, she began to pick out their similarities. Their coloring, their soft brown eyes, even their expressions. When they smiled, each had a dimple on one side that appeared briefly.

No wonder Caden loved her.

The thought made Ellie want to gasp for air, a physical pain spearing through her guts.

Challenge little female for your pack mate. Baby's soft growl as he curled up beside Ellie was obviously meant for her ears alone.

Challenge? What good would that do? No, the best she could hope for was to accept the inevitable. All of this was making her stronger. It was. Somehow she'd free Caden so he could have his perfect little dimple-faced wife, and then she'd go home and find some way to make Ray Stanton wish to hell he'd never crossed paths with her. She would go on. Without Caden.

You challenge. You fight. The thought rolled through her mind again, more forceful this time.

Baby repeated the directive Missy had given her days ago. Even out here, miles away, the bossy little terrier still ruled as far as Baby was concerned.

People don't do it that way. We don't fight. We accept.

Ellie sent the thought to the big dog beside her as she stroked his head. That's what she needed to do. She had to accept and get on with life.

You mean roll over. Expose underbelly. Give up.

Ellie barely stopped herself from answering out loud. She didn't mean that at all. She was simply being practical.

"So . . ." She dragged out the word in the silence that had grown. She needed to face it, to get over it just like she'd told Baby. "Will there be a big ceremony? For the wedding, I mean."

"There's to be a wedding? Who's to wed?" Dair smiled quizzically as he lifted the jug his sister had handed him.

"Alycie and Caden, of course."

Dair began to cough, choking on the wine he'd just

swallowed, and Alycie hurried to his side to pound his back.

"Where did you get such a fanciful notion?" Alycie asked when at last she looked up.

"Well, Steafan told me . . ."

"You need say no more. That explains it well enough." Dair rubbed at his eyes as he shook his head. "Our older brother oversteps himself again."

Alycie returned to her spot near the fire. "I'm sorry if Steafan misled you, Ellie. He canna seem to accept the truth of the matter."

"The truth?" Ellie felt totally confused. Alycie hadn't come back to Dun Ard to marry Caden?

"Aye. In spite of what Steafan thinks, I'm happy with what I've chosen for my life."

"It's no even about you," Dair interrupted. "You ken that as well as I do. Steafan sees it as a reflection on him. He always has. He sees only that yer choice dinna result in the life he'd imagined for himself. You'd think it was him sent to Iona, no you."

Alycie shrugged. "It's no matter. My choice is made. I'd no marry any man and most particularly not Caden MacAlister."

Ellie leaned forward, questions flaring through her mind like Fourth of July fireworks. "Why not?"

Dair grinned, his dimple flashing into view for an instant. "Alycie has given her life over to the nunnery at Iona. She canna marry."

Alycie nodded her agreement.

"You're a nun?" Disbelief rolled over Ellie in waves. "I thought you guys had to wear special outfits and stuff."

"Steafan is not the only family member who has difficulty with the path I've chosen for my life." Alycie lifted the ribbon around her neck and held up an ornate little cross that had been hidden under the high neck of her shift. "I wear only this when I come home because the plain robes bother my mother as well. And since my whole purpose in coming was to comfort her while we waited to learn of Dair's fate, I saw no reason to add to her upset."

Ellie looked to Dair. "You don't seem to have any problem with what your sister has chosen to do with her life."

"I've always believed Alycie and I are opposite sides of the same coin. She follows her heart to Iona and I follow mine into battle. She accepts my decision no to live the life others expect of us and I accept hers." He shrugged and the grin returned. "Besides, even if she could wed, the idea of joining a family of Fae descendants is more than she could handle, is it no, Sister?"

Alycie, eyes wide, nodded her head vigorously as she rubbed her thumb over her little cross. "That it is. Even if I were denied service at Iona, I could no live as the wife of a pagan."

"Another point of disagreement we simply accept in one another," Dair added as he put the cork back in the jug he held. "And on that note I'd say it's time we get some rest. We've an early start tomorrow."

Ellie nodded her agreement and rolled out her blanket. Though she snuggled into the warm wool and Baby cuddled next to her, she doubted she'd get much sleep. Between her worry over Caden's safety and tonight's conversation, she had too much to think about to drift off peacefully.

* * *

"I canna see why you think it a bad plan." Alycie's innocent gaze moved from Dair to Ellie and back again. "You saw them for yerselves when we watched the keep this morn. Surely these are men in desperate need of salvation. Dair could pass for a monk and us for nuns who travel with him. We could carry the gospel to these men and pass inside their gates."

Ellie stared at the woman, wondering how she could say any of what poured from her mouth with a straight face. Was anyone on the face of the planet really that naïve? In the first place, no one in their right minds would ever confuse Dair for a monk. He was no Caden, of course, but he certainly didn't have the look of a man pledged to live a life of celibacy.

And either she'd seen way too many movies or she and Alycie had spied on completely different men this morning. Because while those guys she'd seen might look like they needed salvation, they also looked like the kind who would slit the throats of anyone stupid enough to try and deliver it. Or worse.

As they'd hidden in the trees and watched the men on the wall walk, Baby's warning had been crystal clear. Even Dair had noticed the dog's hackles rise and had reached out a comforting hand to pat the creature.

Baby had lifted his nose, scenting what they couldn't see. *Must use care. Blood Pack inside.*

"You hunt. You probably smell like blood to them, too." Ellie had tried to dismiss the warning at first.

Baby smell of animal blood. Not Hu-man blood.

The very idea had turned Ellie's stomach. And now

Alycie wanted to march through the gates with redemption on her lips? Not freakin' likely.

Fortunately Dair agreed.

He placed an arm around his sister's shoulders and gave her a hug. "The men behind those gates have no interest in the charity and goodness you'd offer, Sister. It's evil they have in their hearts and minds."

"You make a good point," Ellie reasoned slowly as the seeds of a plan took root. "So, if we can't get in by being good, maybe we can get in by being bad." She grinned at the puzzled looks confronting her. "We'll pretend to be traveling working girls. Dair can be our pimp. I'd bet that would appeal to this bunch."

Her companions continued to watch her quizzically.

"I'm no familiar with the work of these girls nor the role of this *pimp* you suggest for me." Dair shook his head, his brow wrinkled.

"Okay, okay, okay," Ellie sighed. The language barrier could be so irritating at times like this. "Working girl. What do you call women who have sex with men for money?"

Alycie gasped, her hands flying to her chest as understanding dawned on the face of her brother.

"Whores? You'd suggest that the two of you pretend to be common whores?"

"Can you think of a better way?" Ellie watched him closely as he considered her idea.

"I'm no sure at all I want to ask what this *pimp* might do." Dair actually looked a bit pale at the thought.

"He's the . . . um . . . girls' manager. Their boss. He sets everything up and collects the money."

"Ah." Dair nodded his head, relief plain on his face. "That I can handle."

"Alycie?"

Ellie waited for a response, watching closely as the other woman took a deep breath and squared her shoulders before nodding her agreement.

"I'll do it. But only because it's my brother's life as well as Caden's."

"Then it's settled."

Ellie started for her horse but stopped as Dair stepped in her path, his arms crossed, a speculative expression on his face.

"What?"

"As yer *pimp*"—he grinned as if he rather enjoyed the word now—"I'm no too happy with the way you look, lass. Dressed as you are, you'd be easy to mistake for a lady, aye?" He stroked his chin thoughtfully for a moment. "But I think I can correct that."

When Dair's dimple flashed again, Ellie reached out for Alycie's hand, not at all sure she was going to like whatever it was her new boss planned.

Twenty-four

Catriona Wodeford Baxter leaned over the basin by her bed and splashed water over her face.

Even the cool droplets hurt.

With shaking hands, she picked up the polished silver hand mirror that had belonged to her mother and looked into it. The sight confronting her made her ill, the surprise of it still as hurtful as the wounds themselves.

Austyn had been angry with her many times, had threatened her before. But in all her years, her brother had never struck her.

Not until this morning.

She could hardly believe it even now. And yet the proof of his fists striking her face, blacking her eye, busting her swollen lips was all too real. As real as the tattered gown that lay in the corner of her room where she'd stepped out of it. As real as the lashes on her arms and back where he'd beat her with his whip.

And for what? The measly bits of cheese and bread she'd taken to Blane and his cousin?

No. Her action was no more than a small breath to the flames of his anger. Over the last few years she'd watched as Austyn had changed. Her brother had grown to relish the violence and the battles and the killing until she hardly recognized him.

Sooner or later, it would have come to this, no matter how she'd tried to please him. He'd come to resent her very presence because she represented the conscience he denied.

She gently patted the drying cloth to her aching cheek and dabbed on a bit of the potion she had made weeks earlier to treat the wounded of Wode Castle. Certainly she had never expected to need it for herself.

Poor Simeon. Her nephew would blame himself for this because he had taken her to Austyn after finding her outside the hovel where the prisoners were kept. It had required three of Austyn's guards to drag Sim from the room when her brother's first blow had landed.

She took a deep breath and laid out her clothing on the bed. She would worry about Simeon later. For now, she had much to do.

Slowly she dressed, biting back the cry of pain that threatened when the linen of her shift settled over the cuts on her back, just as she had refused to make a sound when Austyn had struck her. Perhaps if she'd cried out, begged his mercy, he wouldn't have grabbed for the whip. Then again, perhaps it would have made no difference to him.

She shook her head to chase away the thought and rolled her hair into its usual large knot at the nape of her neck.

Such thoughts were weakness, and in spite of what her brother thought, she was not weak. She was the daughter of a great warrior, the widow of a brave knight. And though she was a tolerant woman, her brother had overstepped his bounds for the last time. In her mind his actions canceled any debt or gratitude she had ever owed him.

But the slate was not cleaned. Not by a long stretch.

Outside, the sun had long since set and the moon was well hidden by clouds this night. She pulled a cloak from the chest at the foot of her bed and wrapped it around her shoulders, carefully lifting the hood to cover her head. She placed each of the items she'd prepared into her pockets before she opened the door and slipped into the dark, quiet hallway.

Yes, this day Austyn Wodeford had crossed over a line and tipped the balance of debt owed in her favor and she intended to see to it that he paid dearly for his error.

Twenty-five

Caden huddled in a dark, damp corner, the moldy bread they'd tossed down to him earlier clutched in his lap. He forced himself to take another bite. He had to keep up his strength.

He had to be ready to seize any opportunity that came along. He would be free of this place. He had to be. Too much depended on it.

Once he was free, he'd deliver the ransom for Blane and Colin, and then he was coming back here. Coming back and finding Steafan.

He wanted answers.

Why would Steafan betray him? The man was his best friend, had been as a brother to him for as many years as he could remember.

Why, why, why?

It had become a litany singing through his mind for

the last few days. It held the wounding sting of betrayal at bay.

He wanted revenge.

An invisible scratching in the inky dark corner caught his attention.

Rats.

Damn, but he hated the vermin. He pushed aside his loathing, thinking instead of Ellie's grin the day she had accused him of fearing the little beasties.

He filled his mind with her as he had over the past days, escaping the rotten food, the smell of sewage, even the rats. He held on to that image as long as he could. It was this that kept him going.

He would admit it now, though only to himself. Only here.

More than answers, even more than revenge, he wanted her.

The wooden slats covering the hole they'd thrown him into were lifted and a pale shaft of light flickered through the opening, invading his cocoon of darkness.

Caden sat very still, waiting for his eyes to adjust to the light, watching as a ladder snaked into view.

"Come on with you, MacAlister, out into the light. I ken yer there. Our laird has some entertainment prepared special just for you." A dirty face peered down over the edge.

Slowly Caden rose to his feet, battling back the dizziness. This was it. His chance had come at last. He had to be sharp now.

One foot after the other, he made his way up the rungs until his head and shoulders breached the opening. The men waiting there grasped him under his arms and dragged him out to his feet.

Up a set of narrow stone stairs where the flickering torch of the dungeon gave way to smoke-filtered daylight. Down a hallway and toward a door at what was presumably the back of the keep.

The frightened screams hit his ears before he made it through the door.

A crowd of perhaps fifteen men gathered, blocking his view, but the stench of blood curled up his nose and straight to his stomach even as the screams pierced his heart.

The guards pushed him forward and the mass parted, allowing him to see a mockery of a throne and Symund MacNab, the so-called laird, sitting there.

"Ah, just in time." MacNab signaled with his walking stick and Caden's guards shoved him forward again, toward the chairs where MacNab sat.

Caden steeled himself. This was good. When he took that stick from MacNab's hands this time, it was MacNab himself who'd feel the brunt of it. Caden's vision tunneled, focusing on the false laird, readying his strength, planning his move.

Until he passed in front of the chairs.

Then his view of what they all watched opened and his footsteps slowed as his horror grew.

There in front of him was a massive pit, perhaps four feet deep and larger than the great hall of this keep. A pole, taller than the height of man, had been driven into the far end. A chain extended from the pole, the end clamped around the wrist of a man who worked desperately at trying to free himself from the manacle, his fingers digging at the iron band.

In vain.

He was the source of the screams.

Two huge dogs stealthily circled him, each dodging in to snap their massive jaws. They were the reason for his screams.

Caden couldn't tear his eyes from the man's bloody hands as he frantically, hopelessly clawed at the band binding him.

One of the guards pushed Caden into the chair next to MacNab and he turned his gaze to the monster sitting there.

"What is this grotesque torture?"

MacNab smiled, affecting a look of innocence. "But surely you must have heard of the sport, MacAlister. It's all the rage with the nobility, I'm told. They call it bear baiting. A vicious bear is placed in the pit and the dogs are turned loose on it. The contest is whether the bear or the dogs survive."

"That's a man, no a bear, down there," Caden grated, the horror of the situation settling over him. "He's no a chance against those beasts."

"Aye, so it is." MacNab shook his head, lifting his hands in a helpless gesture. "And a man you know personally, if I'm no mistaken."

Caden's head snapped toward the man in the pit and he strained to see the poor wretch's face. The set of his shoulders did look familiar, but his back was turned.

One of the dogs dove in, latching his teeth onto the man's leg. The poor wretch fastened his arms around the pole, kicking, stomping at the beast's head with his other foot. The dog let go and backed away and the man turned, just enough to reveal his face.

"Gilberd? You've my shepherd chained out there?" Caden surged to his feet, and was quickly shoved back to his seat by the men surrounding him. "He's hardly more than a lad. Get him out of there!"

The guards dropped a coil of rope around Caden, tying him to the chair.

"Ah, but that's where you come in, my friend. Only you can save the lad now."

The dogs circled again, round and round, tightening their arcs, coming closer with each pass.

"Anything. Tell me what you want of me." He couldn't see one of his people murdered in front of his eyes and do nothing. He'd gladly change places with Gilberd.

"Unfortunately, to continue our sport, we'd need a real bear and they cost dearly. So all you have to do is tell us where to find the silver you carried, and we'll release the lad."

The moldy bread churned in Caden's stomach, threatening to travel up. He had two choices, both equally impossible. If he turned the silver over to MacNab, Blane and Colin would die. If he didn't, it would mean Gilberd's life. Either way, he failed his kinsmen.

A scream ripped through his thoughts accompanied by a roar from the men ringing the pit. Caden looked up, knowing before he did what he would see. Gilberd's body lay on the ground, his head twisted at an odd angle, his throat ripped away by one of the beasts.

What had he done? The blame for Gilberd's death lay at his feet. It was his responsibility. He should have decided faster, acted faster.

"What a pity. Too late to save that one." MacNab made a tsking noise as he patted Caden's arm. "Just as well. He was naught but a dirty little traitor anyway. Brought word of your journey to us, he did. Told us exactly where we might find you so we could escort you here as our guest."

Was it not enough they murdered the man? Did they take some special pleasure in defiling his memory as well?

"I dinna believe yer lies. That's no possible. Gilberd had no idea I traveled this route. He was in the high fields when my plans were set. He could no have done what you say." Caden clenched his jaw. He would speak no more. They'd done their worst.

"What you say may be. Unless, perhaps, someone sent him. Someone who did ken what you planned to do. Someone bent on yer destruction. A man who'd intentionally expose yer animals to disease and then sell you out to the likes of me." MacNab grinned, the few teeth left in his slimy mouth all showing. "You help me by giving me the silver and I'll help you by eliminating yer traitorous kinsmen."

"What?" The strangled words escaped Caden as though he no longer controlled his own will. "I'll hear no more of yer lies and accusations. And now that you've murdered Gilberd, you've no a hold on me. You'll never see that silver."

"I'd no be so hasty to say that if I were you." MacNab leaned over the side of his chair and motioned somewhere behind him. "Bring him!" he called, even as his attention was distracted by the arrival of one of his men leaning in to whisper in his ear.

He sat up, beaming. "'Tis perfect timing for our celebration. Escort them to me at once."

Again Caden's stomach churned, and he strained against the ropes that held him as he watched two guards drag another man out to the pole even as others hauled off what was left of Gilberd.

A man with a cloth sack over his head.

"Who is it?" Caden's words trickled out, barely more than a breath, as a sense of recognition fell over him.

"Patience, my young friend, patience," MacNab counseled.

In the pit, the man's arm was fitted into the manacle, even as he struggled against the process, and the cloth was yanked from his face.

"You can't do this to me!" Steafan screamed. "We had a deal."

A deal?

May the Fae help him, MacNab didn't lie.

Well, it wasn't four-inch spike heels and hot pants, but it would do.

Approaching the gates of the hellhole where Caden was held, Ellie felt a grim satisfaction as she considered their handiwork. Both she and Alycie had pulled and tugged and rearranged until they looked sufficiently sleazy, their shoulders and considerably more of their cleavage bared than was customary for this time. Only her lace bra straps covered her shoulders now, and those should be novel enough to entice the raggedy bunch they waited to attract.

She had to smile as she thought of their preparations. Dair's eyebrows had climbed up his forehead as she'd rearranged her laces and lowered her shift, baring the top of the odd mark on her breast—the rose shape Rosalyn had told her was her Faerie mark.

He'd quickly recovered his composure and grinned at her, nodding his head as if in approval when he turned away. What she wouldn't have given for the ability to read human thoughts in that moment!

Waiting outside the gates, she exchanged glances with Alycie, noting how the woman nervously chewed her bottom lip while Dair carried on a conversation with one of the men standing guard. Ellie adjusted her skirt one last time, making sure to flash some thigh and was pleased to see Alycie follow suit.

Remembering she'd read somewhere how 'good' girls got color into their faces back in the old days, she bit down on her lips and let go her reins long enough to pinch her cheeks. It might not be the makeup counter at the corner drugstore, but it would have to do.

Dair motioned for them to join him, and the three of them waited as the portcullis lifted, their screeching protests music to Ellie's ears.

They were inside!

The gate lowering behind her gave her only momentary pause. They'd come this far. She wouldn't allow herself to doubt their ability to get back out.

A large man, ragged and filthy as though he'd never even heard of washing, helped her down from her horse, his hands lingering unnecessarily long on her bare leg.

That was good. It meant their plan was working.

She gave him a smile she hoped was appropriately encouraging and allowed her skirts to slide down her legs to where they belonged. Slowly. Very slowly.

The man licked his lips and swallowed hard.

This was going to be easier than she'd imagined.

"Here now, what's this, darlin'?" He pulled at the knife belted around her waist. "You'll no be having any use for this wee weapon so I'll be taking it for a time."

He reached around her body, pulling her much closer than necessary to remove the belt, but she leaned into him. Might as well let him think she had no problem with what he did.

The man squatted in front of her and she realized with a start that he planned to pat her down like in some horrible cop movie. She glanced around to find her companions undergoing a similar procedure and tried to relax.

She could play this game.

Ellie lifted her skirts, baring her leg to midcalf and the guard on the ground in front of her sucked in his breath. He latched his hands around her ankle and slowly began to slide them upward.

Somewhere around her knee, she'd had enough.

"Has this man paid for my services?"

His hands froze in their search as she'd hoped they would, and she turned her head in Dair's direction, working to keep her face blank.

"He has not," Dair responded haughtily, playing his role to the hilt. "Kindly take your hands from the merchandise, good sir. Unless yer prepared to hand over the appropriate compensation, that is."

"I'm only checking for weapons, as I must," the man muttered, his hands rising uncomfortably above her knee now.

"Weapons? You took my weapon, you great oaf. And I don't *give* my favors. I *sell* them."

"No wee whores are going near the laird what I dinna check for weapons," he insisted stubbornly.

"Oh, very well." Ellie hoped she'd covered her fright with irritation as she jerked back from the guard and lifted her skirts, clearly displaying her thighs for his inspection.

His and the three other guards' as well. The one in front of Dair wiped a hand over his mouth and nodded his appreciation.

"How's this? Convinced I hide no other weapons?" She dropped her skirts and smoothed them with her hands.

"And you?"

The guard in front of Alycie waited and slowly she lifted her skirts as well, quickly dropping them.

Ellie had to admire the woman. For a medieval nun, she was pretty damn gutsy.

Satisfied the party was defenseless, the guards led them forward to the side of the crumbled stones that passed for a building.

Ellie's heart pounded while they were escorted around the keep toward a mass of men. Caden was in here somewhere. She could feel him.

As they approached the group, heads turned their direction and conversations came to a halt, all eyes on them.

"Bring them to me," a barrel-shaped man called from a gaudily decorated chair that had been placed up on a wooden dais.

Apparently the man in charge.

Exactly the man she wanted to get her hands on.

Ellie narrowed her gaze, focusing on him as she strutted forward, holding his attention with the swing of her hips. This was going to be easy.

He held out a hand and she reached for it, allowing him to pull her up onto the dais. As she stepped up, she glanced past him and her heart started pounding, threatening to burst through her chest.

Or perhaps it stopped beating altogether, she couldn't really tell.

There, next the grubby man who held her hand, in a smaller chair, sat Caden, a rope looped about his body tying him into the seat with his arms at his sides, his face a mask of horror as he stared straight ahead.

Her vision tunneled on him as she fought to catch her breath, searching every exposed inch of him for injury. Her focus was so intent, she barely noticed when Alycie was lifted up next to her.

Only Alycie's strangled "Holy Mother" drew her attention from Caden. The woman's face had drained of all color.

Ellie allowed her eyes to track the direction of Alycie's gaze and found the source of their dread.

Steafan was chained to a pole in the center of a massive pit.

As she watched, the onlookers cheered and two enormous mastiff-looking dogs were brought forward and released into the pit with Steafan. His clawing, panic-stricken attempts to free his hand from the manacle that bound him sickened her.

"Stop it. Stop it now, MacNab." Caden's voice was barely more than a whisper as he faced the monster who still held Ellie's arm. "You must . . ." The words died in Caden's throat when his eyes met Ellie's.

"Pardon, yer lairdship, but this is hardly fit sport for a lady's eyes." Dair somehow managed to control his tone, relaying none of the alarm he must have felt at his brother's predicament.

"I see no ladies," the laird responded. "But I fancy I'll have quite the appetite for what I do see after our sport here is finished." He pulled Ellie's arm to his mouth and ran his tongue from her wrist to the inside of her elbow. "Are you ready to turn over yer silver now, Mac-Alister?"

"I'll see you dead by my own hands for what you do, MacNab," Caden growled, his eyes sparking with hatred.

Ellie fought down the revulsion she felt and stroked a fingertip down the monster's cheek, sliding her arm from his grasp and moving behind his chair. "Let me work on that appetite, your lairdship. I'll help you relax while you enjoy your games."

She placed her hands on his head, threading her fingers into the greasy clumps of his hair and massaged. At his sigh, she transferred her attention down to the pit and the man struggling there.

Opening herself to the thoughts of the beasts in the pit was as gruesome as watching them circle Steafan, darting in to nip at his legs while he screamed and kicked. These creatures were trained to kill. They were crazed with hunger and a thirst for human blood.

Still, she had to try. Steafan might be a lying toady, but even he didn't deserve something this terrible.

She communicated with her dogs easily enough.

There should be no reason she couldn't use that same skill with these animals.

Leave the Hu-man alone, she ordered silently, intentionally using the same inflection she'd heard her dogs use. The larger female swung her muzzle around, as if searching for the source of the noise invading her mind, but with a shake of her head, she quickly turned back to her prey, her need for the kill overriding all else.

Ellie sensed this was the dominant female, the one she needed to convince.

Leave the Hu-man alone, she repeated more forcefully, directing all her attention to that animal.

A snarl of derision was her only answer.

"You want to play rough? We'll play rough." Ellie muttered.

"That we will, lass, if it's what you want," the old laird grunted, his eyes closing with pleasure as she continued to massage his head.

Something. She needed to think of something that would frighten the animal so much she would stop her attack.

As she tried to come up with any idea, she watched the scene below in horror. The animals leaped at Steafan. He raised an arm to protect his face and the alpha female closed her jaws around it as the other dog latched onto his leg, biting, tearing into his flesh.

Now! Whatever she did, it had to be now.

The memory of Missy's fear in the graveyard flashed through her mind. That was it! If she'd been able to send those sounds and pictures to Missy, she could do the same here. It was simply a matter of combining sounds and pictures into thought. But it would have to be truly earth-shattering sounds and pictures to distract these beasts.

What sounds bothered normal dogs?

Ellie pictured row after row of speeding fire trucks, lights blazing, racing directly at her. She added the sirens, thousands of them, pitching the sound as high and as loud as she could possibly imagine. Faster, louder, bigger.

Then she transferred the thoughts to the minds of the beasts.

The animals let go immediately, dropping to the ground, howling.

The men watching went silent.

"What's wrong with the damned beasts?" MacNab demanded, sitting up in his chair, dragging Ellie forward into the wood of the back. "Bring out the other pair!" he ordered before lolling his head back against Ellie's breasts.

She froze, her mind a momentary blank. The mind trick had worked on the first two dogs, but she didn't know if she was strong enough to hold off four.

Once again she forced herself to smile and massage her fingers through the muck of his hair, promising herself that if even one louse crawled out of that slime and onto her skin, she'd find a way to make the bastard pay for it. Big-time.

"Before the fresh beasts arrive, I'll give you one last chance, MacAlister. Will you give me the location of yer silver now?" MacNab kept his eyes closed, pressing his head into Ellie's breasts, rubbing from side to side.

"The only thing yer ever getting from me, MacNab, is yer own death." Caden strained at the ropes, leaning as far toward the laird as possible.

MacNab sighed. "Well, then, lad, since I've no need for that, I suppose I've no more need for you. Yer friend down there tells me you had the silver the morning we captured you. It's more work than I wanted, but we'll scour yer path from yer last camp to the place we trapped you. We'll find that silver, even without yer help." He lifted his hand and motioned to one of his men. "Take him to the pit and chain him there with his friend."

The hand MacNab held aloft fisted onto Ellie's shift, pulling her toward him as his men passed by to take Caden away.

Her mind raced as she leaned in toward his face. She had to think of something. Quickly.

MacNab's eyes were little beads of greedy desire. He opened his mouth and his foul breath wafted up, stinging her nostrils just before he latched onto one of her breasts, his tongue wet against the material of her shift.

When all hell broke loose around her, it only seemed fitting she should take advantage of it.

When he'd seen Baby outside MacNab's hideout, Caden had been convinced the animal hadn't understood his instructions to go for help. Perhaps he'd been mistaken and the animal had simply followed to see where to bring that help.

None of that mattered right now. How Ellie had gotten here, or why, was beyond Caden's reasoning. He knew only that she was here and in danger. Rational thought beyond that one point wasn't within his power any longer.

A haze of red fury clouded his mind, his only desire to get his hands on MacNab's throat and squeeze the very life from his body. Caden watched as the blighted bastard's mouth came down on Ellie's breast. She lifted one hand toward the sky and arched into him.

The red haze around Caden exploded.

The growl emanating from the depths of his soul was more animal than man but he could no more control the sound than he could stop his body from leaping toward MacNab the moment the ropes were lifted.

He surged from his chair, pulling at the arms attempting to hold him back. The elbow to his face wouldn't have stopped him, any more than the hands grabbing at him. His anger was too great to be controlled by mere men.

But the grim smile on Ellie's face, *that* brought him up short.

He suddenly felt as if he watched what happened from somewhere outside his body. Time slowed down, stretched out.

From somewhere she'd gotten her hands on a long, thin dagger, so much like the one he'd given Sallie years ago he would swear it to be the very same one. And she held it poised at MacNab's throat.

Caden watched as the man's eyes narrowed and tiny beads of sweat broke out across his forehead.

Dair had disarmed the guard closest to him. He carried a sword in hands now and at least one of the men was down as he made his way toward them.

None of MacNab's people moved, all of them waiting to see how the drama on the dais would play out.

"You tell those men to get their hands off Caden and back away from him. Now." Ellie tightened her hold on MacNab's hair, pulling his head closer, into the blade.

" 'Caden,' is it? Are you his woman, then?"

"Now," Ellie repeated through clenched teeth, ignoring the question. "Or I slice you a new opening."

"Yer no serious." MacNab's hand slid from his hold on Ellie's shift to his own lap.

"Oh, I'm serious as a heart attack, mister. Now do as I say or you die."

"I've no plans to be dying this day," he answered, his eyes narrowing as he stared out at his men.

The twitch of MacNab's shoulder was the only outward sign.

Caden shouted out her name in warning, but it was too late. MacNab's stick shot up, catching Ellie in the forehead, knocking her head back, loosening her hold on him as a wicked dagger flashed up in his other hand.

Caden clearly heard the ring of metal as Dair advanced, but he couldn't turn to follow the knight's progress. With an almost superhuman effort, he broke free of the men holding him and surged across the narrow space separating him from MacNab, his arms outstretched, reaching.

He hardly felt the metal of MacNab's weapon slice across the arm he threw out to deflect the weapon's path. Closing his fingers over Ellie's, he jerked her hand hard, pulling her dagger up and into MacNab's throat, cutting through the skin and bone under the blade they held jointly.

MacNab's eyes rolled up and a dark red line formed on his neck, but Caden didn't have time to worry about the fake laird. It was the shock on Ellie's face and the swelling pink knot on her forehead that had his concern.

He kicked the arm of MacNab's chair, sending it tipping over the side of the dais. The brigand's body landed with a thud, his head flopping back from his body as a pool of blood formed around him.

Ellie stared at the body, her eyes huge round saucers.

"Oh, shit," she breathed.

"Look at me." Caden grabbed her shoulders, giving her a little shake when she wouldn't look away from the body. "Look. At. Me."

Slowly her head swiveled his direction, her eyes still wild. She gazed down at the knife still clutched in her fist, the blade red with the brigand's blood. "Holy freakin' shit. What did I do?"

"You dinna do anything." Caden grasped her chin and gently forced her face back up to meet his gaze. "Do you hear me? I did that. No you." He wouldn't have that on her conscience. He'd kill the fiend a thousand times over again if given the chance, especially since it had been a matter of MacNab's life or Ellie's. Still, he wouldn't have her blaming herself for the act.

"Let go of me."

"Ellie, dinna do this to yerself. You dinna . . ."

"Let go!" she shouted, pulling away and dropping to her knees.

He couldn't stand that she blamed herself for the villain's death. He was fully prepared to shoulder the responsibility. He was used to that. But her look of horror as she pushed away from him ripped into his very soul.

He dropped to his own knees in front of her, reaching out to grasp her shoulders. "Ellie, listen to me." Caden leaned close, horrified at the fear he saw in her eyes.

She tried to shove his hands away but he was having none of that.

Instead he pulled her closer. "Speak to me. What is it?" he demanded.

In response, she promptly emptied the contents of her stomach down the front of him.

Twenty-six

"Try to sleep, Cousin. You've no any reason to think she's come to harm. And even if she had, yer pacing about like a caged beast will give her no aid."

Colin was right, of course, but that knowledge didn't help Blane in the least. He felt as helpless as the caged beast Colin compared him to, and he would until Catriona showed up at the window just before sunrise and he could see with his own two eyes she was unharmed.

"You'll want yer rest, whatever happens."

Blane stopped his pacing to meet his cousin's brilliant blue gaze; he was the only one of Rosalyn's children to get her eyes, the MacKiernan eyes.

"Whatever happens?" he echoed.

"Aye." Colin remained motionless in the shadowed corner. "I've fashed myself over what's become of Dair long enough. I intend to have my answers from the next guard who walks through that door."

Blane nodded slowly, as if his body acknowledged what his mind could not. The time had come to fight. "We try to escape?"

A low, sinister chuckle was his response. "You do. I'm no leaving until I've my answers about Dair."

Blane stared into the dark corner where Colin lay, hoping to catch some glimmer of the young man's emotions, but nothing betrayed his cousin's thoughts beyond what he had shared.

"Verra well." Blane slid down against the walls of his own corner, leaning his head back against the cold stone. He closed his eyes and wondered how he'd ever manage to pass a night as long as this one promised to be.

And then he heard the noise outside their door.

The quiet scrape of a footfall on gravel followed by the unmistakable sound of a key fitting into the lock.

Though he'd opened his eyes at the first sound, Colin was already at the door, his poised figure highlighted in the moonlight filtering through the little window in the back wall of their cell.

The door slowly opened, and in a blur of movement Colin had pinned the intruder to the wall.

"What in the name of the Fae?" he grunted, stepping back from his captive.

"Please. We must hurry."

"Catriona?" Blane couldn't believe his ears. "I thought you said you'd no betray . . ."

"It disna matter what I said. I've come to set you free. Now follow me." The woman turned back to the door, her hand on the pull.

"Wait!" Colin grabbed her arm, spinning her around.

"What can you tell me of the fate of the knight I traveled here with?"

Though she stood in the beam of light coming in the little window, Blane could see no movement as she answered, her entire form shrouded in the heavy hooded cloak she wore.

"Nothing, I'm afraid. I've no seen yer friend."

"I can give you word of him." The door swung wide, the opening filled with the man who spoke. "But not until you release the lady."

"They dinna hold me, Sim. I've come to set them free and I'll no have you trying to stop me."

Blane stepped forward, putting his body solidly between Catriona and the intruder. It was lunacy on her part to think she could order the warrior about!

"I've no desire to stop you. In fact, when I saw you sneak from yer room, I suspected I'd find you here. I've come to help you."

"And why would one of Wodeford's guards help us escape?" Blane made no effort to hide the sarcasm in his question.

"You could rot in this cell for all I care, MacKiernan. It's my aunt I've come to help. And as to why?"

The young man moved so quickly, Blane barely had time to react, grabbing onto his arm as the young man flipped Catriona's hood from her head.

"This is yer answer."

Catriona stood in the moonbeam, her head bowed. Blane reached out a shaking hand, placing his finger to her chin to lift her gaze to him. Though her beautiful face was a swollen mass of cuts and bruises, her eyes were determined and clear.

"I'll kill the bastard with my bare hands." The growl came from somewhere deep inside him, propelled by a force he could understand no better than he could control it.

She stopped him with a gentle hand to his chest, her touch calming the beast that raged in his soul.

"No. I've a much better way to get even with my brother. Here." She reached into her cloak and pulled out a small cloth bag, which she handed to him. "This is yers. The loss of yer silver will wound Austyn far deeper than any physical injury ever could."

"You said you know what's happened to the knight who traveled with me?" Colin stepped out of the shadows.

"Aye, Maxwell was sent to carry Austyn's demand for additional ransom for yer laird here. It's to be delivered by the heir, riding alone to Wode Castle."

Blane's stomach lurched at the news. "Then I canna go. I'll no have Caden riding into Wodeford's arms."

"It's no a problem." Colin swung the door open, a rare smile on his face. "We'll catch up to Caden before he gets close to Wode Castle."

"But how? We've no idea which back roads he might travel."

"Trust me, Cousin. Now that I ken who it is that comes, I can feel for him." Colin shrugged. "I'm no my mother's son for naught. I'll find him. Dinna fash yerself over that."

"Then we go."

Colin placed a hand against the door barring their way. "I say we eliminate Wodeford first. I've no a taste for a man whose heart is filled with vengeance to be trailing my steps."

Blane looked into Catriona's face, her eyes pleading for words he did not want to speak. His cousin had the right of it. Alive, her brother would always be a concern for the MacKiernan. And yet he could not repay her trust with such an act.

"No. We leave him alive." As much as he personally would wish it otherwise.

Colin tipped his head in acknowledgment. "As you say, my laird."

His cousin was right to doubt him. Still, he was the laird and it was his choice. That Colin conceded the point spoke of his loyalty.

There was yet one matter to resolve.

"And you?" Blane laid his hand on Catriona's shoulder, once again gazing into her gentle eyes. "What will become of you and yer nephew once you've helped us escape?"

"It's no yer problem, Blane," she answered softly. "We'll find someplace to go. Somewhere we'll be safe from Austyn."

He slid his hand down her arm, catching her delicate fingers in his grasp.

His decision was made.

"You'll come to Dun Ard with us. Both of you. I'll have it no other way."

It only seemed right Catriona should have a place in his home. She'd already found a place in his heart.

Twenty-seven

Some great kick-ass heroine she'd turned out to be. And puking all over the guy she had a thing for? Oh yeah, that was some attractive come-on.

No wonder he'd sent her packing back to Dun Ard with Alycie and her brothers.

Still, she had played a part in saving his butt. And Steafan's.

And even the barfing incident couldn't be laid wholly at her feet. After all, it wasn't every day she watched some guy die. Especially not when she had a hand in that death.

Literally.

The memory sent a shiver down her body and she shifted her weight on the horse she rode.

After MacNab's death, his men had scattered. According to Caden, the man had been claiming to be the laird of some local clan. With him gone, the outlaws who had banded together under his leadership feared having to face the legitimate clansmen.

Dair and Alycie had patched up Steafan's wounds as best they could, but getting him back to Dun Ard and Rosalyn's care was apparently his only hope of survival.

Alycie had mentioned taking him to Iona to recuperate if he survived the journey to Dun Ard, but what they'd do with him if he made it back home, Ellie didn't know. Or much care. Since she'd learned he was responsible for Caden's capture, she was finding it hard to be too sympathetic.

"Karma gets you every time," she muttered.

"What's that?" Dair looked back over his shoulder to where she pulled up the rear of their little group.

"Nothing." Ellie shook her head and looked away, knowing Steafan's brother probably wouldn't appreciate her sentiment.

They'd ridden for a couple of hours, though their pace was slow and torturous thanks to Steafan's condition.

Caden, meanwhile, had left them at the bottom of the mountain, heading off in the opposite direction.

Alone.

He'd grabbed her reins as she started to follow him.

"But I want to go with you," she'd told him.

"Yer to go back to Dun Ard and stay there. Dair will watch over you on the journey. You have work to do there, aye?"

"Work? You mean the sheep? I explained to your mother how to prepare the soak. She and Drew can handle it just fine. I'm coming with you."

He'd gone all he-man on her then, growling about how

he'd have Dair tie her to her horse and carry her home that way if she didn't do as she was told. Frankly, after the day she'd just had, it pissed her off, so she'd ripped her reins from his grasp and turned her back on him.

Which was, of course, exactly what the big jerk had wanted.

She could see that now. She'd played right into his hands and missed her opportunity to do what she thought was best.

You alpha female. Your decision. Go to him if you want. Baby walked beside her, turning his head to stare up at her.

"I can't," she whispered, but considered the idea even as she spoke. "I wouldn't have any idea how to find him."

Scent fresh. Baby can find.

"I . . ." She bit off the word that came so automatically to her lips. She was so tired of the *can'ts* in her life.

I can't do anything about Ray. I can't figure out what to do to get home. I can't follow Caden.

Well, why not? Why couldn't she?

Hey, she'd just killed a guy today, hadn't she? Never mind the fact that he was trying to kill her or that she hadn't actually done anything but hold the weapon that had done the deed. She'd been there. Right there in the thick of it, doing things that before today she would have sworn she couldn't do.

If she could do that, she could do anything.

"Are you sure you can find him?"

Waves of reassurance flowed back at her in response to her question.

"Okay, then. That's it." Decision made, she pulled her reins, turning her horse to head back the direction from which she'd just come.

"And what do you think yer doing back there, missy?" Dair brought his own mount to a halt.

"What I should have done to start with."

"Wait." Dair trotted his animal back to her side. He pulled something out of the sporran at his waist and held his hand out to her. "You'll want this."

She took Sallie's little jeweled dagger and fastened the belt around her middle. "Thank you. For this and for not trying to talk me out of going."

He snorted his disbelief. "As if I could change yer mind. I saw the shape upon yer breast when we prepared to go into that keep today. It's a rose, aye? The Faerie mark, if I'm no mistaken. To my mind, that makes you more than a match for our Caden." He grinned and pulled his horse around, rejoining his brother and sister.

Ellie watched them moving steadily away before pressing her heels to her own mount's sides.

"Okay, Baby. Do your stuff."

She could do this, even though she worried a bit about traveling alone out here. Still, she was no city girl. For someone who'd spent as much time alone on the land as she had, riding by herself for a few hours wouldn't be too scary.

Not nearly as scary as worrying about what Caden would do when she showed up.

The silver was exactly where he'd left it, lodged into the rocks at the bank of the river.

Caden had taken it from its hiding place and started forward only to realize he didn't want to face that section of forest this close to dark.

Not after the day he'd had.

He was too tired to face those memories. Both physically and mentally. He'd needed to hold off passing that way until he had a night's rest and a full stomach. So he'd backtracked a mile or so to a place where the river veered from the path, forming a secluded spot perfect for camping the night.

The broth simmering over his fire smelled heavenly, though it was no more than water, herbs and some dried meat. And it tasted even better than it smelled after the diet of molded bread crusts he'd been given over the past several days.

Dair had divided out the provisions he carried, giving half to Caden before they had parted ways this afternoon. The cheese was nearly gone before he'd traveled an hour down the road.

Thinking of that parting, Caden lost what appetite he still had. Ellie had been furious with him. Her eyes had sparked with her anger and it had torn him up to have it directed at him even though her anger had been his goal.

He would have much rather held her in his arms as he'd done after she'd been so ill, stroking her silky black curls away from her face. He'd have chosen to keep her by his side to protect her himself if it had been possible. To tell her of his dreams while he'd been held in that rat-infested hole. Dreams of her that had helped him escape in sleep. To see those beautiful green eyes light with something other than anger when she'd looked at him last.

But none of that was possible.

He wouldn't risk having her face again what she had this day. Or worse. Her anger was a small price to pay to know she was headed toward the relative safety of Dun Ard.

Besides, she belonged to his brother. He had no right to be dreaming of her, much less telling her about those fantasies.

He stood and wiped his hands on his shirt, wrinkling his face in disgust. He smelled like a tavern drunk after a bad night.

And with the thoughts of what he'd put Ellie through this day on his mind, it wasn't like he was going to be able to drift off to sleep anyway.

Instead he headed for the river. It wouldn't be as good as his bathhouse, but at least he'd smell a sight better.

Thank God for the full moon.

Ellie hadn't counted on traveling in the dark when Baby had said he could find Caden. She'd remember to be more specific in the questions she asked before jumping to make decisions next time.

"How much longer?"

Close now. Smell food.

Caden must have set up camp for the night.

Ellie's stomach did that funny little nerve dance she'd been experiencing off and on since she'd made the decision to follow him. They were close. That meant she didn't have long to prepare what to say to him, but so far she hadn't made much progress on that. Her thoughts continued to work in a circle she didn't like.

She knew he wasn't going to be happy that she'd

come after him. But *with* him was where she felt she should be, so she'd better make up her mind about what she was going to do. About why she was even here looking for Caden.

About why she felt the need to be at his side.

Her heart did a double beat as she considered the big question she'd worked so hard to ignore.

What if Rosalyn was right, that she'd been sent here to find that one special man she'd wished for? She'd certainly tried to explain her being here in other ways— saving the sheep, saving Caden.

And yet here she was, still stuck in the Middle Ages, following some overpowering gut feeling to find the man who'd tried to send her away.

Which brought her back to the question: What if Rosalyn was right?

Couldn't be. That path was too scary. It had to be something else entirely. Something so bizarre that it had the power to toss her through seven hundred years couldn't possibly boil down to simply hooking up with some guy, could it?

But if—and it was a big if—*if* it did . . . could Caden be that man?

A deep breath shuddered through her body at the thought. If he was, following her path tonight should give her the answer she needed.

It should also send her home. Home to the life she knew. Home to deal with the stepfather who was even this very minute stealing her beloved ranch.

She physically shook the idea away even as Caden's face danced through her mind.

It couldn't be Caden. Not someone she'd have no

chance of spending her life with. Besides, surely the one person in the whole of time who completed her, her own Prince Charming, couldn't possibly be someone who could make her so insanely angry on such a regular basis.

No, Caden was her friend, the one person she'd trusted with her secret. The one person who'd trusted her with his life.

Yeah. That was it. Her friend.

The friend who was going to be plenty pissed when she showed up.

And that brought her thoughts back full circle to where she had started and no closer to what she was going to say or do when she found Caden. After all, he'd already rejected her once today. What would she do if he sent her away again?

Baby's snort of derision rolled through her mind, jolting her like a slap to the face.

"Exactly. What's wrong with my brain?"

She was looking at this all wrong. Caden couldn't send her anywhere she didn't want to go. She had made up her mind she was going to go where it felt right and the only place that felt right for her now was with Caden.

Unfortunately having made that decision and knowing she'd have to tell him about that decision didn't help the nervous stomach one bit. In fact, the circle her mind traveled felt more like a fast-moving spiral at the moment, leaving her with mental motion sickness but not a single concrete answer.

Baby lifted his nose, scenting the air again before veering from the path and into the trees.

Ellie's cheeks puffed as she blew out a breath and

stiffened her resolve. "Okay. I'm the alpha female. I can do whatever I want." Maybe if she said it enough, she'd convince herself.

A few yards into the trees, Ellie spotted the campsite. Caden's fire burned low, the kettle hanging over it bubbling away. Obviously the source of the food Baby had smelled.

All sat in readiness . . . except no Caden anywhere.

Baby dropped by the fire, his head on his paws, asleep almost before he stopped moving.

The thought *dog tired* ran through Ellie's mind, bringing a smile to her face as she climbed down off her mount and walked him over to where Caden's horse was tethered.

"Hey, boy." She stroked her hand down his horse's neck. "Where's Caden, huh?"

Water.

Unlike the reedy "voice" of the dogs, the horse's thoughts felt deep and reverberated through her mind. The communication was much more clipped and succinct than the dogs' way of speaking, too. All in all, not a very satisfying, or informative, conversation experience.

Ellie stood very still and listened. In the quiet she picked out the sounds of the river nearby. Perhaps that was what the horse meant by its cryptic one-word answer?

Only one way to find out.

She followed the sound, making her way through the new growth of foliage and old underbrush, once again thankful for the full moon that filtered through the branches of the trees.

Just ahead, she could see a glimmer of water.

She pushed past a large bush and stopped at the edge of an enormous flat boulder overlooking a spot where the river turned sharply, forming a pool in the corner of the bend. The water here seemed all the more placid when compared to the flow of the river along side it.

And there, in this idyllic spot, she found the man she sought.

Caden stood in the center of the pool, water streaming down his bare chest in rivulets, glistening in the moonlight like trails of liquid diamonds leading down into the little waves that lapped at his waist.

What was hidden beneath the water Ellie could only imagine. And she certainly had a well-developed imagination.

Her hand flew to her chest as if trying to hold her rapidly beating heart where it belonged.

Just a friend?

What the hell had she been thinking?

Caden had fought them at first. Fought the memories of Ellie's soft lips against his, her gentle hands on his back, her body hot against his skin, driving him mad with need.

But now, alone in the pool, he weakened as he always did when he thought of her.

He plunged under the water, only half wanting the images in his mind to go away. Then he rose, letting the night's cool breeze drive the water from his body and Ellie from his thoughts.

But the waves didn't cooperate. Instead they caressed

his skin like silky fingers trailing around his middle, adding to the fantasy building in his imagination, stoking the fire in his loins he'd hoped to extinguish.

Caden opened his eyes on a groan, only to find the object of his fantasy poised on the boulder at the edge of his pool, one hand over her heart.

Not possible. The moonlight and his imagination conspired against him. He'd sent Ellie with Dair, back to the safety of Dun Ard. Back to wait for her future husband. His brother.

The figure on the shore might be illusion, but the pain he felt at that thought was very real.

What he wouldn't give to have things be different.

"Hey!" she called, and all doubt was erased. "You coming out of there anytime soon?"

The thrill of having her so near warred with his anger at the risk she took in coming. "What are you doing here?"

Indecision danced across her delicate features for only a moment. "You shouldn't travel alone. You need me."

He *needed* her all right, but he'd wager not in the way she was thinking. "I've no a need for companions on this journey. I'm fine on my own."

"Right. You've done such a bang-up job of it so far."

Though he might not understand her words, he had a pretty clear idea of her intent. He wouldn't be pulled into arguing with her. "You've traveled alone?"

"Yep. Just me. And now here I am with you."

Anger was quickly winning the battle over his emotions. When next he saw Dair, he'd have to teach the young warrior a thing or two about doing as he was told. What had the man been thinking to allow Ellie to roam about the countryside unprotected?

"First thing tomorrow, we get you back to Alasdair and on yer way to Dun Ard." It would cost him another day's delay, but how could he do otherwise? The look in her eyes after MacNab's death would haunt him all his days. He never wanted her to go through such as she had in that keep this morning.

"Just you hold on for a minute, Caden MacAlister. We have to talk about this."

Her hands rested on her hips in that particularly bossy stance he'd come to expect from her. It made no difference.

"There'll be no talking on the subject. My mind's made up."

He watched as countless emotions slid across her face so quickly he couldn't decipher them, all ending in a smile that gave him more than a little concern.

"Made up, is it? Well, then, I guess I'll just have to see what I can do to unmake it, won't I?"

He began to shake his head, but any response caught in his throat as she lifted her hands to the laces on her overdress and slowly untied them, letting the dress slide into a tumble at her feet.

The moonlight shone through the soft white linen of her shift, making it transparent, outlining the soft curves underneath. At the very least, he fancied he could see them. Perhaps it was no more than imagination and wishful thinking.

"What in the name of the Fae do you think yer doing?" he managed to croak out.

In answer she kicked off her slippers before grasping

the hem of her shift and lifting. Up and over her head and off to the side it billowed and floated down, as if time and motion had slowed.

Caden swallowed against the dry throat that threatened to choke him, unable to tear his eyes from the vision standing on the boulder. Her bare skin glowed as if a stray moonbeam shone only for her.

For a heartbeat, he felt as if he'd somehow slipped through the curtain separating the Mortal World from the Realm of Fae. Slipped to the other side, where he'd stumbled upon the Faerie Queen herself at the edge of an enchanted pool.

He turned his back on her and scrubbed at his face, knowing that image of beauty would be burned into his mind forever, taunting him with the knowledge of what was just out of his reach.

He was only vaguely aware of a splash and then her hands were at his waist, sending out flickers of fire and shards of ice as they slid up his back to his shoulders.

"I have to be here, Caden."

She leaned into him and he turned, grasping her shoulders as he pulled back from her touch.

"This is no right." It took all his strength to force the words from his mouth.

"No, it is right. I'm supposed to be here with you. I feel it. In here." Her fingers fluttered over her heart, lighting on the dark red mark adorning her perfect breast.

The mark that proclaimed her a Daughter of the Fae, sent into his life by them. The reminder shook him to his very core.

The last time he'd dealt with the Fae, they'd turned

his world upside down, taking with them his dreams and his vision of what his life was to be. This time he felt as though they might very well rip his heart from his body, stripping him of his very soul.

"Tell me you don't feel it, too," she whispered, pushing aside his hands, flowing toward him until her body pressed against his, her cool, wet skin igniting heat everywhere they touched. "You can't, can you?"

Not if his life depended on it. And at the moment it felt as if it very well might.

She slid her hands up his chest, slowing to allow her thumbs to feather over his nipples.

Need burned through him, swelling his manhood to the point of pain. A fact Ellie hadn't missed if the smile on her lips was any indicator.

She ran her hands up his shoulders and around his neck, threading her fingers into his hair, tugging his face down, down inexorably toward her mouth.

Their lips met in a burst of heat and desire and he was lost in the magic of the moment.

He clasped his hands about her waist and lifted her easily, bringing her tightly to him. When she opened herself to him, wrapping her legs around him and locking them at his back, any stray thoughts he might have had about stopping this before it was too late were swept away like leaves in the fast-moving current of the river flowing beside them.

There would be no stopping this time.

Her head dropped back, her delicate neck extended as he kissed his way down. Down to her shoulder, nuzzling aside her heavy wet hair, to follow the beads of water that rolled from her curls down her chest. Down to the mark on her breast and on until he captured the tight bud of her nipple in his mouth, rolling his tongue round and round, sucking gently, insistently, as if he could pull her inside himself.

"Caden," she whispered, droplets of water still clinging to her thick lashes as she looked down into his face. She arched her body into his before reclaiming his mouth with her own, her tongue working across his lips and inside, slowly, tortuously, in and out in a rhythm his body recognized all too well.

He would wait no longer.

He carried her back to the edge of the pool, so lost in the taste of her, in the magic of their kiss, he was barely aware of the steps he took. He knew only that she clung to him as if her need was as great as his own.

As they reached the boulder, he braced her against the edge and she tightened her hold around his neck, shifting against him until his shaft nestled into the warmth of her opening. When he pressed against her, testing, she moaned, and seemed to melt into him, molding her body to his, forcing the tip of his shaft just inside her heat.

He wanted to go slowly, to stretch out the pleasure of this stolen moment to last a lifetime. But once again she moaned and rocked against him, and he lost the thread of his plans.

Instinct replaced any rational thought and he surged into her, filling her, driving deeper and deeper as she pushed back against him, meeting his thrusts, tightening around him until his only thought was to be so deeply inside her they would be as one.

Mine. The word roared through his mind, and he

drove into her again, as if he could lay claim to what he could not have.

He felt her stiffen against him, reveled in her body's series of contractions as they built, each pulling him farther into her heat until the breath exploded from her.

Her sensations pushed him into his own release and he held her tightly to him as the world shattered around them in a burst of emerald light so intense, he knew he would never experience its equal again.

Because even in the joy of this moment, he knew he could never allow this to happen again. In spite of what he might want, in spite of the primal voice screaming in his head, he knew the truth of it.

She didn't belong to him.

And her whispered words, "I don't love you. I don't," reinforced that fact, driving a knife of pain deep into his soul.

Twenty-eight

The blood drummed in Ellie's head, pounding against her ears, all but blocking out any other sound.

The green lightning had come for her again, surrounding her only moments before, robbing her of the joy she'd felt.

Rosalyn must have been right. She was here to find a man.

The man. Her one true love.

And when she'd found him, when she'd given herself up, allowed herself the overwhelming bliss of accepting him, those damned heartless Faeries had tried to snatch it all away, just as Rosalyn had said they would. All because she hadn't wished it right in the first place, hadn't said the proper words.

In a panic, she'd done the only thing she could think to do. Since they'd told her it was the words that held the power, she'd given the Fae words. She'd denied her true feelings, and the light had withdrawn, winking out of existence.

Along with the light, Caden had withdrawn, too. Obviously he'd heard those words. She'd felt him tense, felt the connection between them shatter like an actual jolt of pain.

The poor guy was probably terrified that what he saw as nothing more than a little physical playtime had her babbling about love, even if it was just to deny she felt it.

Apparently men hadn't changed that much in the last seven centuries. Any hint of commitment, and they were out of there.

Had she at last discovered her way home? Was it as simple, and as difficult, as that? She had only to accept her true feelings for Caden and then give him up.

Forever.

And at that moment, after what she'd just experienced with him, leaving him was the one thing she wasn't prepared to do.

But it was all so confusing.

If he were truly The One, the only man in the whole of time for her, shouldn't he have felt the connection, too? Shouldn't he be holding her close, trying to convince her that she did, too, love him?

Instead he rolled off her body, moving just far enough away to avoid any physical contact. Add that to the fact that he said nothing at all, simply lay next to her without a single comment, and his actions spoke volumes. Way more than any pretty words he might have come up with.

And what did it matter anyway? Going home was

what she wanted most. It was. Being stuck in the God-forsaken thirteen hundreds, chasing after some guy who'd made it clear he wasn't interested in anything more than a quick tumble, sure as hell wasn't how she wanted to spend the rest of her life.

Even if what they had just shared had been amazing, unlike anything she'd ever experienced before.

"I'm sorry."

With the quiet words of apology, Caden stood up and walked to the bush where his clothes hung, leaving her feeling both physically and emotionally naked. She sat up and reached for her shift, letting it drop down over her head and into place.

"You don't have anything to apologize for." He didn't. It was all her. She'd totally screwed up. It had been stupid to let herself get carried away with the idea that once he made love to her everything would change.

Although, in truth, everything had changed. Just not the way she'd expected.

"But I do. What we just did should no have happened. I should no have allowed you to do that."

"Allowed me?" She looked up from fumbling with her laces, disbelief at his comment rolling through her mind. "*Allowed?*" As if she needed his permission for what they'd done? It might have been a stupid choice, but it had been her choice.

He kept his back to her, wrapping his plaid around his hips. "I canna even claim ignorance. I'm well aware you dinna belong to me."

"Exactly." Maybe she was just being sensitive and overreacting to his words. She belonged to herself and at least he acknowledged that.

He walked back to the edge of the boulder and reached out, locking his fingers around her wrist and helping her rise to her feet. Immediately he withdrew his hand, placing it behind his back as he continued to stare down at her.

"I'm only trying to say that I'd no intent to dishonor you, Ellie. I accept the fact that you belong to my brother and I'll no ever speak of this night to anyone."

"Just back it up there a minute, cowboy. What the hell are you talking about? I don't belong to anybody, and certainly not to Drew."

Caden looked up and over her head, avoiding her eyes as if preparing to deliver a lecture. "It's Colin I speak of. The Fae sent you here for him. When I return with him, you'll wed. And one day, I will name yer first-born son as my heir to the lairdship of the MacKiernan, just as Blane has done with me."

Ellie stared at the man, only vaguely aware that her mouth hung open. Her shock quickly melted into anger. "Well, you've just got it all figured out, haven't you? Planned my whole life, did you? Did it ever occur to you that I don't even know this brother of yours?"

He grazed her with a look, lips pressed together, one eyebrow cocked. "It's what you've been sent to do. You'll see that he's the one as soon as I bring him back to Dun Ard. You'll be happy together."

He actually sounded as if he believed that load of crap.

Ellie stood, hands on her hips, wallowing in her building fury, letting it roll over her in great whipping waves. When he looked away again, she dropped her shoulder and plowed her body into his chest, much the same move she had perfected in moving stubborn sheep up the ramp and into the back of her old pickup to take into town.

She found the resounding splash he made when he hit the water quite satisfying, topped only by his sputtering and swearing as he broke the surface of the pool.

"You listen to me, you arrogant sheepherder. I'm not marrying Colin or Drew or anybody else in this nightmare. I'm going home. Back to my own time, where I belong. I'm going to get my ranch back or make Ray Stanton wish to hell he'd never been born. And if you know what's good for you, the next time we discuss what's going to happen with my life, you better be asking not telling, you got that?"

Ellie stuffed her feet into her slippers and stomped back toward the campsite.

What an idiot she was.

It couldn't be clearer to her right now that the big oaf sitting on his butt in the water back there couldn't possibly be The One. What had she been thinking? Her true love, the other half of her soul, would never, ever be such a total ass.

And it sure as hell couldn't be his brother—the one she'd never even met—because that green light had shown up for some reason back there by the river and this mysterious brother was nowhere near here.

As soon as she got back to Dun Ard, she and Rosalyn were having one serious sit-down. All she had to do was figure out exactly what had happened to turn the light on and then she was out of here.

Twenty-nine

Ellie hadn't spoken more than ten words to him in the last two days and it was driving Caden mad.

He glanced over at her profile, set with determination as she busied herself laying out her bedding for the night. It didn't escape his notice that she again prepared to sleep as far away from him as possible without actually being outside the circle of the firelight.

In truth, ten words wasn't exactly accurate. She'd spoken hundreds that first morning when he'd told her he wouldn't allow her to go with him, the majority of which he might not ever have heard before, but the meaning of all was entirely clear.

If he took her back to Dun Ard, she would follow. No matter what he did.

And he didn't for one minute doubt her. He'd never met a woman as determined, as stubborn when she had her mind set, as *Elliedenton*.

"Besides," she'd told him, her eyes flashing emerald in her anger, "if this brother of yours is the one who can make me see stars, I want to meet him as soon as possible. I can't wait to get out of this place and back where I belong."

She seemed to think finding her Soulmate would somehow send her home. But that couldn't be. If that were the case, her being here would only make his brother more unhappy, and that certainly wasn't his intent.

He hadn't denied himself the pleasure of this woman only to have his brother's chance at happiness snatched away.

Caden ground his teeth together in frustration at the thought. He hadn't denied himself anything. He'd taken her, as if he had the right, as if she belonged to him.

It was Ellie who had done the denying. Her words had been clear.

"I don't love you," she'd said.

Of course she didn't. He'd been a fool to let the idea enter into his thoughts to begin with. He'd long ago accepted that his life would never include love, just like his cousin Blane. It was their fate, their curse, to bear the responsibility for the happiness of others but to go through life with none of their own.

Having her angry was a good thing. It served to prevent what he couldn't seem to prevent on his own. With her this angry, there was no chance they'd repeat their indiscretion of two nights ago.

But he did have a real problem with her not talking to him. Fury he could handle. This was something deeper. Something he didn't like at all. For even as he'd accepted that she would belong to his brother, the one thing that had kept him going was the hope that she would remain his friend.

Now he'd likely ruined that chance with his rash behavior. He'd hurt her just like he'd managed to hurt everyone else in his life.

And as long as she refused to even speak to him, he had no chance of repairing the damage.

He stole another sideways glance her direction and decided to take the plunge, clearing his throat to see if she might look at him.

She ignored him, turning to her side and presenting her plaid-covered back to him.

He cleared his throat again, stalling for time as much as to get her attention.

"You spoke of returning to a *ranch*." He rolled the unfamiliar word on his tongue, testing it, before he continued. "And seeking revenge on someone named Ray. What is this ranch that it would be so important to reclaim?"

At first he thought she might not answer, but after several long minutes she rolled onto her back, staring up at the night sky.

"My home," she said softly. "The house I grew up in. The land where my family raised sheep for two genera-tions. It's all that I have in the world."

"I see. And this Ray? His clan raided yer keep and occupies it?"

She responded with a short, bitter laugh, a sound un-like any he'd heard from her before. "Something like that. He married my mother a few years back. Thought he'd found himself a sugar mama to take care of him and pay all his bills while he ran around doing whatever he wanted. He cheated on her and she kicked him out. Now that she's dead, the bastard's back, claiming that what was hers now belongs to him."

"And you want yer revenge." That he could understand. He would be wild with the need if someone were to try to take Dun Ard from his people. "Because he threw you out with no place to go."

"Oh, I could have stayed." Another bitter laugh. "All I had to do was be Ray's latest bed partner. And that wasn't happening."

Caden felt a white-hot fury sweep over him. This bastard, this Ray, had dared to dishonor Ellie? "What of the others of yer family, do they no stand up to this man?" If he could but spend a few minutes in her time, he would see to it this Ray suffered greatly for his actions.

"There are no others. Just me." She wiped the palms of her hands down the sides of her face, leaving wet trails that glistened in the firelight.

"I dinna mean to make you cry." Anything but that.

She flopped over to her side again, pulling the plaid up to hide her head, Baby at her side. "Go to sleep, Caden. And don't worry about me. You didn't make me cry. I won't *allow* any man that power over me."

He didn't miss her emphasis on the word *allow*, the same word which had set her off before. Nor did he miss the strangled tears in her voice.

Caden lay down and rolled himself in his bedding, knowing it would be a long time before he slept this night.

This man, her mother's husband, had demanded

her favors in return for lodging in her own home. Was that why she'd given herself to him back at the pool? Because it was what she thought he expected? He'd certainly done nothing to convince her otherwise, completely unable to keep himself from pawing over her at every opportunity.

For all his good intentions and great words, he was no better than that bastard, Ray.

"That's fair odd." Colin perched on an outcropping of rocks at the river's edge.

"Are we no on the right track?" Blane waited behind him, only yards from their campsite.

"No. We're close now. I can feel Caden ahead. Him and . . ." Colin stopped, reaching out with his senses, the gift of his Fae blood. "It's almost as if he travels with someone, but . . ." But not.

"Steafan, perhaps?"

"No."

He knew how Steafan felt and this was entirely different. Though Steafan would have been a logical choice for Caden to have brought along, in spite of the fact that Wodeford had ordered the MacKiernan heir to come alone with the ransom. Colin had learned that much from Simeon.

And since he was thinking of Simeon . . .

"What are yer plans for Lady Baxter and her nephew once we reach Dun Ard?" Colin turned to find his laird stroking his chin thoughtfully.

"I've offered Simeon a permanent spot at Dun Ard. As far as Lady Baxter, I suppose I'll have no choice but to wed the lady. Traveling alone with a group of men will completely compromise her honor, will it no?"

"And so yer going to make the sacrifice and force yerself to do the right thing, is that it?"

The sheepish grin on Blane's face was all the answer Colin needed.

"Blessings on you, then, Cousin, for many years of happiness together. Does the lady have any idea what you've planned for her?"

Blane shook his head, the grin still firmly fixed in place. "I've no yet found quite the proper time to broach the subject. But I will. Soon."

"Aye, well, you might want to drop a word or two about our . . . um . . . unusual heritage." For lack of a better description. More than one person had been put off by the idea of marrying into a family of Fae descendants. As well they should.

"I'm no seeing that as a problem." Blane shrugged his shoulders. "The lady would appear to be past her childbearing years, so it's no like I'd be passing along any gifts to offspring." The frown that flitted across Blane's face was gone as quickly as it came. "Speaking of our companions, I'll go check on them now."

As he watched his cousin make his way back through the trees toward their campsite, Colin suspected it was the madness Blane's father and brother had suffered that kept his cousin from wanting children, not the gifts of their Fae-tainted blood.

But that was only because Blane himself hadn't been cursed with any of the Fae gifts. If he had, he'd know there was more to fear in the world than ordinary madness.

His curiosity piqued, Colin reached out again, searching for his brother's soul with his own awareness, testing.

Yes, it was Caden and one other that he felt. And yet it was somehow different, as if neither one was quite complete. He could feel the jagged edges on each of their souls.

As if it would take both souls to make a whole.

Colin stood, staring into the inky night in the direction he felt his brother. They were within a day's ride of one another now.

He smiled and turned back toward camp.

Whatever it was his awareness was touching on, he'd know before another night fell. Tomorrow should prove a most interesting day.

Thirty

Staring is rude and you were brought up better than that.

Her mother's words rang in her mind as Ellie sipped from her cup, trying her best not to be obvious about the staring she was doing. All the same, she couldn't seem to help herself.

These were the men Caden had risked his life to save.

Just before sundown, she and Caden had stopped to make camp. They'd barely finished gathering wood for their fire when this group had showed up.

She'd listened wide-eyed as Blane had told the story of their escape, sounding like someone recounting the plot of the latest movie he'd just gone to see.

Ellie could almost believe that the case if she didn't have the visual proof of just how real it all was sitting around the campfire with her now.

With the exception of the one named Simeon,

every single one of them looked as if they'd had the crap beaten out of them, even that sweet little Lady Baxter.

Ellie felt as if her heart missed a couple of beats, her breath catching at the realization of what could have happened to Caden if he'd actually made it all the way to that awful Wode Castle. What would she have done if . . .

She stopped midthought, reminding herself she was completely furious with Caden. She would not be worrying about him anymore. She absolutely refused to. A damn good ass-kicking might be exactly what he needed to knock him off that pedestal he lived on.

As if he knew her thoughts touched on him, he walked over to her, offering to refill her cup.

She shook her head in refusal, giving him her best "go away" look. Instead of taking her hint, he sat down by her side, leaning close to whisper in her ear.

"Well? What do you think of Colin? Is it not exactly as I said it would be?"

He looked so serious, so concerned, she hesitated, debating what she really wanted to say.

Whatever magic first impression Caden had expected her to have of his brother, it wasn't there. Exactly as she'd known it wouldn't be. Oh, Colin was handsome enough, in a brooding, big, dark warrior sort of way. If you wanted that sort. Which she didn't.

She reminded herself that she didn't want the brooding, big sheepherder sort, either.

"Sorry to disappoint you, cowboy. I didn't see a single star." She set down her empty cup and stood, suddenly finding that she'd had all she could take of the reunion chatter and needed some alone time. "I'll be back in a while."

Caden grabbed the hem of her skirt, slowing her departure. "Perhaps Colin should accompany you to see to yer safety, aye?"

Colin paused his conversation long enough to give them both a look, his eyebrows raised in question.

"I don't think so. Baby's all the protection I need, thank you very much."

She jerked her skirt from Caden's fingers and hurried to the forest's edge, deciding as she reached the trees to make her way to the river beyond. It wasn't far, and truly, she did feel safe with Baby at her side.

Sitting down on the bank of the river, she stared into the dark water. The moonlight glinted off the fast-moving eddies, shimmering and dancing before her. If she closed her eyes, peeking through just the tiniest slit, she could almost imagine herself home, on the bank of her own river the night she'd been zapped away. As if none of it had ever happened.

A wave of sadness swept over her at the thought, and she rested her chin on her propped-up knees.

If none of this had happened, she never would have met Caden, never would have shared with him the experience at that little pool, never would have shared part of him, if only for such a brief time. And though she still worked to convince herself that she hated, detested, completely loathed him right now for wanting to get rid of her so badly he'd try pawning her off on his brother, she wouldn't have missed that experience for the world.

The glistening water danced before her, only slightly more shimmery through the tears forming in her eyes. The distortion gave the water an almost magical look.

The river! Maybe that was the source of the magic and her way home.

She blinked back the tears, refusing to admit she was grasping at straws.

She'd been by the river when the magic had first swept her away. And when she'd seen it the second time, she was once again at a river's edge.

That had to be it.

Because it wasn't saving the sheep, or saving Caden's life, or even saving Caden's brother.

And the only other alternative was unacceptable. Being in love with someone who didn't want you? No, that was just too painful to even contemplate.

It had to be the water.

"I wish . . ." She stopped and wiped at the tears rolling down her cheeks. Was it just the blur in her vision or had the moonlight on the waves taken on a greenish cast? "I wish . . ."

"Are you well?"

She jumped at the sound of Caden's voice as he came out of the trees behind her, taking another quick swipe at her eyes before she stood. "Of course I am," she snapped.

He grasped her arms and pulled her to him, then let go to wipe her cheeks with the pads of his thumbs.

"Dinna cry, wee *Elliedenton*. To see you so fair breaks—"

He stopped and swayed toward her, as if pulled to her by an invisible string. Or was it her leaning into him, inexorably drawn to the man who didn't want her? His lips parted, and for just that one instant she could swear he intended to kiss her again. If he did, all would be lost because she knew she didn't have it in her to resist him.

Instead he cleared his throat and dropped his hands to his sides. "You'll see yer stars one day. I'm sure of it. Just give Colin a chance."

With that worthless piece of advice, he turned back toward their camp, stopping for only a minute before he entered the trees, speaking without looking her direction. "You'll hurry back to camp, aye? We've an early start tomorrow."

And then he was gone.

What was she going to do?

Rosalyn was convinced it was hunting her true love that had brought her here. Caden was convinced that her true love was his brother. And she was convinced that whatever it was, it all hurt like hell.

Things didn't change and he was all the more fool for thinking they would.

Caden stomped back toward camp, frustration running rampant through his blood.

He, of all people, should know better.

Blane had confided earlier that he planned to wed the Lady Baxter and Caden had grasped onto the news. Not with joy that his cousin had finally, after all these years, found the one woman to share his life, but with a selfish purpose.

If love could happen for Blane, perhaps there was hope for him.

And then, as they'd all prepared to turn in for the

night, Colin had announced his intent to go find the foolish little woman who had wandered away from camp and Caden had seen red. Ellie wouldn't appreciate being called either a little woman or foolish, and he found himself feeling irritation at someone applying those labels to her.

So he'd gone off to find her himself, fresh hope blooming in his heart. If anyone deserved to be labeled foolish, surely it was he.

He'd found her, all right. Venting her sorrow, tears streaming down her cheeks.

He continued as he always had, bringing pain to those who were important to him.

His first thought had been to do whatever, say whatever would make the pain disappear. But then he'd held her close and looked into her eyes, and all he could think of was how much he wanted her, wanted to take her right then, right there at the river's edge.

He'd had to force himself to let her go, a task that had taken everything he had in him. One he now knew he couldn't repeat.

As soon as they returned to Dun Ard, he'd speak privately with Colin. Once his brother and Ellie were wed, they could take up residence at Sithean Fardach. He'd do whatever he could to restore the old castle for them.

Until then, perhaps she'd be willing to stay with Sallie at the MacPherson keep.

Anything to get her away from Dun Ard. Away from him.

Because he feared he could not be strong enough to stay away from her.

Thirty-one

⁓

"No, I willna help you. It's no safe for you to be outside the gates. Especially as we've no idea whether or no Wodeford will come seeking his sister." Rosalyn stood and placed her needlework on the small table between them before heading to the door of her solar.

"But don't you understand? I need to get to a river. I'm sure that's the key to my getting home." It had to be. Ellie couldn't accept anything else.

"It's no the river, lass." Rosalyn stopped at the door, turning. "I've told you. It's yer Soulmate you seek, the other half of yer own self. And when you open yer heart to that, open yer heart to him, that's when the magic will come to you, when yer souls have come together and yer whole."

"Wouldn't this being whole mean he'd have to feel the same way about me?" If she even believed in this Soulmate thing, that is. Which she didn't. Wouldn't.

"It does."

"Well, there you go, then. That's not happening. There's no one here who . . ." She paused as she thought of her conversation with Caden. "No one who makes me see stars. I can't imagine finding this Soulmate of mine, so I can't accept that as the reason I'm here."

Rosalyn's eyes narrowed, her gaze piercing as if the woman looked into Ellie's very heart before she tilted her head and smiled. "It's no stars you want to see, is it? It's the lovely green glow of yer magic. Be honest with yerself, lass, even if you'd no be honest with me. Yer heart's already recognized him, has it no?"

Ellie's pulse pounded in her ears. Was it even possible Rosalyn knew what had happened with Caden? If she did, she should know that he'd rejected her. That he wanted nothing more to do with her than to hand her off to his brother to get rid of her.

It didn't matter.

She shook her head to get rid of the painful thoughts. Her being with Caden had absolutely zero chance of happening. And anyway, she forcefully reminded herself, it couldn't be him. He didn't want her and she couldn't tolerate him. He infuriated her and she hated him.

If only she could make herself remember that, everything would be so much easier.

Rosalyn crossed back to where Ellie stood, placing a hand on Ellie's cheek. "There's a fine line between love and hate that's much like the edge of a well-honed sword, dangerously thin and sharp. A slip off either side of that line hurts as badly as any steel ever could, regardless of which side of the weapon delivers the wound." She leaned in and kissed Ellie's forehead, giving her a little hug in the process. "You've proven yerself no to be a foolish woman, Ellie. Dinna allow yer pride to rob you of yer happiness. You'll think on that, aye?"

Rosalyn turned and quietly left the room, leaving Ellie to stare at the empty doorway for several minutes after her departure, unwilling to fully grasp what had just happened. Was it blind luck or had the woman actually known what she was thinking?

"Blind luck. And even at that, she's wrong," Ellie said at last, her words echoing in the empty room. She had to be.

Or at the very least, Ellie hoped she was. Because accepting the other was just too painful.

"First I try the river, and then, if that doesn't work, I'll . . . no." She stopped herself. The river would work. She wouldn't even consider failure.

Now, if she could just find a way out of the keep.

What a pigheaded, willful lass!

Rosalyn stood in the center of the great hall, her tapping foot the only outward sign of her agitation.

"Making her the perfect match for my Caden," she murmured to herself.

Though both of them seemed determined to go out of their way to waste their one chance at true happiness. Ellie refused to accept what was right in front of her and Caden had taken off to the fields in a mad rush this morning, clearly hoping to avoid any contact with the lass.

Rosalyn chewed at her lip in frustration. All this stubborn confusion and her absolutely helpless to change things, bound by a promise made to her own true love all those years ago.

What to do?

"Might I be of any assistance?"

Rosalyn jumped, her hand flying to her heart. "Catriona! I dinna hear you approach. You fair frightened five years off my life!"

"My apologies for intruding on yer privacy, Lady Rosalyn. You appeared to be in some distress. I only thought to help if I could."

Rosalyn considered the woman as she drew near, her gentle spirit shining about her. She did like this lady who would soon be her niece. Maybe a fresh, unbiased mind would be just the thing.

"Perhaps you can at that," she responded, linking her arm through Catriona's. "Walk with me to the kitchens and I'll explain my dilemma. You see, I've a need to do something to help one of my children, but doing so would cause me to break a vow I made long ago to someone very important to me. I'm torn as to how to proceed."

"Ah," Catriona sighed, her soft brown eyes lighting with a smile. "A problem of perception and details. I believe this is something I can help you with."

They'd reached the kitchen, moving through the bustle of workers to a quiet corner.

"Perception and details?" Rosalyn's interest piqued. Already Catriona framed the problem differently.

Her companion nodded. "Whenever I find what I want to do at odds with what I'm bound to do, I carefully examine the promise I made. Often I find my perception of that promise and the actual words can be somewhat different, leaving me room to act as I felt drawn to in the first place."

"What an interesting way of looking at an inconvenient promise." Rosalyn tapped a fingertip against her chin, letting her mind wing its way back to that long-ago day.

Even at the very last, Duncan's concerns were for her.

"Swear it to me, wife. I canna go on through the curtain of this life filled with worry over what might happen to you. I'd have yer vow."

Though events had worked out exactly as they should when she'd cast the spell to help her nephew, Connor, Duncan had never gotten over the fear that someone would accuse her of witchcraft.

It was such a simple request. Only a few words to keep him happy and she would gladly do anything for her beloved Duncan, even this.

"I promise, husband. I'll no use the magic to interfere in our children's lives, no even to bring them together with their one true love."

"No spells or visits to the Faerie Glen, aye? I'd have yer promise."

"I swear it, my love. I'll no use my magic for such a purpose."

Her magic!

Both the memory and the discovery brought a smile to Rosalyn's face. Catriona had been absolutely correct. She'd been too focused on the problem to see the obvious solution.

She'd vowed not to use her magic. But there was nothing in that promise preventing simple, old-fashioned motherly interfering.

"There's power in words, is there no?" the woman asked.

Rosalyn laughed and threw her arms around Catriona, giving the surprised woman a quick hug. "That there is, my dear. Have I told you what a joy it's going to be having you here?"

Now to get down to the business at hand.

"Bridey, I need you to send one of yer helpers to find my sons and bring them to his lairdship's solar right away."

"But Master Caden's gone up to check on the sheep, Lady Rosalyn. I heard the men speaking of it when I served breakfast."

Rosalyn smiled at the child with the wild red hair who'd interrupted, the same one she'd noticed Ellie had taken a liking to.

"That's right, lass, and all the better for my needs that he's gone for the day. It's Colin and Drew I need to speak with."

The child turned to race away, but Rosalyn grabbed her arm, holding her in place. "Not you, Anna. Bridey will send someone else to fetch my lads. I've a very special task for you. Will you help me?"

"Of course, milady." Anna nodded, her eyes large with excitement, mirroring the emotion Rosalyn felt now that she was free to act.

After all, she'd only promised Duncan she wouldn't use her magic. And even without magic, she still had a few tricks up her sleeve.

Ellie sat in the garden on the lovely little bench she'd discovered, trying to come up with any alternative she might have missed.

There simply didn't seem to be one.

The guards were quite clear in their refusal to allow

her outside the gates. They'd even barred her entrance into the little room where the gate mechanism was housed. Not that she really thought she had any chance of making it through both gates and down the long tunnel in between with all of them so determined she stay on the grounds.

It was probably just as well. The whole river thing was likely no more than grasping at straws. Still, she would have liked to test the theory out.

She looked up to see her little friend Anna running her direction, her tousled red curls bouncing wildly.

"Hey, sweetie. What's up?"

A frown fleeted over the child's face as she glanced overhead, but it was gone in an instant and she hurried to the bench where Ellie sat, dropping at Ellie's feet.

"When you weren't in yer room, I hoped to find you out here. I've a need to speak to you over something important." Anna's head nodded up and down as she spoke, her wild hair bobbing about, framing her huge, excited blue eyes.

"Okay." Anna was just the person Ellie needed to see. Her animated personality always brought a smile to Ellie's heart. "What's on your mind?"

"I ken it to be evil to listen in on other people talking." She bowed her head as if trying for a contrite look, but it didn't last long, the excitement returning as she tipped her face up again. "But I overheard Lady Rosalyn speaking with her daughter and their conversation gave me concern for you."

"Really?" *What on earth?*

"Aye. They spoke of how it was only right that his lairdship should be honest with Lady Baxter about the

MacKiernan magic before he asks her to wed and spend her life here. And I wondered . . ." The child chewed at her lip for a moment before taking a deep breath. "I wondered if anyone had told *you* about the magic? Do you ken the story of them? Of the Fae blood in the MacKiernans?"

Did she ever. "I know a little about . . ." she started, but Anna interrupted, as if once she'd started this story, she wouldn't be stopped.

"My mother used to tell me stories of how when Lady Rosalyn had need to use the Fae magic, she would travel to the Faerie Glen so that she could be at the water's edge when the moon rose and the magic was at its most powerful."

The words struck home for Ellie. She grabbed Anna's hands and pulled her up to the bench beside her. "The water's edge? You mean like a river?"

The child nodded, her eyes fastened on Ellie's face. "At a place where the water slows and pools."

"I knew it!" Both times the magic had come, she'd been by a river, exactly like Anna described. And both times had been at night, too. Excitement blossomed until she realized she still had the same problem that had brought her out to the garden in the first place. "Now, if I could only find a way out of Dun Ard to a place like that," she muttered.

"There's such a place no far from here." Anna sat very still beside her, her little hand tightly clutching Ellie's. "And I ken a way to get there."

"How? There's absolutely no going through the gates. The guards won't open up for anyone to go out that hasn't been approved by the Laird himself." She'd been told that enough times today to know it well.

"No through the gates," the child scoffed. "The way my brother and I sneak out to find berries, through the bathhouse. Come on, I'll show you."

Anna jumped up from the bench and pulled on Ellie's hand, though Ellie needed no extra encouragement to follow.

"Is it far?" She still had a couple of hours before nightfall.

"No really. Just a decent hike, though it would likely be dark by the time you get there."

They'd reached the bathhouse, but instead of going inside, Anna led her around to the side, up against the boulders, where the little stream flowed into the shed.

"You have to crawl through here." Anna dropped to her knees and shimmied under the bathhouse, and right along the bank of the little stream.

"Okay. Here goes nothing," Ellie muttered, getting down on her hands and knees to follow, hoping she wouldn't get stuck in some hole large enough for Anna but not for her.

Instead she found the grated floor of the bathhouse over her head, and though there wasn't a lot of room on the edge of the stream, if she was very careful she could avoid getting wet.

Rocks bit into Ellie's knees as she crossed under the floor of the bathhouse, but she didn't let it stop her. She was on her way.

The opening on the other side was another tight fit, and the ground sloped steeply, but she managed to pull herself through with only her right foot sloshing into the water.

"Okay. Lead the way." She smiled down at the little girl.

Anna chewed her bottom lip, her hands clutching and twisting the dirty apron she wore. "I canna go with you, Ellie. Bridey expects me in the kitchens and she'd be furious if I'm no there. But I can tell you how to go. You canna get lost. You only have to follow the stream until it widens and it will lead you directly to the pool."

She wrapped her skinny arms around Ellie's waist and hugged her tightly before dropping to her knees and disappearing back through the hole under the bathhouse.

Ellie stared at the opening for a moment, a strange sadness filling her heart. She wished she had said something more to the little friend she'd never see again.

No. This was what she'd wanted. With that encouragement, she leaned into the hill and began to scramble down.

This was it. The escape she'd sought. Now she could get back to her own life, back to dealing with Ray and getting away from . . . No, she wouldn't think about that for now.

Just away.

"Come."

Blane's answer to the knock at his solar door cut through the discussion, quieting the voices.

A mass of wild red curls poked through the opening. "Begging yer pardon, milord, but I've come to tell Lady Rosalyn it's done."

Rosalyn stood and hurried to the door, patting the girl's shoulder. "Very good. I knew I could count on you, Anna."

The child's answering grin warmed her heart.

"And you'll remember what's yet to be done, aye? You'll remember to wet yer hands first?"

"Dinna you fash yerself, milady. I'll no let you down." With another mischievous grin, Anna ducked back through the door and was gone.

"I'll send Simeon to follow."

Rosalyn nodded. She and Blane had already agreed on the necessity of the extra precaution.

"Do you think that wise? I'm no sure I trust the man." Drew spoke from his position by the fireplace. "We've no had the time to learn his true nature."

"My decision stands." Blane rose and headed for the door. "Catriona trusts him and that's good enough for me."

"Besides . . ." Seeing the look on Drew's face, Rosalyn rushed to forestall any arguments that might jeopardize her careful plans. "You and Colin must be here for yer parts. With Dair gone to Iona, there's no one else."

"You've no a need to worry. Sim's a good man." Colin spoke quietly from his seat in the corner of the room.

"As you say, Brother. I'll accept yer word and I'll hold my tongue on the matter." Drew bowed his head in a respectful little nod.

Rosalyn returned the nod, a smile playing across her lips as she sat back down. "Then all is in readiness for Caden's return."

And if this turned out as she hoped?

Her smile broadened as she looked from Colin to Drew. There was so much still to be done in this lifetime. Who knew what she could yet accomplish?

Thirty-two

As miracles go, this one had gone quite well.

Ellie's bluestone concoction appeared to be working exactly as she had claimed it would. The *infection*, as she'd called it, hadn't spread beyond the single ewe. And even that animal seemed much improved.

It was all he could ask for.

And yet he was miserable.

Caden ducked his head as he rode under the first gate into Dun Ard, not wanting to wait until the portcullis rose fully. He had an anxiety sitting on him he couldn't quite understand and he simply wanted to be home, to see for himself that everyone was safe. He found himself searching the courtyard for a very specific someone as he entered.

"Have the gates been up since I left?" he called to the guard standing inside the wall.

"Only once."

Caden froze, staring at the man, a hard knot forming in his midsection until the guard stammered on.

"Sir Simeon wanted to ride the countryside. The laird himself gave permission."

A breath of relief puffed from Caden's lungs and he nodded his approval, reining his horse toward the stables.

How foolish of him. Equally as senseless as he'd been earlier this day when he'd prepared to leave the protective walls of Dun Ard. He'd had no reason this morning to suspect Ellie would try to leave. Where would she go? His worry was without cause.

Yet in spite of what he knew to be sensible, the concern had nagged at him when he'd ridden out to check on the sheep. Strongly enough that he'd given specific orders about allowing no one through the gate, in or out, without good reason.

Even now he found himself scanning the bailey for the woman herself or her pack of animals, to no avail.

The apprehension churned in his stomach again as he dismounted and tossed the reins to the lad in the stable.

Gritting his teeth in irritation, he stomped outside, turning toward the back of the keep. There was no point in fighting it. He was tired and overanxious, nothing more. He only needed to know her whereabouts and then he could go inside and relax.

Surely he could locate one woman in this place without actually having to go near her. It was, after all, only to reassure himself. He had absolutely no intent to approach her, only the need to know she was safe.

"It will be a relief when Colin takes on this responsibility," he muttered, but the words brought him no comfort.

He stopped just inside the deserted garden, only absently noting how the setting sun cast a magical glow on the bench his mother loved so. In the distance he found what he searched for—Ellie's dogs, sitting patiently at the corner of the bathhouse.

Odd time of day for a bath, but who knew what mess the woman had gotten herself into this time. Someone would likely fill in the details of her latest misadventures for him before the day was over.

Relieved, he headed into the keep and snagged a fresh loaf of bread as he passed through the kitchens, grinning as Bridey yelled and shook her wooden spoon at him. The old cook had been chasing him out of her kitchen with the same empty threats for as long as he could remember, a ritual that normally soothed his soul.

Odd that now, even with his ridiculous worries put to rest, his anxiety continued to grow.

Rest would change that. He was tired and overwrought.

Up the hallway he headed, toward the stairs, with little more than reaching the privacy of his own bedchamber on his mind.

"Caden! Yer just in time. Join us."

The door of Blane's solar stood open and his brothers sat inside with his cousin, passing a whisky that Caden recognized as one of Blane's finest.

"What's all this?"

"A celebration of sorts," Drew laughed, handing a filled cup to him.

Caden reached for the cup mechanically, feeling as if

the blood drained from his body while he stood there, leaving him cold and lifeless.

This was it.

Colin had come to his senses at last. There would be a wedding.

He dropped into the empty chair in front of his cousin's desk and placed the untouched cup in front of him.

"A celebration?" The words seemed to stick to his dry mouth but the very thought of the liquid in his cup made his stomach churn.

"Aye," Blane responded, a satisfied grin on his lips. "I've spoken to the Lady Baxter this very afternoon. Soon, dear cousins, Catriona will be Lady MacKiernan. But that's not all."

He lifted his cup in a toast and Caden had no choice but to pick up his own. The whisky, his favorite, had the taste of weeds as he swallowed, waiting to hear the remaining news.

"Under the circumstances, we've agreed to dispense with the auld tradition of posting banns. We're to be wed within the week. Should her brother think to reclaim her, I want to make sure he has no the least ground to stand upon."

"I told you we should have done away with him before we left Wode Castle. Then you'd have no need for worries."

Colin's emotionless statement sent shivers up Caden's spine and set him wondering when his brother had become so hard.

Could he have been mistaken about this being the proper match for Ellie?

"Still, yer timing is fortunate indeed for my own

news, Cousin." Colin propped his boots on the desk, leaning back in his big chair.

"And what would yer news be?" Caden forced the words out. This was what he'd waited so long to hear, what he wanted.

Wasn't it?

"I'd no want to miss such as Blane's wedding, but waiting through the posting of banns would surely have delayed it too long. As it stands, I can see that which I thought would never come to pass and still be ready to leave as soon as Dair returns from delivering Alycie and Steafan to Iona."

Colin was leaving? He couldn't do that. Not without Ellie. His brother had to wed the woman and take her away from Dun Ard. Away from him.

Caden leaned forward in his seat, the cup in his hand forgotten. "And where would it be that yer planning to go, little brother?"

"It's rumored that Edward plans to attack Stirling soon. Dair and I will journey there to lend our swords to the castle's defense."

Confusion speared through Caden, melding with a growing anger. "What of Ellie?" The words burst forth as if of their own accord.

"The lass you traveled with?" Colin's brow arched with the question. "What of her?"

"She's to be yer wife, you great fool, that's what. The Fae have sent her, just for you."

"Wed her?" Colin snorted derisively. "I've no idea where you came up with such a foolish notion, but I'll no be wedding anyone. Though a quick tumble may not be so bad, eh? She's no so hard on the eyes as I . . ."

Colin's words were cut away as Caden slammed his body into his brother's, sending his chair and both men tumbling over backward to the floor. In the blur of his fury, Caden fought at the hands dragging him from his brother.

"You'll no speak of her in that manner again, do you hear?" He jerked his arms away from Blane's grasp and straightened his shirt, using the time to regain the control he'd lost.

"I've had more than enough of this," Colin growled as Drew helped him to his feet, a restraining hand placed to his chest. "If you feel so strongly, perhaps it's you should do the wedding." His eyes narrowed as he wiped a trickle of blood from a cut on his lip. "It's you she wants anyway."

"Yer daft," Caden spit, the rage only now ebbing from his body.

"No, he speaks the truth," Drew stepped in. "And more the fool you are for no seeing it yerself. If you go on like this, you'll have no one to blame but yerself for driving her away."

"I've no idea what you speak of," Caden muttered, guilt filling the empty space where only moments before anger had lived.

"Do you no?" Colin shook his head in disgust as he righted his chair and sat back down. "She's done her best this whole day to escape the walls, fair driving the guards mad with her persistence. She's determined to go home, Caden. And if yer half the man I've always believed you to be, you'll act to prevent that. Dinna prove yerself to be the great idiot here."

"I'll hear no more of this." They didn't understand,

didn't know all that had happened. Didn't know Ellie had already rejected him.

"Then yer a greater fool than I ever credited you. I've no desire to waste any more of my time on this nonsense." Colin stood and strode from the room, leaving silence in his wake.

Caden stared at the doorway his brother had stormed out, his thoughts a jumble. He'd been so sure it was Colin she'd been sent for. And if not . . .

"You should go and speak to her."

"I canna!" Caden turned, shouting at his brother. He took a deep breath, fighting for the control that had mysteriously deserted him before repeating more quietly, "I canna. She's already told me she does no love me."

"And you believed her?" Blane laughed, his brow knit in concern. "A woman says many things to preserve her pride. Just as men do."

"In case you've forgotten," Caden reminded, a bitterness he couldn't prevent in his voice, "I've traveled this path once before. I'll no ever again force my attentions on a woman who has no desire for me." He'd ignored every sign with Alycie at a dear cost to his family. He'd sworn never to repeat that mistake and he intended to keep his vow.

"She's no Alycie, Cade." Drew spoke softly, crossing the space between them to lay a hand on Caden's shoulder. "This one's different. You must let the past lie in the past."

This from his brother? He would not be lectured by Drew, especially not with advice the young man didn't follow himself. It was more than he could accept now. He needed time to think. Time alone.

Pushing Drew's hand away, Caden turned and hurried from the room, ignoring Blane's call. Down the hall to the stairs he strode, once again bound for the privacy of his room.

His foot was on the first stair when the poorly muffled sobs of a child found his ears. He stopped and stepped back down, following the sound of weeping until he found its source.

Just around the corner from the stairs, on the floor, huddled up against the wall, he found her, the little red-haired kitchen lass, Anna. She turned her face up to him as he approached, her eyes large, her dirty little face wet with tears.

A desperate glance around the room quickly confirmed there were no women about to assist him. He'd have to deal with the crying child on his own. He couldn't very well walk away from her. Besides, how hard could it be?

"What ails you, lass?" he asked, using his best no-nonsense voice and feeling entirely out of his element.

"I . . . I think I've done something verra bad, Master Caden," the child sobbed, and dropped her forehead to her knees, hiding her face from him.

Perhaps gruff didn't work as well with the wee lassies as it did with his shepherds.

He squatted down next to her and awkwardly patted her little shoulder. "You dinna ken whether or no yer actions were bad? Then what's yer reason for all this bubbling you do?"

Anna looked up and launched her body into his, almost toppling them both to the floor. Her little arms clutched around his neck as she buried her grimy face in his shoulder.

"I've lost my best friend, that's my reason."

"Ah, so that's it, is it?" Nothing more than a disagreement among children. That he could handle. "When I was lad, my mother always told me I should take responsibility for settling arguments with my friends. She taught me to go to them and shake their hand, no matter that I thought I was right, because their friendship was worth much more than my pride. Aye?"

Anna shook her head, grinding her nose into his shoulder. "You dinna ken at all." The muffled words ended another sob. "It's no a fight. It's Ellie."

"What did you say?" Caden grabbed her shoulders and pulled her away from him so that he could look into her eyes. He must have misunderstood her words because there was only one *Ellie* in the whole of Dun Ard. "How is Ellie involved in this?"

"That's what I'm telling you. She's left to go home. I'll no see her ever again and it's all my fault."

"That's impossible. The guards knew better than to let her out the gates." He said the words as much to reassure himself as the child.

Anna hung her head, her whole body reflecting her misery. "It's my fault, I tell you. I showed her a way out and told her how to reach the auld pool so she could use the magic."

No. He wouldn't believe it. The child was mistaken. Ellie was still here. In the bathhouse. He'd seen her beasts waiting for her.

All the same, he couldn't discount what the lass said. If she was right, he had to act quickly. Just the thought of Ellie outside the gates of Dun Ard after dark, unprotected, tightened his chest so that he could hardly catch his breath.

"Show me," he ordered, giving the girl a little shake to stop the infernal weeping. "Take me to the place you say she went out."

She clasped her little hand around his fingers and pulled him along, down the hall past the now closed door of Blane's solar, out through the kitchen, into the garden and beyond.

His stomach tightened as they neared the bathhouse. The sight of the waiting dogs, which before had appeared so reassuring to him, now took on an ominous cast.

They waited for a mistress who would not return.

"There." Anna pointed to a spot under the building before getting to her knees and slipping inside the hole.

He squatted down to inspect the pathway. It was too small for his shoulders to manage, but the child moved through easily. And it was no stretch of his imagination to see Ellie being able to make her way through as well.

"To the auld pool, did you say?"

He waited only long enough for her affirmative reply before running toward the stables. If he took his fastest horse, he might reach her before it was too late.

Thirty-three

Even if the magic didn't work, it certainly was pretty here.

Ellie looked around the pool she'd finally reached. The little stream she'd followed spread out and the water slowed before it hit the rocks and picked up speed again, crashing its way down the mountainside. A small forest of trees grew up around the pool, sheltering the area and filtering the last rays of sunlight as they danced on the water, casting a last pinkish golden glow over the ripples.

This had to be the place.

She dropped to a flat, mossy spot along the bank and eased the wet slipper off her foot, wincing at the blister she'd developed on her hike. This little trip had certainly been another example of the "act first, think later" policy she was getting so good at.

When her foot first slid into the water, she should

have realized right then a walk of any length would be a problem. In fact, now that she took the time to think about it, there were several things she might have considered a little more thoroughly before she'd scampered off down the mountain.

She should have thought to bring her knives along, just in case. Hadn't she listened to Caden and the others discussing the possibility that Catriona's brother might come after them? As she waited for the moon to rise in the sky, a tendril of panic swirled in her stomach, building, sparking every concern her mind could dredge up, her thoughts randomly hopping from one problem to the next.

She hoped Anna wouldn't get in trouble for having shown her the way out of Dun Ard.

Perhaps she should have said something to Rosalyn about leaving. After all, the woman had gone out of her way to make Ellie feel welcome, as if she were actually part of the family. What kind of a guest just took off?

And what about Baby and Missy? Would anyone think to take care of her poor dogs when she was gone?

What if the whole magic-at-the-river thing didn't even work?

It will work.

It had to. Because if it didn't, it would only confirm her worst fears. That Caden was The One. The same Caden who thought her a poster child for improper, inappropriate women. The same Caden who was so anxious to be rid of her, he thought to pass her off to his younger brother.

She wouldn't stand for being treated like some hand-me-down to be discarded when he'd grown tired of her.

The magic will work.

Anna had said the magic was strongest near water when the moon rose. That had to explain it.

This would work.

But when it did, would any of the people she'd come to care for worry about what had happened to her?

Would Caden?

"Stop it!" she ordered herself aloud. This was getting her nowhere. "Shoulda, coulda, woulda. I got to let it go." She shook her head in irritation.

She was not going to talk herself out of this. Going home was exactly what she needed to do.

Be sensible!

Caden wouldn't worry about her being gone. He'd be relieved. He wouldn't have to deal with her grossly inappropriate behavior anymore. And think of the trouble she'd be saving his poor brother, the one Caden had tried to dump her on.

No, working herself up into a fine lather over what she couldn't change was pointless. She needed to put her energies into figuring out what she would do once she got home. Worrying about "what if" did nothing to help.

In fact, all it did was upset her more.

The longer she sat, the harder she found it to fend off her growing unease. She'd made herself so anxious, her imagination was even doing a number on her now, making her feel as if someone watched her from the cover of the surrounding trees.

What had looked sheltering and idyllic barely an hour past now appeared menacing as she peered into the great pockets of dark in their depths, trying to rid herself of the feeling.

Fear shot through her at a sound of crackling underbrush. It might be only an animal, but then again . . .

She left the thought unfinished, fear whipping the adrenaline to flood her system as she rose to her feet, faced the water and looked up at the sliver of a moon rising in the inky sky.

Caden's face filled her mind but she pushed it away, fighting the sense of loss that remained when it was gone. The fear must be responsible for her thinking of him. It was only comfort and safety she sought. Nothing more. Once she got back to her own time, she'd never think of him again.

She wouldn't. Not ever.

Her hands shook and she clasped them to her breast to still their trembling.

Please let those damn Faeries be listening just this once.

"Take me home. Take me where I need to be, where I belong."

Caden followed Ellie's tracks down the side of the mountain until he could be sure she had indeed stuck to Anna's advice to stay by the stream the whole way. Once he eliminated all doubt, he'd be free to take a faster way to the auld pool and could save time.

That was increasingly important to him now that the sun had set.

He had just made his decision to turn away and head straight for her destination when he spotted something unusual. Something that made him climb down from his mount to investigate more closely.

Fresh horse tracks. One clearly on top of the small print Ellie had left behind.

Someone followed her. Someone on horseback.

In his haste Caden had almost missed it. Another ten minutes and there wouldn't have been enough light to have seen the tracks.

He was torn now. If he left the trail to save time, what else might he miss?

He couldn't take that chance. Not with Ellie's safety hanging in the balance. He kicked his horse, urging it to move faster, the familiar old guilt threatening to drown him once again.

If his brothers were right—if she'd left because of him and anything were to happen to her—it would be his fault.

He couldn't live with that.

The fear curdled his blood, eating at him, forcing him to drive his animal harder, faster.

He'd sooner see the Fae take her home than have anyone here bring her to harm.

His need to see her, to know for sure she was unharmed overrode everything else. It was more important even than finding out if she cared for him as his family seemed to think.

That idea was still too large for him to accept.

If she did, why had she denied it? Could it be as Blane had said, only her pride that forced those words from her lips? Pride such as that which drove her need to seek revenge on the man who had stolen her home?

If only he'd opened his eyes to the possibility earlier, perhaps he could have changed this. If only he hadn't been so desperate to avoid her, he would have been there today to prevent her running away.

If only, if only, if only.

The litany beat in his head in time to the pounding of his horse's hooves as the copse of trees surrounding the auld pool came into sight, the forest a darker black against the night sky.

He slowed his horse, preferring to arrive unnoticed by whoever it was following Ellie.

Ahead, at the edge of the little forest, he could just distinguish the outline of a mounted figure, waiting, watching.

Too late for surprise, he moved slowly toward the man, pulling his sword as he did so. When he neared, the figure moved forward into the moonlight, showing himself.

"MacDowell?" His hold on his sword slackened. What was Simeon doing here?

"It's about time you showed up, MacAlister. I've better things to do with my time than nursemaid yer woman."

"She's no my . . ." Caden clamped his teeth together on the denial. His relationship with Ellie was none of MacDowell's business. "What are you doing out here, following her?"

The warrior stared at him hard. "What would you have me do? I saw a lone figure scrambling down the mountainside as I returned to Dun Ard. I followed. When I realized it was a woman, I could no turn away and leave her unattended. And once I got close enough to see which woman it was, I dinna doubt you'd be along eventually."

"She's unharmed?" Caden had to force himself to ask the question at the front of his thoughts.

"I would have allowed nothing else." Simeon sounded almost offended at the question. "Through the trees, she sits at the edge of the water, talking to herself." Simeon shook his head. "Daft female."

Caden's irritation at MacDowell's being there warred with his relief that it wasn't someone else who had followed Ellie.

"You can go. I have this well in hand now." Thanks to his tangled emotions, he couldn't help the gruff dismissal.

The knight snorted his response. "And welcome to it, you are." With a tug of his reins, he and his mount disappeared into the night, following the path Caden had just traveled.

At the tree line, Caden dismounted and led his horse through the forest on foot, looping his reins over a low branch once he caught sight of Ellie by the water.

She turned to stare his direction and for an instant the moonlight glinted off her long black hair, giving her a glow that reminded him of what she was and who had sent her here.

The Fae.

For the first time, it didn't matter in the least.

And just like that, he knew. Knew in the depths of his soul.

Drew had been right about one thing, Ellie was nothing like Alycie.

As of this moment, he didn't care who had sent her or why. She was here. With a Faerie heritage to match his own.

To hell with what his brothers needed. To hell with what he owed them or anyone else. Right or wrong, he wanted Ellie for his very own. And he would do whatever it took to have her.

As he watched, she rose to her feet and clasped her hands to her breast, her voice broken as if she fought tears when she uttered the words that struck fear to his heart, words that drew him forward to the spot where she stood.

"Take me home. Take me where I need to be, where I belong."

Thirty-four

~

"Are you so sure this isna exactly where you need to be?"

Startled, Ellie whipped around to face the one who spoke. With the movement, her bare foot slipped on the damp, mossy bank and she lost her balance, falling backward toward the water.

In the space of a breath, she found herself captured, snug up against Caden's chest, the irresistible scent of him filling her nostrils.

Her heart pounded, beating so loudly it resonated in her ears, but she refused to believe it did so for any reason other than her near fall. All the same, for that one moment, she relaxed in his hold and allowed herself to consider whether or not *this* might be where she belonged. Right here, in Caden's arms.

But it couldn't be. No green lightning sparked

around her this time. Either the Faeries had completely abandoned her, or Caden wasn't The One.

She steeled her raging emotions and pushed away from him, refusing to meet his eyes. His gaze, which she remembered could feel hotter than melted chocolate, would immobilize her, robbing her of the ability to speak, and she couldn't afford that.

Or worse, she feared she might find disdain in his look, accusation painted there on his face. The last thing she could handle right now would be another of his "come home and marry my brother" lectures.

So she stared at her feet and then off to the opposite bank of the pool, desperately searching the shadows for a spot to focus. Anywhere but on him.

When she felt she could speak without her voice giving her away, she held up a hand, hoping to forestall anything he might say.

"Let's get this straight between us right now, Caden. I'm well aware of how you feel about me." She swallowed hard, forcing back the tears that would only make her look stupid and needy.

"I dinna believe you are, lass." His voice was soft, closer to her now than a moment before.

How was she to get through this with him so close? She backed away a step, giving herself room to think, to breathe. "I already know you think my behavior is immodest and inappropriate. You said so yourself. And I know I only reinforced your opinion with what happened between us that night."

"Ellie . . ." He reached out a hand, one finger stroking her hair, and she swatted him away.

"Let me finish. I didn't expect any commitment from you that night and I still don't. What happened . . . happened." She shrugged her shoulders, searching for words to explain without making an even bigger fool of herself.

There was no way she'd admit that she couldn't have stopped herself from making love to him if she'd wanted to. And she hadn't wanted to.

"If this magic thing doesn't work and I'm stuck here, I want you to know I don't expect anything from you so don't worry about that. I understand that you want to be rid of me and I'm doing my best to get away from here."

His hand shot out, snaking around the back of her neck and pulling her to him, so close she could feel his breath feather over her face.

"Yer wrong, woman. I've only one thought about you, and it's no to be rid of you."

He bent his head, crushing his lips to hers.

Only one large hand held her to him. She could easily pull away, but somehow she couldn't make herself take the one small step needed to break the physical contact.

Nor could she stop herself from returning his kiss any more than she could stop the need for him that seemed to hum in her blood in response to his touch.

She leaned into him, reaching for him, twining her fingers in his hair. Her body pressed into his, and she let the want wash over her, through her, until it filled her completely, leaving every tiny part of her aching for more of him.

As if in answer to her need, he kissed her lips, her cheeks, her chin, nibbling his way to her ear.

"Stay with me, *Elliedenton*. Dinna leave me now. No now that I've found you."

His words whispered their way into her heart, into her very soul, as his fingers worked frantically at the laces of her overdress. To her surprise, she found her own trembling fingers doing an equally frantic job of loosening the belt that held his plaid.

He laughed, a short joyful burst of air, as both the plaid and overdress hit the ground at the same time, quickly joined by shirt and shift.

They stood in the moonlight, pressed body to body, their heartbeats echoing, as if calling one to the other. They stared into one another's eyes until again he took her mouth with his own, his heated gaze melting any resistance she might have had.

Not that she'd had any to begin with.

And then she was under him, with no memory of their sinking to the ground, her back flattened into the pile of discarded clothing they'd made in their haste.

She wanted this, no matter what else happened. Even if the magic worked, even if this were the last she'd ever see of him, she wouldn't deny herself this time with him. She wanted to remember him this way, remember his looking at her as if he meant the words he'd said.

He kissed her neck, slowly, as he lifted her arms above her head, running his callused hands down their length and onto her sides, sending shivers through her entire body.

"Say you'll be mine, love," he whispered into her neck as his hands closed over her breasts and the pads of his thumbs rubbed slow circles around her nipples.

She felt her body tense at the words. *Love*, he'd called

her. Was it only a name to him or did it mean more? Was it even her he saw in his mind as he held her close?

As much as she wanted this, wanted him, she had to know it was *her* he made love to, not some stand-in for the one he couldn't have.

She clasped his face in both her hands, drawing his eyes up to hers, holding him there.

"I'm not Alycie. I can't ever be like her." Her breath caught in her throat as she said the words, fear that he would reject her spearing through her midsection.

If he let go of her, rose from this spot and walked away from her at this moment, she wasn't sure she could go on.

She wasn't sure she wanted to.

He didn't do any of those things. He simply smiled. A slow, seductive movement of his lips.

"I ken the truth of that, Ellie, and I'll thank the Fae for it every single day for the rest of my life." Holding her gaze with his own, he shifted his head in her hands and took her thumb into his mouth, nipping at the pad, sucking, shaping his tongue to the digit before releasing it. "Every single day," he repeated.

The smile was still there when he ducked his head, the warm mouth that had caressed her thumb a moment before now clasped to her breast, his tongue working its own brand of magic on her highly sensitive nipple.

The breath she hadn't realized she'd been holding puffed from her lungs, and she arched into him, an unbelievable joy filling her heart.

His hands slid down her sides, around her waist and lower, grasping her bottom and pulling her into him as his knee insistently pressed her legs apart.

"Open to me," he growled, and she gladly obliged, hooking first one leg and then the other over his, sliding the sole of one foot from the back of his knee to his calf and up again.

She threaded her fingers in his silky hair, caressing his head to her as he sucked at her breast, his tongue swirling and teasing, driving her wild.

One hand skimmed its way around her hip, across the flat plane of her stomach, his thumb tracing her belly button as if memorizing a landmark before moving on. Straight down, cupping over her mound and then searching lower, lower until a finger plunged into her depths.

She felt herself tighten and release and a second finger joined the first, moving slowly in and out, forcing her to move in time to the rhythm they set.

His thumb pressed against her sensitive nub and she swore electricity pulsed through her body, short pounding waves spasming around the fingers that moved insistently inside her.

She panted to catch her breath and her pulse pounded in her ears so hard she barely heard his satisfied chuckle as his hands slid under her thighs, lifting her, opening her to him.

The tip of his shaft nestled in where his fingers had been, nudging against her opening. A slight pressure forward and then back, almost entering. So close. She pressed into him, but he held back, teasing her body into a frenzy of need.

Forward and back. Almost there and then denied.

She moaned with the frustration, her breath coming in short, quick pants.

And then his lips were on hers, his tongue plunging into her mouth as his shaft plunged into her body.

Once, twice, three times, she met his thrusts, wanting him deeper and deeper still, wanting him to fill her completely. Needing to be so close she couldn't feel where she ended and he began.

Needing to be as one. Two halves made whole.

When it felt as if time and space around her imploded, she clung to him, riding the waves of her pleasure as he drove into her once more.

"Mine," he shouted as he found his own release.

How long they lay together, his face buried in the crook of her neck, she couldn't say—only that being there, with his weight on top of her, was the only place she ever wanted to be.

She opened her eyes, turning her head to look at him. "Mine," she whispered as she traced the line of his cheek with her fingertip. She pushed a lock of hair behind his ear and watched the corner of his mouth turn up in a tired smile.

It was, without a doubt, the most perfect moment of her life.

Until she realized the darkness around her glowed, her very skin glistened with the green light that surrounded them both.

At last she'd discovered the truth of the magic. It wasn't about finding The One. It was, as Rosalyn had tried to make her understand, all about accepting him into her heart, into her soul.

It had almost happened that first night they'd made love. But she'd denied it then, sent the magic away.

There could be no denying this time. It was too late

for that. Caden was too deeply connected to her now. She couldn't deny him if she tried.

"No," she whispered on a broken sob, the horror of what would happen, the horror of losing Caden choking her.

"What, love, what is it?" In an instant, he was up and crouched above her, ready to defend against whatever threatened her.

But he wouldn't be able to defeat the Faerie magic. It would take her any moment now she knew. Panic pounded at her, constricting her chest.

"I've seen this before. It's the Fae magic, is it no?"

Ellie could only nod her response, tears clogging her throat.

"It's come to take you back to yer own time as you wanted. Back to yer land, back to yer people."

She nodded her head again in acknowledgment, but the thought of leaving him, of going back to the life she had known terrified her.

What did she have to return to?

She had to go home, didn't she? She missed . . . what? She racked her brain, but truly the only things that came to mind were catsup and toilet paper. And there was no question in her mind that she'd gladly trade a forever supply of both of those things for one lifetime with Caden.

"Will you no change yer mind?" He took her hand and clasped it tightly to his chest. "I canna give you the stars, my own *Elliedenton*, only my heart. And I give it freely if you'll but send the magic away and stay with me."

His heart pounded under her fingertips and her resistance broke, the tears she'd held back flowing down her cheeks.

"I don't want the stars, Caden. I never did. I only want you."

"Are you sure?" His free hand stroked down her hair. "Would you give up all you had in yer world, even yer chance for revenge on the man who took yer land?"

"Yes," she whispered. "Nothing, not one thing, is worth as much to me as being with you." She meant every word with all her heart.

"Then send the magic away." He pulled her close, enfolding her in his arms. "Tell them you've chosen."

"I can do that?" Her voice sounded as small and helpless as she felt.

"Aye, love. You can do anything you want." He kissed her forehead before tightening his hold on her. "You've the power of the Fae in you. You control the magic."

"Then I choose you. I choose to stay here with you."

The glow around them sparkled, like thousands of little green lightning bugs all twinkling together.

And then it was gone, leaving only the normal glimmer of moonlight bathing them.

"That was it? That was all it took? Just a couple of words?" The fear of being torn from his arms still hummed in her blood.

"Just words? Ah, love." he wiped at the tears on her cheeks. "Words carry the power of the magic. And we have the most powerful of all magic. We have true love."

She laughed then, the joy of the moment, the joy of being with the man next to her, filling her heart.

He lifted his plaid from the ground beside them and wrapped it around them, snuggling her close under his arm, and they sat together, staring into the night.

"Are you truly happy with the choice you've made?"

She heard the tremor in his voice and understood for the first time that he might feel as insecure as she had.

"Oh yes. I made the right decision." She knew she would never regret staying with Caden. "But you know," she said thoughtfully as she leaned her head against his chest, "I do wish that somehow, some way, Ray Stanton would get what's coming to him for the way he treated my mama. For the way he treated me."

"Be careful how you use that word *wish*. Dinna ever forget the power of it." He kissed the top of her head and rearranged the plaid more snugly.

"Maybe so. But still. I do wish he'd get what he deserves."

Sitting in the dark, safe in the arms of the man she loved with all her heart, Ellie thought back to another night sitting by water bathed in moonlight. Just weeks ago, the night she had sat on the bank of a muddy Texas river, desolate and alone, with no idea of what she would do next.

She shivered at the memory and turned to find Caden watching her, his eyes filled with the look that melted her insides.

His lips covered hers and she wanted to laugh with the joy of how much her world had changed in just a few short weeks. In her wildest dreams she never would have imagined her life would turn out so right.

She, Ellie Denton, living the perfect Happy Ever After with a Highlander of her own.

Epilogue

Dixielee Parker-Stanton shimmied out of her car and into the parking lot of the County Line Bar, sliding her form-fitting miniskirt down as she stood to smooth out the wrinkles. But not too far down. Long shapely legs were one of her best assets.

Yeah, this looked exactly like the kind of place Ray would hang out.

With long red fingernails, she popped open another button on the already dangerously low-cut blouse. Legs weren't her only asset. And as much as she'd paid for the beauties filling out this blouse, she enjoyed showing them off.

The smell of the place hit her on a wave as she pulled open the screen door—stale beer and cigarettes. These places all smelled the same, and she should know. She'd been in more beer joints in her lifetime than she'd care to admit.

But that was all about to change.

Every head in the room turned as she entered, and more than one conversation died abruptly.

Dixielee didn't care. In fact, it was a rush.

And though she loved the power her looks gave her over men, the slow, predatory smile lighting her lips was for one man and one man only. And there he sat. All alone at the end of the bar.

Ray Stanton.

The money he'd come into must be burning a hole in his pocket because that looked like a brand-new Stetson on his head, and shiny new boots like he was wearing didn't come cheap, either.

She'd put a stop to that soon enough.

Flipping a long blond curl back over her shoulder, she began a slow walk down the length of the bar calculated to have every eye in the place glued to her ass before she came to stop.

Every male eye anyway.

"How you doin', Ray, honey?"

He glanced up at her words, his eyes bloodshot.

"Dixielee? I been . . . planning to call you, darlin', soon as I got all settled. You sure are lookin' good," he drawled, grinning and turning on the good-ol'-boy charm that had swept her off her feet once before.

But not this time.

Dixielee didn't have to be taught the same lesson twice.

"I'll just bet you were." She climbed up on the stool

next to him, enjoying the ruckus at the pool table behind them when her skirt slid higher and that joker in the ball cap missed his shot. "But it don't really matter now, does it, honey, 'cause I found you."

She smiled at the bartender. "Just a club soda, please." Drinks and business didn't mix and she was all about business tonight. She'd waited too long for this moment.

Ray continued to grin, stopping to take a swig out of his longneck. "How the hell did something as fine as you end up in a hole like Prairieland?"

Dixielee returned his grin. She could afford to be charitable. She had so loved the way that man's lips curled up in that sexy grin of his at one time. And he wouldn't have much to grin about in a little while, so she might as well let him enjoy himself while he could.

"You, honey. You're the reason I'm here."

He tipped the longneck up once more and then pushed the new Stetson back on his head. "I sure didn't expect to see you again. Not after all these years."

She hadn't thought she'd ever find him, either.

"Funny thing, Ray. I was standing in line at the grocery store, of all places, when I was just possessed with a need to buy one of those cheap gossip rags."

It had been the most bizarre moment of her life. She never read those things. But on that particular day, it was as if some outside force controlled her, forcing her to buy that damn paper. "And when I got home and tossed it on the table, it fell open to a story with a picture of you. A story about how you'd inherited some property when your wife died and your stepdaughter mysteriously disappeared, and then they'd found oil on that property. So I guess you're a rich man now, aren't you?"

"Doing all right. Lonely as hell, though." He leaned in close. "You wouldn't want to do anything to help me out with that now, would you, darlin'?"

"Oh, but that's what I'm here for, Ray. To put a permanent end to your lonely days."

He blinked at her, fighting the beer buzz fogging his brain. "What are you talking about?"

"I've got it all planned. You and me are getting married. Again. Only this time, we're going to sign some paperwork that gives me control of everything you've got. Money, land, oil, everything."

That got his attention.

"You're a goddamn crazy woman. That ain't going to happen." He motioned to the bartender to bring him another beer.

"Oh, I think it is, honey." She waited patiently while his beer was delivered, smiling at the bartender until he walked away. "See, I got me this little piece of paper. One that says we were already married. Over a year before you married that nice lady who died and left you all that land. I saw the dates in the article, Ray. You should have divorced me, honey, if you wanted to be marrying somebody else. As it is, your marriage to her isn't legal. And if people were to find out, I'm thinking you'd have to give all that money back."

The sexy blue eyes went all hard, just like she remembered they could. Just like she'd expected they would at about this point in the discussion.

"You greedy little bitch. You'd be willing to do that to me? Just for money?"

She smiled, patting his hand. "Oh, honey, it's for so much more than money. This is for you walking out on me. Just disappearing without a word. You and every red cent I had to my name and after running up both my credit cards to their absolute limits." She still wasn't sure how everything had just fallen in her lap or how she'd managed to come up with the perfect plan, but it didn't really matter. She'd waited seven years for this, and she was enjoying every minute of it.

"I'll fight you. My brother's a lawyer. You won't get away with it," he sneered.

"You won't do a damn thing but what I already told you, Ray. You'll marry me again and sign the papers I've had drawn up turning everything over to me. Or else."

"Or else what?"

This time she leaned into him, close, running her hand up the back of his neck the way he used to like so much.

"I'm betting half the people in this bar think you killed that young girl, don't they?"

He stiffened under her touch and pulled away.

"I didn't do nothing to Ellie. Last time I seen her, she lit out in that truck of hers just like I told the sheriff. She just ran away or something after I laid claim to her mama's ranch. I never laid a hand on her."

"Would that be the sheriff who also happens to be your brother-in-law?" Dixielee had done her home-work.

When he didn't answer, she leaned in again, running a long manicured nail down the side of his throat.

"It's like this, Ray—if you fight me on this, not only will I see you lose everything by going to the authorities with our marriage papers, I'll see your ass in prison for murdering that poor Ellie Denton."

"But I didn't do anything to her."

"Maybe not, honey, but I'll swear on a stack of Bibles that you told me you did. And how you bragged about how you did away with the body so good they'd never find it."

She watched the blood drain from his face as the realization set in. She had him by the balls and she didn't plan to ever let go.

He was going to pay.

For the rest of his natural-born life.

Not that she really believed he'd hurt that girl. He wasn't a violent man. But he had done plenty of other bad stuff. She was sure there was a trail of women like her across the Southwest, all with broken hearts and empty bank accounts thanks to Ray Stanton.

No, Dixielee wasn't just getting even with him for what he'd done to her. She was getting even with him for what he'd done to all those women, including that poor Denton girl, who must have been just devastated to lose her mama and then her home, too.

This was revenge for all of those women. She felt it in her soul, like some higher power had enabled her to be the one who saw to it that Ray Stanton was getting what was coming to him, what he deserved.